Catalyst

Cat-a-lyst (**kæt'list**) ***n***. a substance which, by its presence, alters the rate of a chemical reaction, but which is itself unchanged by the process.

Ian K. Kent

Catalyst

Tellwell Talent
www.tellwell.ca

ISBN
978-0-2288-1015-5 (Paperback)
978-0-2288-1017-9 (eBook)

Dedication:

For Diana,
my wife, my lover, my best friend.

She asked one day "why don't you write about . . .?"
. . . and thus began this story.

Thanks for the suggestions, encouragement,
the time and space,
Thanks for the ideas, proof reading, and multiple editing,
and . . . for just being there!

All my Love, Ian

Chapter 1

A SMALL BEAD OF SWEAT trickled down his back, starting alone, then joining others with that irritating itch as they fused together in a continuous stream, finally merging into the folds of his already soaked shirt. Craig Porter stared blankly at the cars ahead, the only visible movement was the shimmering heat rising from their metal roofs. Trying to shift to a more comfortable position, he felt his sweat-soaked pants glued to the vinyl seat covers. Again, he looked frantically for an opening in the traffic, savagely pounding the steering wheel as he realized they were totally locked in.

"Oh God, Craig," his wife moaned, "He's getting worse . . . he can hardly breathe!" She held their son close, again squeezing the spray over his nose for his asthma attacks. The small figure in her arms heaved violently, his coughing weaker and his gasps for air becoming more frequent, but shallower. Each Wednesday for two years, Craig and his wife had driven this route, from their home to the clinic for special treatments for their son's asthma. They often thought about moving to a cleaner city, but like many people, were trapped by the restrictions of circumstance, mainly job and money. What had started as a quick drive to the doctor, had turned into a nightmare. Traffic was always slow in this little dip in the road as it approached the main freeway south, but this was the worst they had ever seen. Everything had stopped, blocked by an accident or stalled car ahead somewhere.

The dull ache throbbed through his head, pushing waves of nausea through his system. He rolled down the window, hoping the outside air would somehow be fresher. The heat slammed through the open window, foul, smog-ridden air, thick enough to burn your eyes. He quickly rolled up the window, reaching for the air conditioner he knew was already at maximum. He stared at the machine, knowing that this was just aggravating the problem, everyone running their engines, trying to get their air conditioners to work.

The last week of record heat with no winds added to the inversion over the Los Angeles basin, trapping a week's worth of pollution over the city. A level-three smog alert was in effect, but the public's love for the automobile was winning, adding to an already desperate situation.

He looked helplessly at his wife and son, now both gasping for air. Alarm bells went off. Why is she gasping? He reached for her, his own breathing burning his lungs. He glanced over to the car beside him, looking for help.

"Jesus, the guy's asleep! How in Hell can anyone sleep in this?"

Then he noticed the pickup on his other side, slowly moving. Quickly sitting upright, he thought the traffic had started to move. He watched in disbelief as the pickup slowly gained speed, its driver hunched over the wheel, twitching unnaturally. Locked in the jam, he quickly ran out of room. The bumpers on the pickup crumpled slowly into the rear corner of a long black limousine, rebounded off and headed for one side of the highway. The high curbs at the edge did not budge as the pickup crunched into the concrete. The driver remained hunched over the wheel, now very still. The car's horn added to the cacophony around them.

"God, did you see that?" he turned back to his wife. Her wide eyes screamed to him, her short breaths rasping in the close space. He gaped at the small stream of blood that trickled from the corner of her mouth. His son had stopped moving, he had to do something.

"Stay here" he reached over to kiss his wife, "I'll go for help, try to use someone's cell phone to call an ambulance. We have to do something!" She said nothing, her eyes pleading as she coughed violently, her lungs heaving for more air.

He stepped out of the car, reeling with the impact of the heat and smell of the air. His chest heaved, sucking in more of the foul stuff, scorching his throat. His lungs protested, as violent spasms tried feebly to evacuate the offending material. Each paroxysm hurt more as he spat large flecks of blood over the ground.

Looking ahead, the highway disappeared over the small hill where it joined with the freeway. Nothing moved. Behind him, the same. It looked as if all the cars had settled into this little depression in the highway and couldn't get out. Some cars were jammed against a guard rail or rammed between two other cars. Horns were sounding everywhere, a steady, monotonous blaring. It just didn't feel right, he thought, something's terribly wrong. He'd been through many inversions and smog alerts, but this one was different. Another wave of nausea doubled him over, intensifying the sharp pain in his head. Involuntarily, he gulped larger breaths, sucking the foul stuff deeper into his lungs. He wanted desperately to stop, to sit down and rest, but the agonizing sight of his wife and son replayed in his mind, driving him forward.

He reeled over to a car where the driver had a cell phone to his ear. Craig tapped on the window, gently at first, then louder.

"Hey mister, can I use your phone? It's an emergency, my son's real sick!" He was pounding on the window now, but the driver still ignored him. Temper flaring, he grabbed the door handle, pulling open the door just as it dawned on him that the man wasn't talking . . . in fact he hadn't even moved. His support gone, the man slowly tilted over through the open door, falling awkwardly to the pavement. Dead eyes stared upward into the sun, the spattered blood around his mouth already drying in the heat.

"Oh my God!" he said slowly, gaping at the still figure crumpled on the road in front of him. Slowly turning, he looked around at the other drivers, looking for a reaction, some help. Nothing. They all sat perfectly still, some staring out of their windshields, others fixed on the car's ceiling. Some had run into the car in front of them, and like the pickup driver, were lying across the steering wheel, horn's blaring insanely. Further back, one driver had jammed his car sideways and run into the curb, his body convulsing feebly in the front seat. Most engines were still running, some screaming for attention.

Stumbling awkwardly to the next car, Craig pulled open the door, realizing too late that they were all dead. The road shimmered around him, then started tilting as he slowly lost balance and fell to the ground. He struggled weakly, aware his wife and son were depending on him. Within seconds, he stopped struggling as he welcomed the cold chills and darkness that surrounded him.

A TV-news chopper circled above, not sure what to report on the confusion below. There was no visible reason for the traffic jam as the highway ahead was clear. An armada of sirens slowly approached the site, blocked by the jam from behind, eventually reaching them from the freeway in front of the mess.

Unknown to the rescuers at the time, both the news helicopter and subsequent rescue helicopters had luckily whisked away the cause of the problem with their down-drafts. Later, the Porter family would be counted among the forty-three dead. No apparent cause or reason was immediately given for the tragedy. Government officials and bureaucrats clammed up with a "no comment", or "an investigation is underway". The press, however, were fast to offer their theories, especially the crews that had been following the main news items for the past few days. Of course, with the threat of terrorism constantly in everyone's mind, the most popular theory was an attack by some of Bin Ladin's boys, or possibly a home grown fanatic cult. Most of them had expected a bomb, but the possibility of a mass poisoning seemed to fit, in the form of a noxious gas attack.

Chapter 2

THREE DAYS EARLIER, JAKE PRESCOTT'S Monday morning flight from Vancouver was on its final approach into LAX, Los Angeles' main airport.

" . . . and place your seat-backs and tables to their upright position" the announcement droned on. He finished his drink, then closed up his laptop computer and slipped it under the seat. He leaned back, relishing the closing bars of a Chopin piano concerto on his earphones before they landed. In his late thirties, Jake was physically fit, a quiet, gentle man just over six feet tall. He had a rugged, yet intelligent face with an unruly mop of brown hair, recently greying around the edges, flipped forward over his dark blue eyes. He flicked it back with his hand, reminding himself to get a haircut as soon as he could free up some time. Not yet used to the luxuries of first class travel, he took advantage of the large seats and ample room by stretching out his lanky body. Working out the kinks in his long legs was always a complicated procedure for Jake, especially his left leg and knee, which still exhibited the scars and residual pain of a major car accident years before in which he lost both of his parents. He leaned over to the window to study the city below.

Los Angeles had always fascinated him, mainly the sheer size, the spread of it. Each time he flew into the city, he watched the miles of houses and freeways roll by beneath him. He wondered things like "who lived in that house", "what did that person down there do for a living", " what's going on in that house right now, what kind of happiness, worry, sorrow?" He played the same game in every country and city he visited, but Los Angeles offered so many houses to consider.

"Seat belt buckled up, Mr. Prescott?" the attractive little flight attendant leaned over, checking him once more. "Staying in L.A. long?" she asked. Jake got the distinct feeling she might be offering an opportunity for some additional service, on the ground. He had been on several of her flights before and although he had never given her the slightest encouragement, she kept trying.

"Just for the week," he replied, shying way from her advances. To make sure, he added "I'll be tied up in a convention, meetings, that kind of thing."

"Oh! Well have a nice trip!" she continued to the next passenger.

He relaxed, feeling almost relieved. Although confident and capable in his own field or with other professionals, his relationships with women were cautious, almost pathetic. He often wondered how he even got married, but knew it was because of the direct approach and unrelenting efforts of his wife Lori. She died after a brief battle with cancer, leaving Jake alone again, still scarred from the loss of his parents. The loss was devastating for Jake, and he lost all poise and confidence with women, almost turning into a recluse.

He looked out the window again, his practised eye evaluating the scene before him. The curtain of smog had been visible for many miles. Now, as the aircraft dropped nearer the ground, he could smell the distinctive odour of ozone creeping into the ventilation system of the aircraft. Nearing the airport, the smell mingled with the oily stink of jet exhaust. Descending into the brown cloud that covered the landscape, he thought about his own city of Vancouver, Canada, and how they were fighting the same war between the automobile exhaust and the need to breathe. This brought his thoughts right around to the paper he was planning to present at tomorrow's air pollution conference.

After many years in the business, Jake Prescott was a recognized expert in the field, eagerly sought after for these conferences. He had officially "retired" two years earlier, still in his thirties, after a large corporation bought him out. He now enjoyed travelling, doing the lecture circuit, and taking on special jobs as a consultant for his own interest rather than just for the money.

It had really started almost eight years ago, when he was barely recovering from the loss of his young wife. After months of mourning and depression, he directed his anger and energy into his work, pushing the limits of both mind and body. By the end of almost three exhausting years, he had developed a revolutionary analysis procedure for continuous air monitors and the detection of trace gases. After a lengthy period of field testing, the company finally acquired the highly sought after compliance certifications from the U.S. Federal Environment Department. For a Canadian company to attempt to obtain EPA Equivalency Certification, the red tape was endless. Perseverance and persistence paid off, and once he had received the government certification, the company went into production. Initially it was tough. Every step was agonizingly slow, raising capital, finding suppliers, beating the technical bugs, and then finding customers. Once the systems were operational in the field, word of their success got out, and the orders started rolling in.

After three very successful years of turning out analyzers, one of the giants in the industry made him an offer he couldn't refuse. The small fortune thus gained virtually guaranteed he would never have to work again. Always an active person, Jake was not the type to be idle, and within a year he was back in the business, this time on his own terms. First, he built one of the best analytical labs in the northwest, sort of a "play room" full of toys where he could go and play when he wanted to. He then added computer power, the latest hardware and software in the industry, for both analytical and dispersion modelling predictions. By "stealing" a couple of his ex-employees and friends, he also had the best in manpower to run the operation. They loved him for it. Jake had always been popular with his staff, his quiet manner and soft voice commanded respect in almost every situation. When he asked his old buddies to come and work for him, they jumped at the chance.

For Jake, his new found wealth was a challenge, one he felt he scarcely deserved, and had to live up to. The research lab was the first step. Once equipped, he then wandered the world. Travelling was his first love, after getting a taste of it during a three year stay with friends in Bavaria, as well as a few years travelling the world with Canadian Foreign Affairs. Initially, his travels were for the adventure alone, just to get away, but it soon developed into a game, the challenge of finding yet another interesting environmental problem to solve. Eventually, his fees for lecturing and problem solving more than covered all his costs.

The paper he was presenting at the conference the following day was in the field of air pollution dispersion modelling. The subject had been worked over for years, with hundreds of computer models in use to predict the impact of air pollution on the public under certain conditions of emissions, wind, temperature, sunshine, etc. Most predictions were moderately accurate, depending on the variability of winds, terrain, and other inputs. Together with today's incredible computer power, Jake's new techniques added a new dimension to the predictions, resulting in accuracies never hoped for before. Initial tests in the greater Vancouver area had proved very promising and he was hoping to be able to try it in Los Angeles.

The bump of the landing-gear on the runway snapped him back to the present. The plane quickly came to a halt, turning to taxi to the ramp. Already he could smell the exhaust fumes of other planes mixed with the ground level ozone as the air intake system sucked in local air to ventilate the cabin. Unconsciously, he was running the photochemical smog formulas through his mind as he picked up his briefcase and his cane and limped toward the exit. Before long, he had claimed his luggage and was heading for the rental car agency.

"BE FAIR, SAVE THE AIR" read the placards waving in front of him as he stepped out of the terminal. A small group of unkempt protesters milled around by several of the exits, obviously targeting members of the environmental industry arriving for the conference. He paused, trying to figure out what their purpose was. Why do they picket and protest the people who were involved in the process of "saving the environment" every day of their lives, people who were dedicated to that goal? His curiosity aroused, he stopped to ask one of the picketers.

"Yeah, man, like all you corporate bums gotta get withit man!"

He knew somehow he was talking to the wrong person. Looking around, he spotted a man watching him, a curious look on his face. As Jake tried to figure where he had seen the face before, the man approached him.

"Hi there, aren't you Jake Prescott?"

"Yes" he answered, surprised the man knew him. "And you are . . ."

"Frank Haywood, local president of W.A.S.T.E.", he offered his hand.

"WASTE?" Jake queried, lowering his briefcase to shake his hand.

A couple of flashes went off, surprising both of them. Jake turned around to see a reporter snapping another shot of the two men shaking hands.

Haywood recovered first. "W.A.S.T.E., World Army to Save The Environment" he answered Jake's question. "We're here to take in the conference, keep you guys in line, so to speak."

Jake estimated the man was in his late forties, tall and slim with a very pleasant face, glasses and carefully groomed hair. His smile was disarming, and Jake felt himself liking the guy, even though he was usually repelled by these "green hippies", as he called them.

"World Army" he repeated, laughing. "Why in hell do you guys always come up with some kind of army thing, like you were going to war or something?"

"We are at war, Jake", Frank answered, "War against the corporate and government bureaucracy! You know as well as I do, if our system doesn't change, we're all going down the tube! What with CFC's, ozone depletion, global warming . . ."

Jake cut him off. "Sorry Frank, I can't get into this now," as he picked up his briefcase again and shifted his weight to his good leg, "I've got to meet somebody over at the hotel . . . maybe some other time."

"Sure Jake, any time! We'll probably see you over at the conference. If not here, then call me next time you're in L.A. . . . here's my card."

Jake thought about their meeting as he turned on to the freeway and headed north to the hotel. The man looked vaguely familiar, although he couldn't place him. Jake thought it was odd that the man knew him, even though he hadn't been in L.A. for several years.

He was astonished as he pulled up in front of the hotel. Another large group of picketers were gathered on the street, walking up and down the sidewalk, waving their signs as they chanted weird slogans to the beat of a ghetto-blaster. Reading a few of the signs, he saw that this group also belonged to WASTE, the World Army to Save The Environment.

After checking in, he made a quick phone call to an old friend, another conference delegate he knew was also registered in the hotel.

Chapter 3

STEFAN SCHILLER WAS MORE THAN an old friend, he was almost a father to Jake. A respected scientist specializing in physical chemistry relating to atmospheric studies, Stefan had watched Jake grow up since his early school days. He and his wife had known Jake's parents for many years, after a chance meeting in Germany. The Schillers were attending a conference in Cologne, during the time when Jake's father worked at the Canadian Embassy in Bonn. Jake's parents also attended the conference, standing in for a government representative who couldn't make it. The chance meeting developed into a life-long friendship, a life span cut short by yet another twist of fate.

A horrendous autobahn crash was a major turning point in Jake's life, killing his parents and leaving him close to death. The Schillers had watched over him for months in the hospital as he slowly recovered, followed by months of rehabilitation at their home in Germany.

Although he did not realize it at the time, this was the beginning of a whole new chapter in the story of Jake's life. Nestled in a little village near the Bavarian Alps in southern Germany, the Schiller's house was a quintessential Bavarian home. To Jake, everything was like a post-card; the odd steeples on the old churches with golden rococo interiors; the colourful market-place that came alive with music and food every week-end; the clean, picture-perfect homes with cascading flower boxes at every window and balcony; all framed with a background of snow covered peaks.

It was all so strange and new to Jake, arousing his curiosity enough to dull the pain of grief and his healing legs. Even after many difficult operations and months of restful healing, his left leg and knee never did return to normal. With expert physiotherapy and advice, Jake managed to learn how to walk again, helped along with his ever-present cane. The most frustrating part of this was that his knee was not dependable, failing when he least suspected.

Then the language offered another first challenge. Although Jake's childhood had exposed him regularly to German through his parents' friendship with the Schillers, his formal training was lacking. This early exposure went a long way to develop his sound and sentence structure recognition, as well as vocal skills not usually available to older students. The Schillers soon realized their young charge had an ear for languages, so they arranged private tutoring to hone his skills further. What started to be a summer recovery period turned into a three year stay, enough to pick up another degree at the university and a lot of experience in local field work.

By this time, Jake's German passed as native, able to handle not only excellent *Hoch Deutsch* or High German, but also the distinctive southern Bavarian dialect, and yet comfortably switch to a conversation with a local Austrian or a Swiss German in their own vernacular. His good ear, language skills and a few rough colloquialisms made any remaining accent undetectable.

He discovered he loved travelling, and wanted to develop his natural talent for languages further. When he returned to Canada, he signed up with the Armed Forces, knowing it was the only way he could afford to travel. After his months of convalescing and regular hiking in the Alps, he had thought he was in reasonable shape, but a few weeks of Basic Training humbled him, showing what he could really do with his body. Even with his bad leg, he learned how to compensate for this weakness by drawing upon inner strengths to redirect the loads and forces to his good side.

As it turned out, his best subjects were martial arts, computers and communications, the latter skill being the key to an assignment in Europe with the Canadian Foreign Affairs Department. The next three years honed those skills, as well as rigorous training in counter-intelligence and foreign languages. Although he was very good at the technical and intelligence parts of the job, he was not a diplomat, and he eventually realized he couldn't stomach the political duplicity and devious operations required for a career in the diplomatic service, so as soon as he received his discharge, he returned home.

His electronic skills and keen technical intuition quickly landed him a job with the environmental department of a local government office. Initially, he thought there was a great future in environmental regulatory work, but the political inertia and lack of concerted action in the Canadian environmental industry turned his stomach even quicker than the foreign service. Within a year, he had struck out on his own, realizing he would have to concentrate on the thriving U.S. and European market in order to survive. He found himself like many others in the business, often the 'starving artist', but at least independent.

Stefan Schiller waved from his table as Jake walked into the restaurant, leaning on his cane as he looked around. In his late sixties, Stefan had an oval, friendly face with a large nose and deep-set eyes covered with dark brows that contrasted with his white mane of hair. The two met in an emotional embrace, both men almost in tears. Backing off slightly, Stefan held Jake at arms length, looking him over.

"*Wie geht's* Jakob? How are you?" He shook his head, spotting the silver streaks in Jake's hair. "*Mein Gott*, you have changed, my boy! I have forgotten how long it has been."

"Almost eight years, Stefan . . . since Lori's funeral." The words rolled out easily enough now, eight years of healing soothing the pain of his wife's untimely death.

"Ah yes", the older man said, slowly stroking his beard, the memories saddening his face. "I am thinking that is a bad thing about these telephones, we take . . . accept a telephone conversation as a substitute for a real meeting." After years of international lecturing, Stefan still struggled with some of expression of ideas in English. "Now it is even worse, people now are satisfied with their mindless e-mail, or some other *Abfall* . . . garbage on the Internet." He paused, looking closely at Jake. "And how is your leg Jakob, I see you are still using your cane?"

Jake studied the wrinkled face of his old friend and mentor. He had always thought of Stefan Schiller as a kind of modern day Albert Schweitzer or Einstein, a typical German scientist, complete with long white hair. His dark piercing eyes peering over a pair of reading glasses completed the image, together with his small, perfectly groomed goatee.

" My leg is fine Stefan . . . or at least no worse. I depend on the cane to survive because when I least expect it, the leg folds up!" He sat down, motioning the older man to do the same. "Come on, Stefan" Jake said, "No doom and gloom . . . we have a lot of catching up to do! How are things with you?"

"*Gut*, Jakob, although my Christa tells me I am spending too much time on my research." His voice dropped slightly as he quickly glanced around the room. "I must tell you about this work, it is very important you know."

"How is Christa?" he asked, missing the second part of Stefan's comment.

"Good also. I know she does not talk to you, but I am sure she sends her love. She works in Frankfurt now, not far from where we used to visit in the *Alt Stadt,* the old town, here's one of her cards." He paused for moment of thought, then continued. "You know Jakob, she really never got over you. I think she thought you might come back after Lori's death . . . and I am thinking maybe you should have!"

As he pocketed the business card, Jake's thoughts were a world away, recalling the long days of recovery, helped along by Stefan's daughter, Christa. During his three year stay, they had become very close, but more like an older brother and younger sister. She was still in high school, while he had already graduated from university. At the time, he was too wrapped up in his own adventures, not aware of the feelings of others, especially those of a young high-school girl. He did not learn how deep her feelings were for him until years later when he married Lori. Stefan had come to the wedding, with excuses from Christa who apparently had sworn off men for life.

"That's a long time ago Stefan, I'm sure she has her own life now."

They both paused a moment to order their meal, Stefan selecting a full-bodied Franken wine for their dinner.

Jake laughed when he heard Stefan order the wine.

"Still going for the robust ones, Stefan."

"Of course! If you are going to drink wine, one must select one with body, some character. There is an old German saying; '*Frankenwein ist Krankenwein . . .*'"

"I know, I know . . . you taught me that years ago, remember?" Jake interrupted, "'Franconia wine is for when you're sick' . . . etc."

"That is correct . . . or to prevent sickness. I've always said, a good Franken or Wurttemberg for a full-bodied man's wine, not one of those ladies' wines from the Rhinepfalz or heaven forbid, the Mosel!" Jake laughed again as he recalled other conversations when he and Christa had argued their favourite wines with her father.

"This is California, Stefan, you're lucky you even found that on the wine list. You should try one of the wonderful wines they make here." Jake's suggestion was answered with a disgusted snort, typical of many European opinions of North American wine.

The waiter arrived, performing a brief wine opening ceremony for the two men. Stefan accepted the wine and they both had a toast to remember old times. Jake picked up the cork, inspected it in detail, then slipped it into his pocket.

"Still collecting corks Jakob?" Stefan asked, laughing.

"Not really Stefan, just the old habit I picked up years ago. I keep saying I'll do something with them some day . . . but I haven't so far."

Their conversation continued into the evening, covering subjects from atmospheric chemistry to favourite old Weinstubes along the Danube.

"So Jakob . . . tell me about your paper" Stephan asked. "What new and *wunderbar* theories have you come up with now?"

Jake spent the next hour immersed in the technical jargon of atmospheric chemistry and computer modelling, one of Stefan's favourite subjects as well. The two men were well suited, repeating a scene that Christa Schiller had seen many times, temporarily shutting her out of their lives completely.

"I'm sorry Stefan" Jake finally realized, "I've monopolized the entire evening. You mentioned something earlier about your work, what have you been up to lately? Isn't this the same project you were working on about eight years ago, and couldn't tell me anything about it then?"

The older man nodded, about to speak, then looked around quickly again, leaning a little closer to Jake. He started once more to say something, then changed his mind, looking at his watch.

"*Ach, Mein Gott,* look what time it is, and we have that conference tomorrow!" he said, quite loudly. "I must get to bed Jakob, I'm not as young as I used to be you know!"

Taken off-guard by Stefan's sudden puzzling behaviour, Jake agreed, signing the check and leaving the restaurant.

"I'll see you at the conference tomorrow Jakob." he said as he headed towards the elevator. Jake watched him go, wondering why their evening was cut so short. He walked across to the newsstand to pick up a newspaper, thinking about Stefan's comments. 'Must get to bed'? He had never seen Stefan give up this early before, and although it had been eight years since their last meeting, he was convinced Stefan had not really changed that much. It was usually Jake that had to cry 'tired' or 'enough' and head to bed early. He was still baffled as he left the elevator and walked to his room.

Chapter 4

THE WORLD AIR & WATER Association held their international conventions every two years. As host city for this year, Los Angeles was definitely a desired destination for many members world-wide. The variety of entertainment, the glitter of Hollywood, the sunny beaches and the family fun of Disneyland attracted a large number of delegates from countries all over the world. Business-wise, the history of air pollution problems in the huge city attracted many of these scientists who wanted to experience it first-hand. They also wanted to discuss with their Los Angeles colleagues the great steps that they had made in recent years to cut the pollution.

Leading scientists, meteorologists, chemists and government officials attended, the conscientious ones to present their latest research or theories, others just for the vacation, and yet others just to be seen in the company of such a distinguished group. For some countries, it was important to have their government leaders at least appear to be interested in environmental matters. Unfortunately, this type of international exposure also attracted a variety of self-interest groups and bizarre cults, both foreign and domestic.

For the first day of the conference, Jake decided to take the courtesy shuttle bus the hotel provided to the convention centre. After a quick breakfast, he met a group of other candidates in front of the hotel where they all squeezed into the mini-van and headed into the morning traffic. As the driver skilfully fought his way through the horrendous mess, he was glad he left his car back at the hotel. When the shuttle pulled up in front of the centre, he was even more pleased with his decision, as the entire street was a circus.

"Do you know what's going on?" he asked the driver when he saw flashing lights of police cars and fire trucks.

"Yeah, it just came in from dispatch . . . another nut call . . . a bomb threat or something . . . early this morning" the driver chomped out between handfuls of "cheezy" snacks. He shook his head, swearing at the jammed traffic in front of the entrance. Several delegates rose from their seats, hoping to get off the bus and walk in.

"Relax folks," he yelled to the back of the bus, "We'll be here for a while! Once it's clear, we can get into the parking area, but it doesn't look like anyone can go into the building yet." He continued to mumble profanities about " . . . goddamned A-rabs and Jews."

"Do they know who it was or what they wanted?" Jake asked.

"Two versions - one of course was killing as many American imperialists as possible, the other was they mentioned getting even with some of the middle east delegates here at the convention. Those guys have more old grudges and scores to settle, I don't know why they can't do it at home." He paused a moment as he swung the van into a gap in the traffic. "There will probably be more on the news, especially the TV station they phoned. No telling what those nuts will do . . . things are a lot different since 9/11, they don't give a damn how many other people they kill!"

"Unfortunately," added Jake, "That trait isn't necessarily held only by nuts from the middle east", referring to the Oklahoma bombing.

After almost an hour, they were finally off the little bus and heading into the building, their enthusiasm for the conference considerably dampened. Jake followed the group in, looking around in interest as he entered. The police had cordoned off a walkway to the entrance, holding back onlookers and protestors milling along the sidewalk, the large picket signs of the W.A.S.T.E. organization waving high. A smaller group was being held back by additional police, several swarthy looking men, holding pickets declaring them as the Arab Freedom Corps, seeking justice for their countrymen in the middle east and an end to American military involvement in that area.

He spotted Frank Haywood standing off to one side, almost distancing himself from his own group. Not wanting to get involved with him again, Jake looked away, limping quickly into the lobby, anxious to get to the first event, the opening ceremonies, already postponed two hours.

He didn't catch up to Stefan until they all broke for a late lunch, hundreds of delegates milling around in the lobby. Some delegates were attending the official luncheon ceremonies, which involved long, dragged out official speeches and flowery predictions about the future of the environment industry. The usual result and bottom line of the predictions was the fact that as long as everyone kept polluting, they all had a job.

"Stefan," he called to his friend, "I missed you at breakfast this morning."

"*Guten Morgen* . . . Good morning, Jakob" was the solemn reply. "I'm sorry, I had an early meeting, so I missed my breakfast and could not attend the opening ceremonies. I hear there was a little excitement around here this morning."

"Probably nothing new for LA" he replied. "Let's grab some lunch, I'm starved! I want to hear about your latest work, remember?"

Stefan looked around, his gaze hesitating briefly on a man sitting to one side of the lobby, reading a newspaper. Jake glanced at the man, at first thinking he was a delegate or associate of Stefan. Rather short, but built like a weight lifter, the man wore a generic "Visitor" name-tag, rather than the usual registrant or exhibitor tag most of the others wore. Something in the back of Jake's mind nagged at him, something familiar, not about the man, but his manner, his presence.

"I'm sorry Jakob, maybe later", he replied quietly. "I have another meeting." He turned and left, once again leaving a baffled Jake Prescott standing alone.

Jake turned to see again the man Stefan had glanced at. He had already folded his newspaper and was walking toward the entrance where Stefan had just left. Old habits from years past took over and Jake followed, watching the man closely to see what he was up to. From inside the lobby, he watched as Stefan got into a cab and headed out into the street. The other man walked briskly to the curb, waving at a car parked up the street. The car pulled up quickly, picking up its passenger, then pulled out into the traffic, following Stefan's cab.

Jake watched through the window of the lobby, puzzled by the events, worried about his good friend.

"I must be getting paranoid!" he thought, thinking of a dozen scenarios that could explain Stefan's behaviour.

He walked across the lobby, heading for a coffee shop to grab some lunch. As he sipped his coffee, he looked around at the now familiar room, replaying the scene the previous night when he had dinner with Stefan. As he reviewed his memories, he suddenly remembered where he had seen the stocky man before. While they ate dinner, the man had been sitting alone at a table in the corner. Jake hadn't paid much attention to him at the time, only to notice that Stefan had glanced over there a couple of times, especially just before they separated for the night.

A television set in the corner of the coffee shop was tuned to a local news broadcast. He watched, fascinated as they covered the bomb threat that morning, and the resultant traffic problems. The news anchors then switched to coverage on other groups that were using the WAWA convention as a base for their protests. They played a brief interview with Frank Haywood from WASTE, then others with GreenPeace, SPEC and the Sierra Club. Each group had its own slant, its own agenda to cover during the convention period. Jake listened to all of them, shaking his head as he wondered at what kind of direction these groups were under. They always wanted to do everything, right now! If only the answers were that simple! Many of the groups had demands or answers to problems that looked good on the surface, but had never been thought completely through. If most of them had their way, we would all be back to the horse and buggy days tomorrow, but then someone would be picketing the horses about the mess they leave on the road! Very few of the groups would select one, reasonable goal to achieve, then attack it. GreenPeace had come close a few times and had probably accomplished more than most, but the organization still attracted militants and nut-cases to its folds. Judging from the picketers Jake had seen at the airport yesterday, WASTE was even worse. He thought of their leader, Frank Haywood, and wondered again why the man seemed so familiar.

Chapter 5

ARRIVING BACK AT THE HOTEL late that day, Jake picked up a newspaper and headed for the bar. Exhausted from the day's events and technical overload, he just wanted to relax. He picked a small table near the back of the room, away from the noise of the game on TV. He ordered a double Demerara rum, then turned his attention to the newspaper. The front page was full of coverage of the WAWA convention, with special emphasis on the bomb-threat and related sidebars. He sipped his drink, scanning the articles with interest.

"Well, Mr. Prescott, you didn't quite make front page." the voice declared from behind the newspaper.

" I beg your par . . . " he began, dropping the newspaper slightly. A short, stocky man stood in front of him, the same man that he had seen earlier, following Stefan! A few locks of his dark, unruly hair flipped across his forehead, a perfect match for the heavy brows and smouldering eyes.

Jake felt uncomfortable as the man's gaze burned into him. Before he could reply, the man continued, "Check the next page . . . page two."

Slightly startled by the encounter, Jake turned the page. The photo jumped off the page at him. Spread out across the page was the shot of his arrival at the airport, the environmental protesters picketing in the background and him shaking hands with Frank

Haywood. The heading above the picture declared "Leading scientist welcomed by renegade!"

"What . . . Who the hell are you?" Jake asked, quickly recovering from the initial shock. "What's this all about, and why are you following Stefan Schiller?"

"Hold it Mr. Prescott, one question at a time" the man held up his hands. "The name's Butler, Paul Butler . . . N.S.O. in Washington. We're just covering the convention, working with the F.B.I. and local police, checking out some of these threats, as well as the actions and activities of a few people."

"N.S.O.?" Jake asked. "Who the hell is the N.S.O., and do you have some sort of I.D.?"

"National Security Organization" he replied impatiently, obviously more used to asking questions than answering them. Almost reluctantly, he showed Jake his identification. Even with his experience in the intelligence business, Jake was constantly amazed at the number of government security organizations and special police groups there were in the United States, with their love affair with 'alphabet soup' nomenclature. He often wondered how they kept them all straight.

"So what's this got to do with me, Mr. Butler?" he asked again, his distaste and impatience with government bureaucracy starting to show.

"Considering the events of this morning, I just wanted to ask what connections you have with the WASTE organization."

"Connections?" Jake asked, astounded. "I don't have any 'connections', as you call it. This photo was taken as I walked out of the terminal building, looking for my rental-car shuttle-bus. This Frank Haywood came up and introduced himself. That's all there is to it!"

"Didn't you know Frank Haywood before?"

"No . . . well, actually, I'm not sure. He did look familiar when I first saw him yesterday, but I've met a lot of people in this business. Why . . . do you know something I should remember?"

"Actually, Mr. Prescott, if you reach back a few years, you'll probably remember." Butler seemed to enjoy himself now, as long as he was controlling the interview. "Frank Haywood was one of the top men at the Federal Environment Department for several years . . . until the Millwood incident."

The Millwood incident! The name hit Jake like a blow to the stomach. Why are some of the most serious events in history called "incidents", like it was some minor quarrel down at the corner store? Millwood, like the infamous Love Canal, a victim of circumstance and stupidity . . . an innocent village that had the unfortunate luck to be located near an old hazardous waste disposal site, a site used for years with never a thought of what went into it, or what might happen after the containers rusted or rotted away. Nobody was concerned about either air or ground water contamination, the weird compounds formed as the leaking contents combined and drifted away. It was a disaster waiting to happen. When it did, it was aggravated by one of the biggest screw-ups and bureaucratic bungling in recent history, costing many lives, various forms of cancer and countless birth defects, probably for generations.

"Millwood . . . right!" he repeated to the agent, vaguely recalling Frank Haywood's involvement. "Didn't Frank fight that thing, try to expose some of the cover-ups? If I remember right, he got into a lot of trouble."

"Yeah, he fought it, but he was tilting at windmills, didn't have a chance against the FEDS. That's why he quit, turned to the press for help. He made a lot of enemies, but took a few down with him. Actually, during that fracas, he also made a lot of friends, allies in Washington. Now he spends all his energy fighting the establishment, working with nut-cases like this WASTE organization."

"Now I remember" Jake mumbled, recalling some of the unpleasant details that made headlines at the time. "But to get back to your original question, the answer is no . . . yesterday was the first time I had actually met Frank Haywood."

"Thank you Mr. Prescott, I figured that's all it was." he replied. "We have to ask, you understand." He paused, his dark eyes watching Jake closely. "You do a lot of travelling Mr. Prescott, are you familiar with the A.F.C., the Arab Freedom Corps?"

Surprised at the question, he felt his anger starting to rise. Jake had already developed a dislike for the man, but his arrogant, almost amateurish approach to questioning were really starting to grate on him.

"Other than what was mentioned on the television reports and in the paper today, again the answer is no, I am not familiar with the A.F.C.!"

"Thank you Mr. Prescott, have a nice day" he said as he turned to leave.

"Hold it, Mr. Butler," he called after him. "Could you explain to me again just how the hell the N.S.O. is involved? For beginners, how about my other question . . . why are you following Stefan Schiller?"

Paul Butler turned around reluctantly, a slight scowl on his face. He seemed to gather his thoughts before he answered Jake.

"I'm afraid Mr. Prescott, that I can't answer that question completely, as it is somewhat of a classified nature."

"Oh come on, Butler, don't give me that 'national security' bullshit!" Jake scolded, "Stefan's a well known environmental scientist, as well as an old friend of mine. What in hell is the U.S. government following a German scientist around these days for? He's not into rockets, warheads or nuclear devices. Are you afraid that if he got his way, some clean air might break out?"

Butler almost smiled at Jake's question, but did not answer it. "I realize that, Mr. Prescott, but please believe me, I cannot discuss the matter. I can set your mind at rest, however, we will not let any harm come to Mr. Schiller." With that he turned and left the room.

Jake sat there, stunned . . . "not let any harm come to him"? Who are they talking about, who would want to harm Stefan, he wondered? Butler's reply raised more questions than it had answered.

Chapter 6

THE DAY OF THE FIRST "incident" started like any other day. It was Wednesday, and the sun was already very hot when Jake went down for breakfast. The forecast on television that morning included a severe smog alert, asking people to use carpools or public transit wherever possible. In Los Angeles, a common term used for carpooling was "ride-sharing". As a student of languages, Jake was fascinated by the different words and expressions that were coined and used in the English language, words that many times were generated from the situations and conditions of a specific location.

He was scheduled to present his paper during the first hour in the morning, so he was a little nervous. By the time he headed down to the coffee shop downstairs, he was quite excited and anxious to get on with it. Spotting a couple of old friends and business associates sitting across the room, he quickly shuffled across the room to join them for breakfast.

"Looks like another hot one today, guys." he commented as he sat down, mentioning the smog forecast for the day. The local guys nodded, the heat, smog and related air quality problems a regular part of their day-to-day life.

"Brent" he asked, "I hear you guys got some federal funding for some new analyzers for studies up in north LA." He was talking to Brent Willis, one of the top technical people in the South Coast Air Quality Management District.

"Yeah, I'm sure you heard," Brent laughed, "We bought a whole truckload of your analyzers! We've been working around the clock to get them hooked into the data grid before this convention."

"Whoa!" cried Jake. "Not my analyzers . . . I sold out, remember? If you guys are getting federal money now, maybe I should've hung on to the company."

"O.K., O.K., you know what I mean Jake. Actually, this is the first time we have got this much federal money. You know how the SCAQMD works, it's all funded from permit fees, licenses and fines. All I know is the FEDs came to our boss one day and said they were doing some kind of study, and wanted extra monitoring stations around the north end . . . up near Burbank, Glendale, Pasadena way, and were willing to pay for them all. The only condition was that we install them, maintain them, and we could keep them later."

"Wow, that's great!" Jake said, "That's the area I wanted to try out my new computer model. It deals with complex terrain, hilly territory. With the extra stations in place, the results of my model can be validated that much quicker. Remind me before the end of the convention Brent, I'd like to get a copy of some of your topographic grid data that you use for that area. We can load it into our system to try our latest version."

The breakfast continued with environmental war-stories and ended with some rude remarks and a quick shuffle out the door for one of the group who wanted to light up a cigarette after his coffee.

The first reports were sporadic, rumours picked up during the break between sessions. At the half-way point during the next session, most presentations were interrupted to bring the news bulletins about the highway disaster further north. Isolated reports were incomplete, both the exact location and the nature of the problem kept changing, from just a massive traffic jam to large numbers of dead. By this time, most of the delegates had lost interest in the technical presentations, and eventually the meetings were cancelled for the afternoon.

Jake immediately sought out his luncheon partners, knowing they would be some of the first to find out the truth, especially if any of them lived in that direction. He found Brent Willis and Linda Seymour from Seymour Labs huddled together in the hall. Brent was talking on his cell phone, his face pale. Jake approached them, anxious to hear the real story.

"Jesus!" Brent exclaimed as he pocketed his phone. "It's worse than I thought!" He looked around quickly, not wanting to spread the bad news. "They're just getting to the site now with rescue teams. They figure at least twenty or thirty dead . . . no obvious reason! Some of the press are already calling it a nerve gas attack like in Japan."

"I'm phoning Ed to see if he's heard anything on this." Linda said, pulling her own phone from her purse. "We often get called in for analysis work on things like this."

The two men watched Linda Seymour a little too attentively as she leaned against the wall slightly, casually talking on the phone, her lithe body twisted in a seductive pose. She noticed them watching, quickly straightening up, blushing slightly. In addition to a gorgeous body, Linda had one of the best brains in the business. She and her brother Ed ran Seymour Labs Inc., one of the area's most respected analytical laboratories. Jake had used their services several times during some joint projects in California.

Linda joined them again, her face grim. "Ed says it's getting worse, more dead, injured. They still haven't asked us for any sampling or analysis help. He asked if CDC was being called in from Atlanta, just in case it's a virus or something, but nobody is talking. They're really tight on this one!"

"Where did it happen?" asked Jake, "If they were going to attack someone, you'd think it would be in a more likely place like a hotel or the convention center, not out on the highway somewhere." He paused a moment, then continued as he remembered the first day's events. "Remember the other day, the bomb threat? If they were after us environmental types, it would have been here!" The thought was not comforting to any of them.

Brent continued, explaining the location as reported to him. "It's somewhere up near the hills, almost to Glendale or Pasadena somewhere." His words rang a bell in Jake's mind. They were just talking at lunch time about the extra monitoring stations that had been set up in that area.

"How were the smog levels?" he asked Brent. "Do you think the new stations will show anything?"

"I doubt it, those stations aren't set up to monitor nerve gas or anything weird, just the usual NOx, SOx, CO, Ozone and particulate, etc. They will show all the components that contribute to photochemical smog, along with temperature, wind etc."

"Good, let's go take a look" Jake suggested, heading for the door.

"Hey, hold it Jake!" Brent yelled after him. "First, you're not going to get anywhere near that area right now! The police and emergency response teams will be there half the night, maybe longer. Second, the traffic will be so bad out there that you wouldn't get to first base." He paused a moment, a large smile forming on his face.

"What . . . do you have a idea?" Linda asked.

"Yeah, I sure do. Jake, do you have your lap-top with you?"

"Sure, it's right here, what have you got in mind?"

"All those stations are logging data, and are polled constantly from headquarters, down-loading the data into the main-frame. We can tie into any station via modem and down-load the data for this afternoon. We do it all the time to check the system."

Intrigued by the idea, Jake agreed.

"O.K., let's all go back to my hotel, this place is a little too public. We can set up in my room."

Before long, they were back in Jake's room, setting up the computer. While they worked, Linda turned on the television to get the latest reports. They watched, mesmerized by the broadcast as the news chopper flew over the site. Cars appeared bunched together in one small area, some jammed together, some up on the curb. The location was a low section of the highway, where it crossed a little coulee just before joining the main freeway. Medical teams had already taken away most of the injured, surprisingly few considering the situation. The TV crews interviewed one man as he was being carried to the ambulance. From what he told them, the cars had already stopped on the highway when he arrived, so most of the injuries were not caused by an accident, but related to heat stroke and respiratory problems. They were now removing bodies from the site. Some of the rescue crews were not taking any chances, covered in bulky suits, air-packs and sealed face masks.

"That's funny" Linda commented, "Look . . . why are some suited, and others not? And how come that guy they interviewed was O.K.? Remember, they carried him from the back of the jam right through that mess to the ambulance." They all watched closely, unable to explain the discrepancies. "By the way, I just called Ed again, he still hasn't heard a thing from anyone on site, so obviously they're doing their own lab work."

By this time, Jake had finished the computer set-up, connecting through the hotel's wireless high speed WI-FI internet access. He quickly configured the system, accessing the SCAQMD website and into the first remote station. After he heard the digital-buzz of the computer handshake, the connection was made and they were then asked for a password. Brent gave them the password, swearing them to secrecy not to reveal it.

"If that gets out, we'll have every nut and hacker in the country trying to log into the system!"

As the data started pouring in, Jake configured the system to log all incoming data to a file, so they could browse through it later if necessary. They quickly scanned the rows of numbers, looking for extremes, high peaks, or other anomalies.

"If anything, most of the numbers look low, especially NOx" observed Brent. "Ozone is high, but not as bad as some I've seen . . . probably because the NOx is so low." The NOx, or oxides of nitrogen, was one of the by-products of combustion, in this case, the automobile engines. With the help of the ultra-violet rays in the sunshine, the oxides of nitrogen contributed to the production of ground level ozone, which in turn helped to oxidize more nitric oxide, hydrocarbons, etc., continuing in a chain reaction that eventually produced the photo-chemical soup called smog, contributed to acid rain, and who knows what other noxious products.

They disconnected, moving to the second station. Before long, they had down-loaded the afternoon's data from all of the relevant monitors.

"Well," said Brent, stretching himself upright. "It's a little early to say . . . you know, until we've graphed this and looked at it in detail, but initially, I don't see anything significant there at all. Like I said, if anything, the numbers are a little low for this kind of day."

"Maybe that is significant" suggested Jake, his mind trying to find a pattern. "Well, I've got the data, and I can graph it later to see if there are any trends we couldn't see." He opened his email program and sent himself a note with the data files attached. Out of habit, he then copied the files to a little backup memory stick he carried around his neck just before he closed up his computer. Flipping the memory stick back in his shirt, he said "Let's go have some dinner, and we can plan our next step."

Chapter 7

THE SPECULATION CONTINUED THROUGH DINNER, each of them offering wild theories as to what group was responsible for the disaster. Speculation ran from the AFC, PLO, IRA, Red Brigade, Iraqi's and other paramilitary organizations with Al Qaeda at the forefront, to outlandish suggestions of religious cults, a renegade remnant of the KGB or environmental activists like the WASTE organization, or possibly a group similar to the one in the Japan nerve gas attacks.

Linda Seymour sat quiet most of the time, not contributing much to the conversation. During a pause in the conversation she finally opened up.

"Air samples" she said quietly, her eyes wide. "Air samples."

"Air samples?" Brent repeated, "What do you mean? Our stations continuously sample the air, we've already got that data."

"No, don't you see?" she replied, "Ed said nobody had called, so he assumed they were doing their own samples. If so, then how come none of those guys were taking air samples at the site, did you see anyone doing that? If there was some sort of poison, they should have been taking air samples to analyze later."

"You're right!" they agreed, not able to offer an explanation. "Well, maybe we can go out and take some samples, check them out ourselves."

Brent answered, killing their enthusiasm. "No, like I said earlier, that area will be locked up for a while, . . . besides, with all that activity, helicopters, etc., there won't be a trace left for analysis."

"The bodies!" Jake shouted. "If there is something there, it will still be in or around the bodies, probably in their lungs."

"Great!" Brent answered, "And who the hell is going to go sample some bodies?" he asked. One look at the others told him immediately who would be doing it. "Oh no, you guys, not me!"

"But you're the obvious one Brent. You have the authority, you can gain access to the victims. From the news reports, they are all over at the hospital, just down the freeway from here!"

"You get us in there," Linda injected, "and I'll take the samples. I took a couple of years of pre-med at college, so I'm used to working on bodies." The two men stared at her, amazed, yet glad of the reprieve. "Let's go, we'll stop by the lab to pick up some bombs, maybe some bags and a pump. We usually have a stock of clean ones ready, and I think we even have a new batch scheduled for some PAH tests."

"Bombs?" they both asked, gaping at Linda.

"Sorry guys," she laughed, "sample bottles," she explained. "Most labs refer to the glass sample cylinders as 'bombs'."

Within minutes, they were on the way, practising the routine they would use at the hospital. Stopping by the lab, Linda picked up some canisters, bags and evacuated cylinders for samples, as well as some lab coats for them to wear. By the time they entered the hospital, they each looked quite official, with their convention I.D. badges pinned on their white lab coats.

"I must be crazy" Brent mumbled as they entered the hospital, "to let you guys talk me into this!"

"Come on, Brent, it's not like you were pulling off some sort of crime! After all, air quality sampling is your job, that's all you're trying to do."

They were not prepared for the scene that greeted them. It was a circus, a melange of concerned family and friends of the victims, reporters, staff and police. The noise level was high, an overall clamour of hundreds of voices punctuated by occasional screams of grief and mourning from relatives. The stale odour of hot, sweaty bodies in close proximity permeated the hall, mingling with the antiseptic smell of an emergency room. The worst of the surviving victims were isolated in intensive care, while those in better shape were sprawled out on beds lining the halls, some still sucking precious oxygen from a mask. Smaller groups of friends and families stood in remote corners, weeping softly, their worst fears realized. Policemen were still interviewing victims as they recovered enough to talk, photographers hovering for that classic shot.

Taking advantage of the confusion, they mingled with the staff and headed down to the morgue. Linda's knowledge of the hospital procedures and Brent's SCAQMD identification helped their progress. A few quick inquiries got them the answers they needed, and before long they were directed into a large, cold room, temporarily overloaded with carts and beds holding more bodies than the morgue was designed to handle.

"Are we sure we want to do this?" asked Brent, looking a little pale. "What if the residual poison or whatever is still dangerous, or even fatal?"

"Well then," responded Jake, not feeling too confident himself. "We'll soon find out . . . I'm just hoping there is enough left for us to measure, or at least analyze to find out what it is."

The traffic in and out of the room was now minimal, but they wasted no time, wanting to get out before anyone asked any embarrassing questions. Linda went quickly to work, while Jake helped her. All of the bodies were bagged, trapping any local gases inside, as well as slowing down any further loss from the body itself. The started by unzipping some bags, bracing themselves for the morbid task ahead. By holding or shaking clothing, pushing rib cages, they extracted air from both the lungs and the clothing of the victims. Using a small battery powered air pump, they filled a couple of glass cylinders and some special plastic bags with a variety of air samples. Brent gladly stayed to one side, keeping guard by the door.

"Look at this," Linda observed, "cyanosis . . . blue lips, indicating circulation or blood problems. And look, Jake, at their mouths and noses, a lot of bleeding, probably from the lungs." She paused a moment, staring at the bodies. "These people did not die easy!" Jake agreed, stifling a wave of nausea that swept through him.

Slipping the final sample bottle into a small carrying case, Linda straightened up. "O.K. guys, let's get the hell out of here!"

Just as they were leaving the room, they spotted a group of three doctors and two men in business suits walking down the hall towards them. They quickly turned their backs and huddled off to one side, apparently comparing notes on a clip board. Jake held his breathe as he recognized one of the men . . . it was Paul Butler from the N.S.O.! The man had glanced at him, but Jake was hoping he had not recognized him. As the group went into the room, the three conspirators immediately headed down the hall to the exit.

"Mr. Prescott?" Jake heard the voice behind him.

Without turning, he said quietly "You two head back to the car, I'll try to stall this guy. He's from Washington, some security organization." He quickly added "And keep those samples out of sight!"

Jake turned, facing Paul Butler as he caught up to him. "Well, Hello, Mr, Butler. What can I do for you?"

The agent stopped to talk, quickly glancing around for Jake's associates. "What are you doing here?" he asked, visibly agitated. "This area is off limits. That means no visitors, no press, and certainly no aliens from Canada!"

Jake had always cringed at the Americans' use of the word "alien" to describe any foreigner in their country. He thought it always made him feel like he was from outer space or somewhere. He thought quickly, remembering some of the cover stories they had thought up on the way over.

"I realize that Mr. Butler, but I managed to convince an old friend of mine to let me in to check one of the bodies." His voice remained calm, his old training and self-control taking over. "I thought one of the victims might have been an old business associate of mine. Luckily, it wasn't." He held his breath, hoping he would buy it.

Hesitant at first, Butler finally relented, his associates were calling him from the room. "I think we should talk again, Mr, Prescott." he added, studying Jake's lab-coat as they separated.

Jake gripped his cane firmly as he quickly walked out of the hospital, visibly relieved. Meeting the others in the parking lot, they wanted to know about Paul. Jake briefly explained his earlier meeting with the man, not mentioning the incident with Stefan. Stefan! Wrapped up in the conference, then the highway disaster, he couldn't recall seeing the scientist all day. Making a mental note to call him as soon as he got back to the hotel, Jake turned his attention back to his friends. Looking at their lab-coats, he suddenly realized what Butler had noticed inside the hospital.

"Damn . . . the logo!" he hissed. The others turned, surprised.

"What are you talking about," they asked, puzzled.

"Your logo and name on the lab-coats, right beside our name-tags, I'm sure Butler noticed . . . that's what he was looking at!"

"Well, we'll soon know." was the response as they pulled into the parking lot of Seymour Labs, Inc.

Seymour Labs was a very successful sampling and laboratory analysis company the two siblings had started right after they left college. Initially filling a niche requirement in the market, they succeeded, eventually expanding into the general air and water quality analysis market.

Linda quickly checked their equipment, wanting to run the sample as quickly as possible.

"Damn!" they heard her say, reading a note on the desk. "It's from Ed, the GC's down until tomorrow," referring to the large analyzer they were going to use. "He's picking up some parts for it in the morning."

Disappointed, they all agreed to pack it up for the night. Before they left, Linda put the samples in the large refrigerated cabinet used for sample storage.

"Linda, just before you put them away, can you transfer a portion of the samples to a couple of smaller Tedlar bags. I think I'll take some back to our lab, just in case nothing shows up here. I know . . . it's not the best field sampling protocol, the sample will probably change between now and the time they get to the lab, but I'd like to have some all the same."

Linda agreed, knowing Jake's facility was a chemist's dream, equipped with gadgets she could only dream of. Portions of the sample were then transferred to some small bags, made of a special inert plastic, widely used for air samples requiring super clean care and minimal contamination. He then slipped them into a plastic shopping bag, which he would later put into his brief-case for carrying home.

Back in his room, he called Stefan, but there was no answer. He packed the samples in his brief-case beside the lap-top computer. He felt the side of the small computer, thinking how odd it was that it was still warm, as they hadn't used it for several hours.

Chapter 8

THE CONSTANT RINGING CONTINUED, HE fought to avoid it. He tried covering his head again, but suddenly realized it was his telephone ringing.

"Hello . . . " he mumbled, picking up the receiver. After laying awake half the night trying to make sense of it all, he had finally dropped off into a deep sleep. Peering at the little clock-radio beside the bed, he was surprised to see it was after eight, a rare occurrence for him.

"Jake, they're gone! All of them, gone!" he recognized Linda Seymour's voice.

"Wha . . . what are you talking about?"

"The samples! That Butler guy showed up early this morning with a couple of his 'associates', confiscated all our samples, "for national security reasons" they said." She paused a moment. "Who is this guy Jake, what the hell is going on?"

Jake's mind was now up to full speed. "Does he know about the samples I have?" he asked.

"No, he never asked, and I didn't volunteer. What'll I do?"

"Good, Thanks Linda. Don't do anything, you'd better stay out of it. If he asks any further questions, just tell him the truth, that we were curious, etc. He'll probably buy that. Just don't let on that I have other samples."

"O.K., Jake" was the tentative reply.

"Say Hi to Ed," he added as he swung out of bed. "I'm heading out today, I'll see you both next time I'm down here, probably very soon."

He headed quickly for the shower, formulating his moves for the rest of the day. He couldn't believe they had already been to the lab and confiscated the samples. This group has a real agenda, he thought. He admired their thoroughness, indicating a very high degree of organization and control, but on the other hand he hated any type of government organization that goes off half-cocked, almost to the point of harassing citizens, when they should be out somewhere "catching the bad guys". The problem was, who were the bad guys?

He had just finished dressing when the phone rang again. It was Brent.

"Good, I'm glad I caught you!" he said, a note of relief in his voice. "I'm downstairs, need to talk to you. Are you heading to the convention or do you have time for a coffee?"

"Sure Brent, want to come up first?"

"Thanks, but no. I'd feel better if you came down, I think we have a problem."

"Oh . . . O.K." he answered, noting the urgency in Brent's voice. "I haven't had breakfast yet, so I'll be right down." Something was definitely bothering Brent, something he didn't want to discuss over the phone or in Jake's room.

As he arrived at the coffee shop, Brent waved him over to his table. A frown creased his forehead as he started to speak, glancing around the room.

"I just talked to Linda, she said she already told you about the samples."

"Yeah, I just talked to her before you called, is that what's bothering you?"

"No . . . yes . . . shit! I don't know Jake, those spooks from Washington give me the creeps! The samples aren't the only thing . . . they arrived at headquarters this morning with a federal warrant and confiscated all our data for yesterday afternoon, then erased it from the main-frame! They're smart, I'll give you that. Then they checked our system and erased all of our back-up files as well."

Jake listened, astonished and baffled by these actions. These were the actions of a desperate, almost paranoid mind.

"It's a good thing you have that data in your computer Jake, we can take a look, see what the hell everyone is getting so paranoid about!"

"The data!" Jake hissed, leaping to his feet, heading for the door. "Stay there, I'll be right back!" he yelled over his shoulder as he left.

He headed straight for the stairs, not wanting to wait for the elevator. Cursing his bad leg, he tried to take full advantage of his cane to assist him. He took the stairs two at a time, he was on his floor in less than a minute, hobbling down the hall to his room. He pulled the laptop out of his briefcase and turned it on, anxiously waiting for it to boot up. At last the system settled down, and he switched to the communications program directory they had used yesterday. Scanning the computer's contents, he could not find the files. He tried a search with no results. Desperate, he switched to DOS mode, typing in DIR.DAT, he watched as the system told him what data files were in the directory. Nothing! He knew what happened, but tried again, this time typing in just DIR. The system again listed the files, this time everything in the directory. He watched as the file listing scrolled up the screen . . . nothing but the usual program files, all data files had been deleted!

"Jesus, they worked fast," he mumbled, trying to figure out when somebody could have worked on his computer. Then he remembered, the computer was quite warm when he arrived back in his room last night . . . they must have been in his room just before he returned. They? Who in hell is "they".

He quickly called up another program, a special utility program he used for recovering lost or deleted files. As he called up the commands, the system responded with "file not found" and other cryptic messages.

"These guys are good" he thought, "they've thought of everything." His mind jumped back to a night in Berlin, when he was on an assignment with a senior field operative. He rarely did field work, this time along strictly for his communications and computer abilities, doing exactly what had just been done to him, extracting data files and eliminating all trace of them! The question remained, what the hell is going on? He patted the front of his shirt, feeling the small memory stick on the cord around his neck, his back-up from the previous evening. "Not quite everything," he thought.

Returning to the coffee shop, Brent looked at him, a question mark over his head.

"Just as I feared, they've been into my computer, erased all the files."

"God Jake, what the hell is going on? I don't like this, why are they getting rid of all this data, what are they doing?"

"I don't know," Jake answered, specifically not mentioning his back-up. He figured the less Brent knew at this point, the healthier it might be for him. "They're your government Brent, you should know more about how they operate than I. Considering your position, it might be better if you just back off, let the authorities work on their investigation."

"Investigation?" he blurted, disgusted. "How in hell can you investigate something like this if you go around confiscating or destroying the evidence? Besides, if anyone wants to interpret that data, they will have to call us in anyway. I don't see the point!"

Jake couldn't see the point either, but he knew he wanted to get the hell out of town, probably back home where he could analyze both the samples and the data.

"Look Brent, I've got to go, I wanted to talk to Stefan before he finishes at the conference. I'll call you next week, I want to keep in touch about this thing." He got up from the table, trying to act casual and unconcerned. It worked, Brent seemed to relax, agreeing to call him the following week.

After Brent had left, he shuffled quickly over to a house phone and called Stefan's room. A strange voice answered, so he quickly hung up. He then checked with the desk, asking about Stefan, explaining he was an old friend and associate.

"Of course Mr. Prescott," the efficient little desk clerk answered. "As I told the other gentlemen, Mr. Schiller checked out late last night. He just phoned in, asking that his bags be sent to Lufthansa at the airport." He paused, pleased with his own importance. "Of course we followed his instructions, as I told the gentlemen who just came by now . . . they asked the same questions."

"You say these men are here now?"

"Why yes, of course. They had some official from immigration or some other government department, said Mr. Schiller was only on a limited visa and had to return to Germany immediately."

Jake almost laughed at the pompous little ass. "Limited visa?" What in hell was that, and who were these guys in Stefan's room now? Of course he knew who they were, and he didn't feel like getting involved with them at this point, otherwise he might find himself with a "limited visa".

He settled his account and told the man he would be checking out later that day, after the conference. He specifically repeated it, suggesting if anyone asked for him, to leave a message or drop by later to see him.

He then headed for his room, anxious to get out as fast as he could. He took the stairs again, carefully entering the hallway from the stairwell. The hall was clear, and he was in his room in seconds. Most of his gear was already packed, so he just closed up his bag and headed for the door. Again he paused, checking the hall. He quickly walked down the other stairwell that headed to the rear of the building and the parking lot. Throwing his gear in the car, he headed out into the traffic, heading for the 110 Freeway south. He didn't relax until he was well on his way, checking his rear view mirror every few minutes. He knew that if they wanted, they could be following him and he wouldn't know it, but he felt more comfortable not being able to see anyone.

Soon, he turned on to the 405 Freeway, heading south to LAX airport. He kept running the problem over in his head, trying to figure out who was involved, what was their motive, why the government interference? The local news coverage provided little more information. The final death toll now stood at 43, with only a few left on the critical list. Most of the other injured were either still recovering or had already been released. Interviews with local officials were useless, the usual rambling about nothing, no responsibility taken for anything.

He turned off the 405, turning back and along Century Boulevard toward the rental car lot. He wasn't prepared for what happened next. Just as he was going to turn into the lot, he spotted Paul Butler and his buddy on the lot, talking to the rental return agent. Stunned, he corrected his turn and continued without pausing, his hands sweating on the wheel, wondering what he was going to do next.

Chapter 9

BY THE TIME HE REACHED the end of the block, Jake had decided what to do. Butler's actions had surprised him, but he still couldn't figure out why, or even if the N.S.O. was after him. There was the possibility they were looking for somebody else, but somehow Jake knew the men back in the hotel had already checked his room and radioed ahead to Butler. He then wondered about Stefan, did they already have him and why, or had he really left the country as the clerk said? Knowing Stefan, he was probably one step ahead of Butler all the way, but what triggered the chase, why did they want him?

He swung around back on to the 405, the San Diego Freeway heading south. Accelerating out into the left lane, he matched speeds with the faster cars, both to blend into the traffic, and put as much distance as possible between himself and those determined government agents. Knowing a little about the business, he knew that time was important . . . as long as they thought he was still in the area, or heading to the airport, their efforts would not be too serious. His only priority now was to get both the data and the air samples back to his lab to be studied.

Familiar landmarks passed by as he thought how many times he had driven this route, on his way to some of the high tech firms down in the Irvine area. As he passed the signs leading to Long Beach, he was tempted to turn off to the Long Beach Airport, but he felt they might have someone watching that one as well. Now paranoid about someone following him, he tried changing lanes a few times, as if he were planning to exit the freeway. He then watched the cars behind him, to see if anyone matched his actions. A white sedan had stayed behind him for the last twenty minutes, and appeared to change lanes when he did.

At Westminster, he took the first exit, swinging off the main highway, turning into a shopping centre parking lot. The white sedan kept going down the freeway, making no attempt to leave. He waited a short time, watching cars that were coming and going into the lot. Satisfied, he started rolling again, turning back to enter the freeway again, heading south. Nobody else appeared to be following him as he accelerated back into the fast lane.

He stuck to his original plan, continuing south past Costa Mesa, finally turning off on Newport Boulevard and headed over to the Orange County "John Wayne" Airport.

Still cautious, he parked the rental car far out in the parking lot, planning on sending the keys and paperwork back to LAX later. The extra time and pickup charges were unimportant at this time. Recalling some of his basic training, lesson one on "how to disappear", he quickly packed his jacket into his carry-on bag along with his tie, opened his shirt and rolled up his sleeves for a more casual appearance. Slightly rumpled hair and sunglasses completed his "disguise", a meagre attempt to look less like a concerned businessman, and more like a casual traveller.

He approached the terminal building with caution, pausing beneath the large statue of John Wayne near the entrance. He watched other people, especially their eyes. He could tell if they were really catching a plane, or if they were there looking for somebody else. He kept moving, not wanting to attract attention to himself. His first stop was an automatic teller machine, where he withdrew several hundred dollars for his plane fares. He knew that it could be traced as well, but again, he calculated he had some time on his side, as it should be hours before they even checked it.

Limping slightly, his leg started to bother him, aggravated by his desire to move a little faster. Moving to the nearest airline counter, he checked the departure times to San Jose, a regular commuter flight.

"Can I help you Sir?" the perky little clerk asked.

Sweating slightly, he tried to control his nervousness as he asked for a ticket to San Jose.

"One way or return, Mr . . . ?"

Almost caught off guard, he quickly recovered "Prescott . . . Jake Prescott," using his real name. "Just one way today, thank you," acting as if he did this often. With all the new Homeland Security rules in place, he could no longer use false names like they used to do years before. He could only hope that his name had not been flagged in the computer system yet. She told him the price and he handed her the cash.

"You can make this flight if you hurry, Mr. Prescott. You just have carry-on luggage, so head right over to that gate now." She handed him his boarding pass and he was on his way through the final security gate. He glanced around one last time before he boarded the aircraft, almost convinced he would see Paul Butler walking towards him.

The flight was short and uneventful, but it put some distance and confusion between him and his pursuers. Arriving in San Jose, he headed for a phone booth and called the office back in Vancouver. Alan Cook, his lab manager, answered.

"Jake, where the bloody hell are you, mate? We've had all kinds of calls for you! They said you are wanted for questioning in LA."

"Wanted for questioning? Who called, who told you that?"

"Ed Seymour called, said there were some federal blokes hanging around the lab again, looking for you. They had already checked with the hotel, but you had checked out." He stopped, wondering how to word the next question. "Are you in some kind of trouble Jake, anything you can tell me?"

Jake laughed, thinking how ridiculous this whole thing had become.

"No, I'm not in any trouble, Al." He stopped, thinking about what he had just said. "Not real trouble, just fighting government bureaucracy again, as usual. You know, I just can't keep my mouth shut!"

"Oh! Anything you want me to tell them, anything you want me to do?"

"Don't tell anyone anything, they probably have our telephone bugged already. Check my email and see if some data files came through, maybe they've even stopped that. In the meantime, just keep the GCMS warmed up and calibrated. I'll be back later today, so plan on burning a little midnight oil tonight." The GCMS was a Gas Chromatograph Mass Spectrometer, their number one tool for laboratory analysis.

He hung up the phone, knowing for sure he had to keep moving, as those federal types were seriously after him.

He repeated his earlier moves, this time catching a flight to Portland, then another that continued on to Vancouver, Canada. The last flight was the tricky one as it was an international flight and when he handed over his passport for scanning, he fully expected alarms to go off. He was worried about clearing customs in Vancouver, thinking about the air samples in his brief case. He piled some technical brochures on top of the bags, making them look like additional samples from the trade show part of the convention.

At the Vancouver Airport, he forced himself to relax as he walked from the plane into the new international terminal. His limp and slower walk became a good reason to isolate himself as the remainder of the passengers moved ahead of him. As he continued through the terminal, he glanced down on to the new Vancouver Aquarium display area of the airport, scanning the faces of the people walking through the area. Soon, he approached the Canada Customs clearance area. He handed the agent his passport, trying to act casual. Customs agents seem to have a built-in radar for detecting someone who is trying to act casual.

"Anything to declare, Mr. Prescott?" he asked, watching his face closely.

"No, nothing," he replied, "I've just been to a air pollution convention in LA." He was hoping the authorities had not contacted Canada Customs about him, to hold him at the airport.

"Good place for it," he joked, then added "bring back any sales literature, samples?"

"Well, not really," he replied, knowing they were looking for sales people who loaded up on brochures and sales literature while they were away. "Just a few brochures on some new equipment, and a couple of samples of new style plastic bags." Truth is always the best defence, he thought. By declaring the bags, at least they would not be confiscated if they checked his bag. He needn't have worried, as he was passed on through without inspection.

"God, I'm getting paranoid!" he thought, as he had been reviewing a dozen scenarios in his mind where the N.S.O. were on his tail, ready to arrest him at the slightest chance. A slight twinge of panic hit him as he thought maybe he had cleared customs too easy . . . maybe they wanted him to get away . . . but then maybe they really didn't give a damn and he was dreaming all of this up. He wasn't familiar with the N.S.O. and he did not even know if they had the authority to arrest him.

As he walked out of the terminal building, he gulped in a few breaths of fresh, cool air, marvelling at the difference between Los Angeles and Vancouver. Normally, Vancouver had the advantage of enough cooling in the evenings to develop brisk sea-breezes to help clear the air. It was only during certain summer periods when the breezes stopped that the city was faced with a problem similar to Los Angeles. When an inversion, or warm air layer developed over the city, it acted like a cap or lid over the area, trapping the normal pollutants, car exhausts, and industrial emissions underneath. These emissions would continue to build up, sometimes for a week or more, getting progressively worse as each day passed. The average Vancouverite usually thought of his city as a clean one, but during recent years, Vancouver had, at times, become worse than Los Angeles on a per capita basis.

He hopped on the next shuttle bus to the parking lot to pick up his car. Within a half hour of arriving, he drove into his parking spot in front of Prescott Technologies, Jake's proud realization of a dream. The large, white building stood out among the others in the light industrial park complex, its mirrored glass facade reflecting the surrounding scenery, from the snow-capped mountains in the distance, down to the river and low farm lands nearby. As soon as he walked into the lab, the familiar surroundings immediately eased the tension of the past two, very hectic days.

"Well, I say . . . look who's here" Alan Cook's Australian accent greeted him. "Should we lock the door and turn out the lights, or are those Yank blokes that close on your tail?" he laughed. Peter Wong, his computer expert stood back, also laughing at his good friend and boss.

"Don't even joke about it Al", Jake returned. "Those idiots are like a bad dream, they keep coming back! Problem is, I can't figure why they are after me." He continued straight into the lab, opening his briefcase on a side counter.

"Here," he said to Alan. "I think this is what all the fuss is about! Run some of this through the GC and whatever else you need to find out what the hell is in there." He explained to both of them the events of the past couple of days, and how they got the samples. "I'm afraid we broke every rule in the book, Alan, as far as the sample and storage protocol for those samples. I just hope there's something there you can figure out."

"O.K. Jake, I'll have a gander," Alan said as he took the samples. "You're lucky to be here, you could have been included with those poor buggers that died on the freeway!"

"Yeah, or caught up in the bureaucratic nightmare of Washington, trying to explain your actions to a grand jury!" Peter added.

As Jake finished his account of his visit to Los Angeles, he suddenly remembered the data.

"Did you check my email, the data files?"

"Sorry Jake, nothing there. They must have access to that stuff and deleted it. I can't believe they want that stuff so bad!"

"Well they're not infallible," Jake said as he pulled the cord out from his shirt and unclipped the little memory stick from its cord and handed it to his colleague. "Here Peter, this one's for you. You'll recognize the format, you should be able to bring it into a standard spreadsheet so we can look it over. Play with it for a while, make some graphs, see what you come up with. I'm beat, and my leg's aching something fierce, so I'm going home to crash for a few hours! I'll see you guys here in the morning." As he left the two men he felt confident they would have some answers for him by the next day, but something else was nagging at him, another missing piece of the puzzle he needed.

Chapter 10

THEY ALL MET FOR BREAKFAST the following morning, a regular procedure they had found to be both enjoyable and productive. When Jake had the building constructed, he specified certain aesthetic and functional features built in. The one they all enjoyed the most was a spacious "lunch room" or lounge area, facing east to accept the morning sunlight as they had their morning meeting sessions. This morning was spectacular, as the sun rose over the distant Cascade and coastal range, lighting up the lounge with a warm glow.

Both Alan and Peter arrived with a fistful of papers, each one anxious to share his findings with Jake. They enjoyed their breakfast first while Jake recounted a few more stories about his trip, discussed some of the papers and technical details presented at the convention, and handed them each some brochures on new equipment.

"Here, these looked interesting to me. Look them over, see if it's something we could use in the lab." The two men eagerly took the information, knowing that on their say alone, Jake would buy whatever new equipment they wanted.

"So what have you got for me?" he finally asked, turning first to a slightly wrinkled Alan Cook. "Did you guys get any sleep last night?"

"Just a tad . . . I crashed on that couch in the reception area . . . didn't want to miss this meeting this morning." Alan answered. He spread out some charts from one of the GC's in the lab. "Interesting stuff, Jake, very interesting!" The GC, or gas chromatograph, was a laboratory analyzer that could detect and quantify many compounds in a mixture, at extremely low concentrations. "I must say, it eluded me for quite a while . . . I think a lot of the sample had deteriorated during your trip back. Also, there was so much other stuff in the sample."

"'Other stuff' . . . ?" laughed Jake, "Alan, you're starting to sound like the rest of us . . . you'll have to watch that!"

Alan ignored the comment, totally involved in his work. "Yes, you know, all the normal car exhaust stuff, carbon monoxide, oxides of nitrogen, as well as certain compounds from the body, clothes, etc. I had to get a little tricky to find it, but I think I got what you're looking for!"

"Good, let's have it!" Jake leaned forward, anxious to hear Alan's findings.

Alan spread out some sheets of the recording paper, some with a couple of the traces circled in red pen, some very small peaks in a series of squiggles in the recorder trace.

"It's small . . . very, very low concentrations at this point, but something that shouldn't be there at all! Nevertheless, it's there, and it's the only thing that could cause that much damage if were in high enough concentrations. The only reason I noticed it was by comparing these figures with some other exhaust readouts. I then had a devilish time finding what it was, an example signature. This stuff is just not supposed to be there . . . in any concentrations."

"What . . . what's there?" they asked.

"I'm pretty sure it's nickel carbonyl" he announced proudly.

Total silence permeated the room, each person staring at the others with a bewildered look. Nobody had expected such a strange compound, something never found under such circumstances.

"Nickel carbonyl?" Jake finally repeated, only slightly aware of its existence, a vague memory stirring. "Isn't that formed during nickel refining or something . . .? We had an inquiry about that from a nickel company years ago. All I remember is that it's real poisonous!"

"Bingo, mate! You said it! Nickel carbonyl or sometimes called nickel tetracarbonyl, a colourless, volatile gas." He referred to his notes. "It's listed in one of my chemical handbooks as: '*poisonous! . . . one of the most toxic chemicals encountered industrially. Inhalation of vapours may cause pulmonary edema with focal hemorrhage*'." Alan paused, enjoying dropping his little bomb. "In case you're wondering what that means, it causes fluid build-up in the lungs, and bleeding . . . I looked it up." He smiled at their reaction, then continued. "The OSHA Chemical Information Manual also mentions 'acute lung edema' along with serious effects on the central nervous system! There are all kinds of nasty symptoms with this stuff too . . . headaches, vertigo, nausea, coughing, stomach pains, delirium and convulsions!"

"Stop, we believe you!" they cried.

Jake continued, "I think you're right, Alan . . . I saw some of the bodies . . . not a pretty sight!" He paused a moment the added "But what kind of concentrations are we talking about, what levels would do this to those people?"

"OSHA lists their limit as 0.001 parts per million, but it would have to be a lot higher than that to do the kind of damage you witnessed. The LC50 is 35 ppm, so take your pick."

Jake thought back to the TV news coverage and Brent's description of the general area of the disaster. He thought out loud "The area was low, a dip in the freeway . . . stalled traffic, no wind, inversion, minimal dispersion . . . stagnation, build up to higher concentrations . . . ideal conditions to release a gas for maximum impact."

Alan continued "It also oxidizes in air, especially at the temperatures you've been through, so you were lucky to get these samples at all . . . that's probably why they were so low level and hard to find. It probably wouldn't have done you any good to sample at the site later that day, as the material would have been all gone.

As it was, you were lucky to get what you did, probably the body bags and the cooler temperature in the morgue slowed down the oxidation, but the trip home almost killed it all."

They all sat there, digesting the new information. Many had suspected nerve gas or some other industrial agent, pesticide or herbicide compound.

"So where did it come from?" Jake asked first. "I didn't even know nickel carbonyl was available."

"That's it, Jake, it isn't available!" answered Alan. "At least not anywhere I checked. I've looked through about every gas supplier catalog we have . . . bugger all! I can understand why, the boiling point is about 109 degrees Fahrenheit, up to that point, it exists as a 'colourless liquid with a musty odour'. Don't ask me who the stupid bloke was that smelled it to find out it had a musty odour! Like I said before, OSHA lists the limits on this stuff as one thousandth of a part per million, or 1 part per billion! I'd love to know what the level was on the highway that day."

Peter interrupted, "maybe we can use the levels you have, plus the oxidation rate, and extrapolate back to find out what the levels were."

"That's good Peter, but I still figure we have to find what the source is. It's got to come from somewhere," Jake said, "If it's an industrial compound, how is it made and where is it used?"

Alan again flipped through his notes. "The chemical source-book I checked said that it is an intermediate in nickel refining, made by passing carbon monoxide over finely divided nickel. From what I could gather, it's used in organic synthesis. It has a molecular weight . . ."

"No that's fine Alan," Jake interrupted. "We don't need all of the details now, just enough to try to figure out where it came from." Jake's thought processes took over, cranking through all of the possibilities of chemical reactions, how a poison like this could be made or delivered to the site. "The only common denominator I see is the carbon monoxide." he announced.

"And lot's of it" added Peter, spreading out his notes on the table. "Take a look at this. These are graphs of the ambient air stations you brought back from LA." He paused, looking at Jake. "By the way, if you could get some data from what would be classed as a 'normal' day, I would appreciate it. These data are fine, but we don't have a normal baseline to compare them to."

"O.K., I'll ask Brent next time I talk to him." answered Jake. "Maybe he can email a few files".

"From what we have for that day, if you watch these NOx levels and CO levels, they do things a little different from stations I've seen before." He pointed out the time scale on the graph, starting with early morning. "For that morning, they look quite normal, the ozone starts to build up as the sun rises, then the NOx and CO as the traffic builds, and the usual cycle starts." He pulled out another graph, spreading it on the table. "But watch here, see? Just after noon, the temperature is still rising, CO is still rising, but quite suddenly the NOx starts to drop! Some of the other compounds also start doing things that don't look right, but I'll have to compare them to a normal day. It almost looks like somebody suddenly changed the rules, and a different set of photochemical reactions took over!"

They listened to Peter, fascinated by the data, puzzled by the results. All of them had worked on smog problems and dispersion modelling long enough to be intimately familiar with the normal photochemical reactions expected in a heavy traffic, hot day combination. These started off in the normal way, then suddenly start deviating from the norm.

Jake wrapped up their breakfast meeting, suggesting they all return to the lab to do some more research and investigation.

"Good morning, Jake, have a good trip?" his secretary, Shannon Hall asked as they came in the door.

"Well, Shannon, it depends on how you look at it." Jake laughed, then explained the happenings of the past two or three days.

"Oh my God! You were involved in that?" she asked.

"Only as an innocent bystander. Although now we are being hounded by bureaucratic zealots that don't seem to be playing by the same rules." He told Shannon more of the confusing events and results of the tests, as well as the illogical actions of the agents.

"The big question is, what . . . or even WHO is changing the rules?"

As soon as he was in his office, Jake phoned Brent Willis in LA. He wasn't in his office, but picked him up on his cellular.

"Jake! Jeez I'm glad you called! Those federal guys have been crawling all over us here. I thought they were supposed to be out catching spies or some other bad guys.

"That's what I was just thinking Brent, but who are the bad guys? Why are they bugging you? I thought they had taken all of your data and all of your samples."

"That's true, they seem to be hanging around a lot, as if they are expecting something to happen . . . maybe another attack!" Brent paused, the laughed, "Boy, that Paul Butler fellow was sure pissed when he found you had skipped town!"

Jake thought for a moment, then asked "Brent, why don't you ask a few questions, maybe check out these guys. Watch yourself, but I feel you should have your boss check with Washington, find out what they are here for."

"Good idea, I'll send out a few feelers." Brent answered. He continued "The press are having a field day, what with speculation on which group was responsible, etc. The city is full of FBI, NSO, Homeland Security and God knows how many other agents, pulling in every member of every cult, fringe group or environmentalist they can find." He paused, suddenly remembering that Jake had the other samples. "I almost forgot! What did you find in those samples? Anything interesting?"

"For sure Brent! We're not completely sure, but the preliminary analysis shows the presence of nickel carbonyl." They continued to talk, Jake supplying the details of their findings. "Sorry I didn't tell you yesterday, but I had a back-up memory stick of your station data with me . . . another reason why I wanted to get the hell out of town! The numbers don't follow the rules, that's why we need a copy of what you would consider a normal day. If you can get a few data files for all the same stations, and email it up to me as soon as possible."

"You got it! I'm at one of the stations now, so I'll start here. It'll go out later today. I've also got that topographic map information you wanted for that area. I'll email that to you as well and you can try out your new model." He paused then added "Actually Jake, I'll do both, just to make sure you get it. I'll e-mail the data and send copies by courier as well."

"Thanks Brent . . . got to go, talk to you later" he quickly ended the call as he saw Peter frantically motioning him to take the other line.

"Hello, Jake Prescott here . . ." he answered, not sure who it was.

"*Wie geht's* Jakob?"

"Stefan! Where the hell are you? Are you O.K., and what's going on between you and those Washington creeps?" He couldn't get the questions out fast enough.

"*Langsam,* slowly Jakob, please" Stefan continued in German. "I'm afraid I cannot discuss anything right now, there are too many ears listening."

"*Was bedeuten Sie* . . . What do you mean . . . ? Jake interrupted, also in German, "Why are you speaking German Stefan?"

"I know this is being recorded and will be translated later, but this might give you a little time."

Jake's head was spinning, all of the unanswered questions and now Stefan's actions colliding. "Time for what Stefan? Does this have anything to do with that mess in LA . . . why are the N.S.O. following you, what do they want you for now?"

"Jakob, please, not now! We should have talked at the convention, I wanted to tell you then."

"Stefan, does this have anything to do with nickel carbonyl?" Jake asked, a wild guess.

There was silence at the other end. Slowly and quietly, Stefan started talking again.

"*Ach, mein Gott,* I should have known you would figure it out." He paused, his voice dropping further. I'm sorry you did, now they know that you know."

"Who knows?" Jake said patiently, getting more frustrated by the minute. "Who are you talking about?"

"Jakob, I cannot talk. I strongly suggest that you do not talk on the phone about this as well, it is not safe. Please come, then we can talk. Ask your old hiking partner to find out where I will be. *Auf Wiedersehen.*" The line went dead as Jake sat there, staring into the receiver.

Chapter 11

HE SAT AT THE DESK for a long time, not moving, just staring out of the large window at the distant mountains. Everything was piling up, the questions he had were not being answered, and there were still more questions being asked. He felt like a player in a game where the rules were being kept secret, or a game where there were too many players, all on the other team.

Jake had always approached life casually, with a devil-may-care, almost cavalier attitude. Under most conditions, this approach to life helped maintain not only his sanity, but mainly his sense of humour and well-being. The down side was that he was sometimes slow to respond to the negative comments or actions of others. This was why he always seemed to have problems with politics and negative diplomacy. Conversely, if he could solve the problem logically, or in a way that required some straight forward action, he usually could handle it.

In this case, he realized that he had only been reacting to external pressures for the last few days, pressures caused by the events and actions of others. He had not thought things out . . . made any conscious, rational decisions, or felt he was in control of his own actions. He thought back, many years . . . he had been there before, reacting to the grief of Lori's death, wandering, lost, useless, until he had taken control of his life again. By turning the force of his grief around to help drive his creative powers, he found new direction and purpose in life.

His left leg was aching, a common symptom whenever he came under stress. He consciously slowed down, forcing himself to relax and try to recall some of his training from years past. He knew he must use his logic and scientific reasoning to work on the problem, the reasoning that had pulled him out of trouble before, reasoning that had made him a fortune. Act, rather than react.

Stefan had said 'come', that could only mean to Germany, the only place where they could drop out of sight, get lost. "'Ask your old hiking partner' . . ." he repeated, mumbling to himself. "What's he talking about? I never had any hiking partners. None except . . . of course! Christa! Who else? The perfect go-between to set up a meeting, someone that an eavesdropper would not recognize." He stopped, remembering what Stefan had said about their conversation being recorded. If that was true, he had to make sure they only heard things he wanted them to know!

For the first time he began to realize that he was involved in something a lot larger than it had originally appeared. A terrorist attack or environmental disaster should have brought some of these responses, but not all. What are these government agents trying to learn, or what are they trying to cover up? From his experience, they were not acting like they should. When it all started, he visualized a scenario where he and his associates would be asked to act as a consultant to the authorities, helping them pinpoint the problem, discover the source. At the very least, the experts in Los Angeles, experts in air quality monitoring should be heavily involved in this. Instead, he and his associates were being hunted and tracked down like criminals, evidence was disappearing.

Slowly, a plan began to form, and with it, a completely different style of action. He could now see that these agents had their own agenda, and it certainly didn't fit well with his. Every time he moved a step closer to the solution, they tried to remove one more piece of information from the game, put up one more obstacle. It was almost as if . . .

"Of course!" he yelled, leaping to his feet, almost collapsing on his weak side. "They don't want the puzzle to be solved!"

"You O.K.?" Shannon's voice timidly asked from outside his office.

"Yeah, sorry Shannon. Could you ask Alan and Peter to come in please, right away?" Jake replied, now totally occupied with his new line of thought. He grabbed his cane and shuffled around the office anxiously until the two men arrived and sat down. Jake leaned out the door near Shannon's desk. "Maybe you should be in on this Shannon, I think you should know what's going on." Shannon picked up a notebook and joined them.

"What's up Jake?" a timid voice asked, seeing the determination in Jake's face.

"I think I've figured out some of this puzzle . . . not very much, but a little . . . unfortunately, the biggest question remains, why? I still haven't figured that yet." He paced some more, not speaking, making his associates nervous.

Peter Wong finally took the bull by the horns and asked, in a pseudo-Chinese dialect, "Ah so, Mr. Prescott, I have studied some of the old oriental philosophies, but I have not yet mastered the reading of minds. Are you going to let us in on this great secret?"

"Sorry" Jake answered, suddenly aware of the three. He quickly summarized the events of the past few days, hinting at the new slant he was thinking of. He then repeated the actions of the N.S.O. agents and described what he knew of Stefan's actions. The next part was not as easy.

"I've got to tell you, if you don't want to get involved with this, that's O.K. with me. I don't even know what I'm going to get into if I keep this up, what things might be under the stones I overturn."

"We're with you Jake, you know that!" the two men assured him.

"How about you Shannon?" he asked.

"I can't see any problem Jake. I'll just continue to do my work, it's not as if you are asking me to do something illegal or immoral."

"Good! And thanks to all of you." He paused momentarily, gathering his thoughts. "I guess what's bothering me is there doesn't seem to be any motive, a reason why these people are acting this way. There's something or somebody important we are missing, someone else in the loop somewhere." He pounded his desk, impatient at his own confusion. "Well then, from this point, we go into an action mode, rather than just a reaction mode. We must take decisive actions, find out what the hell is going on, and try to stay at least one step ahead of whoever is trying to stop us." They all agreed to that.

"What kind of action, Jake?" was the first question.

"First, I'm heading out to Germany. I've got to talk to Stefan, find out how he is involved in this . . . it must have something to do with the research he has been doing for the last couple of years." He paused, thinking again of what Stefan had said. "Secondly, all future phone calls between us will be in some kind of code . . . we'll have to set up something we can all remember, something simple, yet effective. I wish we had some of the scramblers we used in Foreign Affairs. Third, after today, all sensitive conversations will be held either outside, or we'll mask them with external sound, music, or whatever. Maybe we can meet in the shop, with some machinery running. Stefan seemed to think they were recording our telephone conversation, but I don't think they've had time to bug the office yet, so this conversation should be safe."

"I've got a friend in the security business, Jake." Peter interrupted. "I can ask him about some counter-surveillance equipment, anti-bugs or whatever they use."

"Good, get whatever you need . . . on second thought, I'll make a list of items for you . . . I've been in the business before! Also Peter, I'd like you to run some of that data through our model, see what you can come up with, only this time, you won't have the source point. Maybe you can run the thing in reverse to find out where it's coming from. Brent Willis is e-mailing some baseline data later today, as well as the topo data. He's also sending a backup by courier later with the background information you wanted."

"I'll watch for the emails and the shipment, and run interference when I can." Shannon offered.

The four of them continued to discuss their plans, aware that this would most likely be the last time they could talk freely, without the fear of being bugged. They planned their telephone code, as well as a fax code, using a copy of the latest bestselling novel as a code book. Nobody would be suspicious of a copy of the novel if they found it in his briefcase. By using a combination of page number and sentence or word number, they had a simple and commonly used but unbreakable cipher.

"That's it then!" Jake announced as he rose from the desk. "Don't be surprised if the R.C.M.P. or the Canadian Security guys show up. I'm sure the N.S.O. has contacted them with some cock and bull story about me. They have no reason to stop me from travelling, but I know they can make things difficult."

They wrapped up their meeting, each one intent on his own plan of action. Jake looked around, thinking about what he wanted to take with him, not knowing how long he would be away. He packed his laptop computer together with additional copies of the data and Peter's graphs and printouts. He then headed home to pack. He didn't notice the plain sedan that pulled into the parking lot just as he was heading out. Fortunately, they didn't notice him as well.

After he had thrown a few clothes in his carry-on, he then stopped at the local shopping centre, using a pay phone to call the airport. He had packed his cell phone, but decide to use anonymous pay phones until he knew it was safe.

There was a direct flight to Frankfurt that afternoon. The flight had lots of space, so he didn't bother to reserve a seat, knowing that as soon as his name got into the computers, it would be flagged. He considered his actions, knowing they were bordering on paranoia, but it was all part of their new plan of action, a plan of survival.

He then stopped at his bank and withdrew a few thousand dollars, again not wanting his movements traced through his use of credit cards or bank machines.

He left his car in the shopping centre parking lot and took a cab to the airport. As soon as he arrived, he stopped by the airport book store to buy a copy of the bestseller they all had agreed upon. He then headed over to the airline check-in, handed the agent his passport and purchased a ticket in his own name. Chances were pretty good that his name wouldn't be red flagged before he had a chance to take off. The two agonizing hours before his flight was just a taste of what was in store for him.

Back at the office, Shannon had stalled the two men from the Canadian Security Intelligence Service or C.S.I.S., confusing them with misunderstanding and misinformation. They had just left when Brent Willis called from LA.

"Where's Jake?" he asked breathlessly, "I got to talk to him right away!"

Shannon's mind was quick, trying to figure out how she could tell Brent something without doing it over the phone. "Just a moment Mr. Willis . . . I'm sorry, he's really tied up right now, can I have him call you back right away?"

"Yeah, sure, just tell him it's real important" he replied, hanging up before she had a chance to ask him anything.

"Alan!" she called, heading out to the lab, meeting him halfway. "Come-on," she said firmly, grabbing his lab coat and ushering him out the back door. Alan was at first confused, then realized what Shannon was doing.

"What's up Shannon?" he asked.

"I think this is important Alan, Brent Willis just called from LA . . . something's bothering him, so I think you should call him back . . . here's the cell number Jake left. If you use your own cell or go down the corner to the pay phone, then nobody will listen in."

"Thanks Shannon, jolly good! Let's call him right now" pulling a telephone from his lab-coat pocket. The call went through in seconds, an agitated Brent Willis answering at the other end. "Brent, it's Alan Cook in Vancouver. I work with Jake and he's filled us in on the LA thing. Jake's going to be out of the country for a short time, but I might be talking to him soon. Anything we can do for you, pass on a message?"

"Just tell him it's happened again, in a parkade downtown, God knows how many people killed this time!"

The driver of an unmarked car parked a block down the street hesitated, his face ashen as he glanced over at his partner. Their high-tech scanner continued to record the conversation.

Chapter 12

Brent Willis was having a bad day. In fact, his entire week hadn't been that great. It had started out O.K., the WAWA convention was a welcome break from his routine, a break that he needed. He looked forward to these meetings, an infrequent chance to meet with his peers from other jurisdictions, other countries, as well as meet and compare notes with old friends. It also provided some relief from the usual stress of the day-to-day problems with the massive Los Angeles air monitoring network.

The terrorist gas attack, as it was now called, had changed all that. Just at a time when he could have made a difference, provided some real information, some idiots from Washington moved in and confiscated everything they had. He had gone over the events of the week many times, trying to figure what went wrong, why they were acting as they were. He still couldn't come up with a reasonable explanation.

The press were having a field day, interviewing every individual or group that would give them time, either legitimate or fanatic. Every fringe organization or cult in the city took advantage of the possible press time to air their theories and pontificate their views. No organization had come forward to claim responsibility for the attack, but many expressed the view that it wasn't over yet. As soon as one of the groups viewed that opinion, they were usually carted away for further questioning by the authorities. Brent and his staff were constantly trying to avoid the press, not wanting to get between them and the Washington agents.

The convention had wrapped up by Friday noon and Brent was enjoying a long lunch with Linda and Ed Seymour. The little seafood place was one of their favourite haunts for a Friday lunch, its dim, quiet interior a balm for their tired bodies and stressed nerves after a week of work and driving in Los Angeles traffic. They had met again several times since the 'attack', comparing notes, trying to analyze the problem. This Friday was another blistering smog generator, so none of them was anxious to abandon the dark, cool interior of the restaurant.

Brent's cellular phone buzzed in his pocket. Answering it discreetly, his face went white as he nodded a couple of times, then hung up.

"What the hell was that Brent?" Ed asked. "You look like shit!"

Brent moved closer, lowering his voice. "That was Betty, back at the office, she's been monitoring police frequencies since Wednesday. There's been another attack!"

Their shocked looks told him his words had hit home.

"This time it's in that big parkade just around the corner, only a few blocks from the convention centre and here! The word just came in, so nobody's there yet!"

It was all Ed needed. "See, Linda, I told you! You head back to the lab, get things warmed up, Brent and I are going air sampling!"

Brent stared at him. "What the hell do you mean . . . going sampling? I'm not tired of living yet!"

"No, come on, I got suits, air packs, the whole thing. Like I said earlier, I'm ready for this thing and I want to get some good samples this time. My stuff is in my car, just out in the parking lot, we can get suited up there and be at the parkade in fifteen minutes."

Brent reluctantly agreed, following Ed from the restaurant, a concerned sister watching them go.

As Ed had estimated, they arrived on site as the first of the fire/rescue and Hazmat crews were entering the parkade, also wearing sealed suits and air packs. The police and fire crew were already stringing tape around the entire parkade, making it a no entry area. Their own suits and sampling gear marked them as "official", so no opposition was encountered. Access to the large building was easy, what they encountered was not.

Their first impression was the heat. The second was the air. It was a large, concrete building, built for parking cars. The design was basic, simple construction, with almost solid walls. Rather than the normal open design used in warmer climates, the owners had wanted a more discreet appearance, rather plain walls with very few windows for ventilation. Without any natural ventilation, they depended on additional fans to prevent the sunlight on the grey concrete from turning the interior into an oven. Later investigations found that the ventilation system had kicked out earlier that day, allowing the exhaust gases and heat to build up in the building. The air was thick, the far wall of the parkade barely visible. Cars had come down from the upper levels, only to be held up in the ramps by a stalled vehicle below. As the blockade became longer, drivers became more impatient, gunning their engines, honking their horns. With the fans off, the build-up escalated, making the air impossible to breathe, the heat stifling. There was no indication of when the poison entered the cycle. As the first victims perished, their cars either coasted or were driven into the car below, or in some cases, the walls of the ramp. The first thing rescue crews did was to reach in and turn off the engines, many racing at full speed from the heavy foot of a dead driver. Brent and Ed walked around, quickly taking the samples they needed, filling several plastic sample bags from what appeared to be the worst areas. They watched in horror as the crews started disentangling the victims from their cars. Faces were frozen in agony, blood trickling from blue lips. Further up the ramp, several survivors were found, coughing, vomiting, and others convulsing violently before they died.

Ed finally signalled to Brent for them to leave. They packed their samples in a case with the pumps and started to leave the building.

Walking quickly around the back of a pickup truck, Brent felt his hip catch on a piece of chrome trim. The loud tearing sound penetrated his helmet with ease, paralysing him. He looked down, fearing the worst. The large tear in his suit immediately allowed the poison air to enter, pumping in and out with each movement of his body. Panic filled his mind as he turned quickly to move towards the entrance, only to catch his air hose on a large, overhanging rear-view mirror on the side of the truck. His forward motion ripped the hose from his mask, exposing him to the deadly atmosphere. Almost instantly, he could smell the smoky, oily smog, overladen with a musty flavour.

Ed noticed his plight immediately. "Hold your breath!" he yelled. "You'll have enough to get out of here, let's go!" He grabbed Brent, leading him quickly to the exit.

A few seconds later, they left the building to the rescue crews, Brent coughing violently as they headed up the alley. Both men were silent until they returned to the parking lot, knowing how close they had come to tragedy. They removed their gear, throwing it into the trunk just as a TV crew descended on them, wanting information on the disaster.

"No comment" Brent kept repeating as he pushed them away, hoping his picture wouldn't end up on the six o'clock news. They were persistent, swarming around them, trying to figure out why they were leaving. Brent locked the doors, and pulled out his phone, dialling Linda's number.

"We're on our way!" he announced as she answered the phone. Fighting traffic, they swung around to Macy Street and up Broadway, trying to avoid the crowds and traffic that had already built up. Luckily, they were back at the lab within a half hour.

"You start running the samples," he called to Ed, who was already in the lab, "I'm calling Jake." It was several minutes later when Alan Cook called him back. After he had blurted out his news, he went into more detail with Alan, describing the scene they had just witnessed and almost been part of.

"Thanks for calling Brent, I'm sure Jake's going to want to know this. You say you've got some good samples this time?" he asked.

"Yeah, I'll let you talk to Ed, maybe you've got some ideas for him on the analysis, seeing as how you've already been there." He passed the phone to Ed, letting the two analysis experts discuss their approach. Brent listened to part of the conversation as they reviewed the procedures for using the Gas Chromatograph, Mass Spectrometer, OSHA test methods, and bubbling sample through midget impingers, the little glass bottles used in analysis work. The one-sided conversation soon lost him.

Linda joined him from the lab. "Let's have a coffee . . . the first run is in the GC, Ed can check it when he gets off the phone." She watched Brent closely as she poured the coffee. "I understand you guys had a pretty close call, especially you."

"Yeah, I guess you could say that." Brent replied, his mind on another problem. "I just can't figure it! They're running around looking for terrorists, nut cases, etc., . . . I think it's got something to do with the smog, some reaction we're not considering. It was just too damn thick in there today!"

"Well, we'll soon know . . . something at least. We'll find out if Jake's original findings hold up. Let's hope they don't come and confiscate all of our samples again. Then . . . we might learn something!"

Chapter 13

JAKE SPOTTED THE MAN SHORTLY after leaving the plane. He was a tall, dark haired man; his dark, very European style suit too large for his lanky frame. As Jake coasted along on the moving sidewalk in Frankfurt airport, he glanced back occasionally at the man, also riding the belt about a hundred feet behind him, reading a newspaper. Jake had been watching carefully as they left the aircraft and headed towards passport control. Luckily, he spotted the man just as he turned to follow Jake, his slight limp exaggerated by his height. He had been waiting at the gate, obviously expecting Jake to be on that flight!

Jake didn't waste energy trying to figure out how he knew, he just accepted that somebody was following him. He remained confused as to why, and also how the man had managed to get that close to the arrivals gate, inside the passport control area. Were they after him, or were they still trying to get to Stefan? If they were after him, they could pick him up any time, so it had to be something to do with Stefan.

Jake could feel himself changing into his 'European mode'. Years ago, as a young trainee with Foreign Affairs, he was still young enough to be fascinated by the thrills of the espionage and counter-espionage business. Even before he was an operative himself, on his days off his imagination and insatiable appetite for spy novels would transform him into the country's number one agent. He would walk the streets, through the shopping areas or to the theatre, spotting potential foreign spies at every street corner. After a few years of experience, a lot of study and discussions with senior people in the business, he learned a few of the important techniques of surveillance, how to follow people without being spotted, and how to spot someone following you.

He proceeded through passport control without any hold-ups, and turned to visit the newsstand and gift shop, using his cane and his own limp to slow his actions, watching to confirm the intentions of his pursuer. The tall man limped over to another kiosk, watching Jake's progress as he bought a newspaper and left the shop. As he walked calmly over to the escalator to descend to the train level, Jake noticed the man pick up the trail, following at a discreet distance. He decided to ignore him until the right moment, the theory being that if you knew where your enemy was, you had better control of the situation.

He continued down to the train station, located under the airport. Jake enjoyed coming into Frankfurt airport, a fascinating combination of the old and new. To most visitors, the visible part of the airport was the ground level area where the planes landed and unloaded their passengers. In addition to dozens of restaurants, bars and souvenir shops, the airport housed a large supermarket, several other types of retail stores and several movie theaters. Beneath the large complex was the airport train station, a hub of transportation for most of the area. Although the central, larger, main train station in Frankfurt handled the majority of the European travel, the airport station was extremely busy, for both long distance and local trains.

He paused shortly to purchase a ticket, then headed for the platform to take the S-bahn, or local commuter train into the downtown area. Within minutes it pulled into the station. He quickly walked on, casually glancing behind him to make sure his pursuer had also made the train. The doors closed and the train silently picked up speed, racing along the tracks through both residential and industrial areas towards the centre of town. The trip was short and uneventful, packed with early morning commuters and students heading into the city. Mistaken for a normal, English-speaking North American tourist, Jake casually listened to the conversations around him, smiling at one point as one student revealed rather intimate details of her latest affair.

He left the train at the "Hauptwache" station, named after the historical old sentry house on ground level above the modern rail station, shopping and restaurant complex near the old part of Frankfurt. The underground shops were just opening, preparing for the onslaught of commuters, tourists and travelling public they would deal with for the remainder of the day. He paused at a small kiosk, buying a coffee and a bratwurst-on-a-bun for his breakfast. After the ten hour flight with very little sleep, he felt it was still late evening. As he munched on his German "hot-dog", he casually watched around him, noticing the tall man had stopped at another kiosk, looking over the selection of magazines. Jake smiled to himself, thinking how easy it was to spot the man.

"How easy . . . " he thought. "Of course!" It suddenly dawned on him that maybe he was supposed to notice him! He quickly looked around again, berating himself for letting his guard down so easy. He couldn't see anything obvious, but the lesson suddenly came back to him; if there was a second man, he would not be easy to spot! He left the kiosk quickly, almost catching his pursuer off guard. The man followed at a distance as he walked up to street level and strolled slowly down the Zeil, the wide, pedestrian-only shopping streets in central Frankfurt. Killing time, Jake stopped at several shops, either just window shopping, or sometimes entering the shop to check out something that caught his eye. This also gave him a chance to keep track of his stalker, and also watch for the possible second man.

After almost an hour of stalling, Jake decided to make his move and try to lose the man. Turning right off the Zeil on Fahr Gasse, he headed quickly down towards the river. With another couple of turns he doubled back and walked into the Kleinmarkthalle, a large, covered market-place, normally packed with shoppers and tourists at this time of day. He wasn't disappointed, and he quickly mixed in with the shoppers, looking over the fruit and vegetables for sale. He took his time, idly browsing through the market, checking the produce and talking with the shop keepers. He knew that with his cane and visible limp, he was an easy target to follow and he would have to be very clever to lose them. He changed directions several times until he was about halfway through the market, when he made his move. Stooping down as if to tie his shoe, he slipped into the back of one of the stalls. The proprietor was surprised, and started to protest, until Jake offered him a hundred Euros for his white smock. The deal closed, Jake quickly donned the smock, put his carry-on bag into a potato sack and slipped out of the stall, head down, shuffling towards the exit with his cane hidden under the smock. He waited until he was just leaving the building before he glanced back, just long enough to spot number one pursuer conferring with his colleague, the second man that had eluded Jake until now. Both were looking nervously around, knowing they had been duped.

He quickly tramped down to Berliner Strasse, his white smock and potato sack over his shoulder labelling him as another shop worker or delivery person. He doubled back east again, eventually turning down Domstrasse towards the river into the cobblestone streets of the Römerberg, an old, very picturesque section of Frankfurt. Slipping into a small side-street, he stopped at a phone booth to make his call. Pulling Christa's crumpled business card from his pocket, he read the name more closely as he dialled the number.

The company of *Sicherheit Steinbock GmbH* was located on small street near the Main River in Frankfurt, close to the main train station. He asked for Christa and soon a familiar voice answered. Speaking German, he announced who he was.

"*Jakob*! *Wo bist du,* where are you?" she almost yelled at him. Her voice sounded good, deeper, more mature, but still unmistakably the girl he knew years before. He told her he was in Frankfurt, explaining briefly about his flight, not mentioning the other problems or the men following him. From Christa's comments and questions, he got the impression she already knew most of this, and also was aware of her father's situation. Not knowing how far the "ears" had extended, he decided to keep playing it safe.

"How about dinner tonight?" he asked. "Besides getting caught up with about eight years of news, there's a few things we have to discuss."

"Yes, I know Jakob, I . . ."

Before she could answer or suggest anything, he quickly added "Remember the last place we had *Schweinehaxe*, many years ago?

"Wasn't that . . ."

Before she could say more, he added "Don't mention names Christa, just tell me if you remember the place."

"Yes."

"Good! I'll meet you there . . . what, seven o'clock this evening . . . does that give you time?"

"Yes, perfect! See you then, *Tschüs*!"

Jake hung up, Christa's words still echoing in his ears. With the first part of the plan in place, he slipped off his smock and stuffed it into the sack, leaving both of them in the phone booth. Joining a group of tourists, he followed them partially around the Römerberg, gazing at the old half-timbered burgher's houses along one side of the plaza, including Frankfurt's historic old Town Hall. Opposite, another row of historic family houses looked over the square, many now converted to shops or restaurants.

As they approached a cafe, he slipped away from the group, walked in and took a seat near the rear, and ordered a meal. The food was good and the coffee excellent, raising his spirits and boosting his energy. He relaxed over the meal for over an hour, hoping to discourage his followers. After finishing his meal, he ordered more coffee and a newspaper from the waiter, hoping to catch up on the latest news. He almost choked on his coffee when he opened the paper, the large type over one column catching his eye. "21 DIE IN SECOND GAS ATTACK". Dated the day before in Los Angeles, the short article covered the early reports of the second disaster in downtown L.A. He read quickly, hoping to see some new information, knowing there would not be any.

He quickly paid the waiter and left the restaurant, heading for another phone booth near the museum. It was shortly after noon local time, after 3 A.M. in Vancouver. He hoped the authorities had not bugged everyone's personal phone yet, so he called Alan at home. It rang seven times before he answered, a foggy, irritable "Hello?"

"Alan . . . it's Jake. Sorry for the poor timing, I just saw the news about L.A."

Alan quickly woke up, explaining to Jake how they had worked late on the gas samples, as well as his conversations with Brent Willis. "Brent and Ed have some excellent, on-site samples . . . so close to the event that Brent almost bought it!" He described how Brent had come very close to becoming one of the statistics. "If you call Ed tomorrow, I'm sure you'll get some interesting information."

Jake digested this news, trying to figure out the next step. "Thanks Alan," he said. "Knowing what you did with the first sample, Ed will get everything we need on these samples. Call him first thing in the morning and have him email or fax the results to you, maybe even copies of the GC charts. Then ask Brent to send us the data files via e-mail for any stations in the area, maybe Peter can run some simulations or something. I'm sure Brent down-loaded the data before anybody had a chance to erase them."

"How are you making out Jake?" Alan asked. "Any progress so far?"

"Hell no, I just got here," he answered. "And I've already had two guys on my tail!"

"Who . . .?"

"I don't know . . . I can't figure the N.S.O. chasing me over here, so I have no idea who they are . . . it doesn't make any sense! If the police were after me, especially Interpol or Europol, I would never have made it through passport control." He thought back, visualizing the first man to follow him. Definitely European. . . . but did the Americans have agents in Europe, or did they have some sort of reciprocal agreement with a similar agency in Germany? His lack of sleep was catching up to him, hampering his reasoning power.

"I'll call again tomorrow if I get a chance . . . this time at a more humane hour."

"Thanks Jake, take care, cheerio!"

Jake moved quickly, knowing the call might have been traced. He took off his jacket, slinging it over his shoulder, his arm partially obscuring his face. Hunching over slightly, he dropped his normally tall stature by several inches, making him a little more difficult to spot. He then shuffled up the sidewalk, hiding his cane as much as he could manage. He continued, wandering in and out of shops with many of the tourists. After crossing Braubachstrasse, he continued up Neue Kräme, a short pedestrian street, packed with shoppers and tourists. He ducked into a small hotel he had used before, hoping they would have a room. He was lucky, and within minutes, he was in his room, collapsing on the bed for a few hours sleep before his dinner meeting with Christa.

Chapter 14

SATURDAY MORNING FOUND LINDA AND Ed Seymour trying to catch up on the week's work. The conference and the gas attacks had taken up a lot of their time, so they were playing "catch-up ball". After some initial analyses, they had called a press conference and released as much of the poison gas details as they could to reporters the day before. The complexity of the chemistry and analytical methods involved appeared to be too much detail for most of the reporters, and they could not even guess as to the source of the gas or reasons for the attack. Even so, he wasn't surprised when another reporter arrived at the lab the following day to ask some more questions.

"But I've already told you guys about our test results, we handed out copies to the press yesterday." Ed thought the man looked vaguely familiar, but could not place him.

The man returned Ed's stare with a steady, sincere look that immediately made Ed feel at ease. Unlike the young reporters he had seen the day before, this man looked like he had been around for a few years and had seen more than most. Well into his thirties, Scott had the body of a younger man, but the face of an older man. His features were soft and rounded, but his brown eyes were alert and probing.

"Excuse me, what was your name again?" asked Ed.

"Scott Anderson, WBC" the man answered in a quiet, disarming voice. "I'm sorry I missed the press conference yesterday, but I've been tied up on another assignment, and just flew in from Washington this morning."

As he spoke, Ed noticed him looking around the office, reading the certificates on the wall, cataloguing and analyzing everything. The combination of the man's name and affiliation suddenly struck a chord.

"WBC . . . of course! Aren't you that investigative reporter that digs out all that shit . . . I'm sorry . . . has all those exposés on T.V.?"

The reporter laughed, enjoying Ed's candid appraisal of his work. "Yes, Mr. Seymour, guilty as charged!" The laughter relaxed his manner and softened his countenance as he reached up, running his fingers through a mop of curly hair.

"Please, call me Ed, we only get Mr. Seymour around here when I'm in trouble!" Ed immediately felt more comfortable with the man, recognizing his work as some of the best in the media today. After an exhausting journalistic apprenticeship that lasted through several presidents, Scott had grown into a demanding, hard-hitting journalist with an unequalled tenacity in the search for the truth. As an investigative reporter for the WBC network, Scott Anderson had started his career covering military coups and counter-coups in a half dozen countries, not for the military actions themselves, but the corruption and political power struggles that caused them in the first place. Closer to home, he had exposed some of the dirtiest political scandals of the decade. Recently, his reporting leaned more and more towards environmental issues, Kyoto, global warming, some of the hottest subjects of our time. Ed now realized he was talking to a pro, and someone he could probably trust to help find the truth. It didn't take him long to reach a decision. "I think we should go back into the lab, I'd like you to meet Linda."

They found Linda running yet another sample of the parking lot gas through the GC. Scott gaped, fascinated by this beautiful woman totally at home in this high-tech environment of analyzers, gas chromatographs, and mass spectrometers. They watched closely as she pulled a sample from one of the special plastic sample bags and injected it into the GC MC unit. As she finished the first step, she realized they were watching her.

"Linda, this is Scott Anderson, from WBC . . . you know . . ."

"Why yes, I remember . . . one of my favourite programs." Linda approached the reporter. "How do you do, Mr. Anderson?" she asked, her cheeks slightly flushed.

"Now it's my turn," he responded, "Please call me Scott. I get the feeling we are going to spend a little time together."

After adjourning to their little lounge room with a coffee, Ed started the conversation. "How do you want it Scott?" he asked. "Do you want to ask questions first, or shall we just tell you what we've told the others?"

"Actually, neither, Ed . . . let's just start by telling me about yourselves . . . how you two got into this business." He turned to Linda, a disarming smile wrinkling his eyes, "Or as the old cliché goes, 'how come a nice girl like you is working in a place like this?'"

Thus began a long session that lasted most of the day. Both Ed and Linda grew to like Scott's easy manner, his direct, yet honest way of digging out pertinent information, cutting to the main issue, the important information. At first they were a little surprised as he did not take any notes. Only later when Scott asked a few questions for clarification did they realize that he had been logging every detail with almost total recall. They described their early efforts, how they had started the business and struggled to survive. After lunch they continued with their account of the events in Los Angeles as they had unfolded the previous week, including their visit to the hospital to sample the cadavers from the first attack.

"That must have been interesting!" Scott interjected. "How did you manage that, how did they allow outsiders in at that point? It must have been a zoo in there!"

Linda agreed, then explained how they had worn lab smocks and blended in with the hospital staff, bluffing their way to the morgue. "It didn't do us any good though, that government guy came the next morning and took all of our samples!"

"What do you mean . . . what government guy?" Scott's interest suddenly peaked, his journalistic alarm going off.

"The guy from N.S.O., what's his name Ed . . . Paul Butler? He said it was for national security or something, they didn't want the samples to be lost or get into the wrong hands."

Alarm bells continued to ring in Scott's mind. "You said he took them the next morning? How come he was here that fast after the event, and what the hell is N.S.O. doing here in the first place?"

"He was here before that . . . since the beginning of the week. He told Jake that he was here to keep his eye on the protestors, all the fringe groups. Jake didn't totally believe him because he saw him following Stefan on the first day of the WAWA conference, and Stefan definitely is not a protestor!" she laughed.

"Whoa . . . wait a minute! Back up a little, please . . . who's Jake and Stefan?"

Both Ed and Linda then filled in additional details of the week, explaining about Jake Prescott and Stefan Schiller. Scott's attention was now totally centred on their account, processing and filing the information. He knew there was a story here, but felt somehow it was different than what he initially thought.

"You said Jake took some sample home with him . . . I assume this was where the original analysis came from as you just said that Butler had taken all of your samples."

"Yeh, that's right." Ed added. "They were lousy samples to begin with, and handled with every violation to sample protocol in the book. There was probably hardly anything left by the time he got home, but there was enough trace material left to start us on the right track." He continued "So when the second event happened, Brent and I went in for some excellent, on-site samples. This time we knew what to look for, and had them analyzed within hours.

Although we knew what we were dealing with . . . " his voice tapered off " . . . we still don't know where it's coming from!"

"Do you have any theories on that Ed?" Scott asked. "Where would some of these fanatics get this kind of stuff . . . how would they make it?"

"I don't think a fringe group was involved in this. There's something different about this, something or somebody else is involved and we can't quite put our finger on it!" he paused, then added "That's why we are running as many tests as we can on the second samples . . . maybe something different will show up."

Scott asked "How come Butler didn't come again and take your second samples? If was important the first time, it should have been even more important after the second event. Have you talked to him again since the first time?"

"That's what we thought, but no, we haven't even seen him or talked to him since." Ed laughed as he explained " . . . probably because we were a couple of steps ahead of him this time. First, we had better samples. Second, we had them analyzed and called a press conference before he even knew we had them. I think that blew him out of the water! Third, we had backup samples stashed, so we didn't care this time if he did come." He stopped for a minute, thinking. "Besides, that black guy, that FBI agent had been here as well, maybe they got together and decided we weren't the bad guys after-all."

"How about the monitoring station data . . . has he taken any of that?"

"Not that I know, but you'll have to ask Brent Willis, over at the Air Quality office."

"Have you heard from this Jake Prescott . . . since the original analysis?"

Ed and Linda looked at each other, not knowing just how much to tell Scott, how much they could trust him. Linda nodded slightly, giving Ed the go-ahead to tell the reporter what they knew.

"We don't know everything, but I must ask you to keep what we do tell you in confidence . . . at least for now." Ed started.

"Of course, but what kind of information do you have?"

"Actually not much . . . " Ed recalled as much as he could of his discussions with Alan Cook, describing their plans and actions to date. He continued "The latest we've heard is that Stefan is hiding out somewhere in Germany, and Jake's gone to find him because he has some of the answers to the cause of this mess!"

"In Germany?" Scott asked. This was definitely taking a different turn. "Do you know where?"

"No, you'll have to talk to Shannon Hall or Alan Cook at Prescott Industries, maybe they can tell you."

Scott's mind continued to process the data, more than he had hoped for on his first day on this story.

"One other thing, please. You mentioned an FBI agent . . . do you remember his name?"

Linda went into the other office, returning shortly with a business card. "Here it is, his name is Bert Jackson, out of Washington."

"Washington?" Scott blurted out. "Why Washington, the FBI have agents all over California?" A new twist, he thought. Why would Washington send an agent out from headquarters, unless he was working on something before, something they didn't want spread around.

Chapter 15

LOUD CATHEDRAL BELLS A BLOCK away yanked Jake from a deep sleep. With no air conditioning, the room was hot and stuffy. He had closed the outside shutters on the windows to cut out some of the street noise, but the loss of air circulation was the price he had to pay.

Six o'clock . . . he had slept for over four hours! When he peeked out the window, the sun was already low in the western sky, promising a lovely warm evening. First the shower, and the sheer pleasure of the hot stream of water rinsing off the residue of the ten hour flight and the tension of the past thirty-six hours.

Refreshed, he dressed and left the hotel and walked quickly down the little street toward the river. Not sure if they were still following him or had given up, he remained alert, stopping occasionally to check behind him. The cobblestone plaza in the Römer section was a magnet for visitors, even lone tourists like himself, wandering from shop to shop, window shopping or stopping to buy a post card for friends at home. A casual walk around the Justice Fountain in the middle of the square provided a chance to scan the area for followers. Further down he passed the historic museum and continued to the edge of the river. He climbed the steps up to the Eiserner Steg, an iron pedestrian bridge across the river to the old town of Sachsenhausen. From his higher vantage point on the middle of the bridge, he could look back with a clear view of the

Frankfurt end of the bridge to see if he was being followed. He paused, killing more time, watching the river barges chugging up and down the river, travelling to and from ports in a dozen cities in almost as many countries.

By the time he reached the Sachsenhausen side, he was sure nobody had followed him. It was Saturday night, and the debris from that morning's flea market was still strewn along the south bank, from the river up to street level. It was probably Jake's favourite *Flöh Markt*, or flea market that he had visited in his travels. In full swing, the tables, stalls and mobile shops spread out over a mile along the banks of the Main River. It was a great place to hang around, picking up interesting articles and an occasional bargain from all over the world.

Once he was off the bridge and back down to street level, he walked quickly up Schiffer Strasse, crossing over and back via some smaller side streets, until he reached the old quarter. *Alt Sachsenhausen,* or Old Sachsenhausen was a picturesque, funky old section of town, confined to a relatively small area along the south shore of the river across from Frankfurt proper. Almost an anachronism, the few streets of half-timbered houses and old inns had held off the invasion of steel and glass common in the centre of this twenty-first century city. Picking his way along the narrow, cobbled streets, the memories of other times floated back, times when Stefan, Christa and a much younger Jake used to visit Sachsenhausen when they came up from his Bavarian retreat on business. They would wander around the old section, among the stone and half-timbered houses and crafts shops, eventually stopping in the medieval *Ebbelweil*, or Cider Quarter. They would finish the evening in one of the old *apfelweinstubes*, or apple wine houses. The area was well known for its apple wine, a rather potent cider that was best drunk with the huge German meals.

The old building was a classic, old, half-timbered house dating back at least two or three hundred years. Like many similar buildings, the quality of the original work, together with the occasional renovations every hundred years or so, kept the structure in excellent shape. Huge, dark wooden timbers crossed the ceiling of the main dining room, supporting the floors above. Typical *weinstube* adornment covered the walls; pewter plates, wine flasks and barrel-ends, artificial grape vines and various *Wappen*, or coats of arms from around Germany. The tables were fashioned from heavy, hand hewn planks, now well-worn from countless customers that had enjoyed the food and drink for generations.

Jake was waiting in a booth near the rear of the old *weinstube* when Christa arrived, out of breath. Her long blond hair was pulled back behind her head, accentuating the glow of her cheeks. He watched her walk towards him, scarcely believing what he saw. The last time he had seen her, she was a grown woman, but just barely. At that time, she was just out of high school, an innocent girl in her late teens. Now, in her mid-twenties, she had blossomed to an incredibly beautiful woman, filled out in all of the correct places. He grabbed his cane and rose from the table, unsure of what to say.

"You can close your mouth now, Jakob" she chided as she approached, his mouth gaping in surprise. "Oh, you do look good!" she cried as she threw her arms around him, planting a wet kiss directly on his lips.

He returned the kiss, revelling in her passion, pleasantly aware of her warm body against his, full breasts challenging his own. His body started to respond, confusing him more, as he stammered a reply.

"Christa, my God! I had no idea!" he finally blurted out. Recovering a little, he continued "God it's good to see you again, how are you? Your father said you were doing well at your new job."

"New job?" she laughed, her eyes flashing sapphires. "Father still calls it my 'new job', even though I've been working for the company for about six years now. In any case, it's just fine, and I enjoy the work. They treat me very well, every need is taken care of." She paused, looking at Jake with appraising eyes. "I see you still need the cane - is it still bothering you?"

"Not as much as before, but I still use it for a little backup."

Christa continued "I hear you've done well for yourself Jakob, made millions on that deal a few years ago."

"Yes, I can't complain. I can pretty well do what I want now . . . spend a lot of time travelling, freelance work, that kind of stuff."

"Like this Los Angeles thing?" she asked.

The reality of the present descended on him, and he remembered why he was there. "This Los Angeles thing . . ." he repeated, "Did you see today's paper . . . it's happened again."

"Yes," she replied, "I feel so bad about that," as the waiter came to take their order.

"*Schweinhaxe und Apfelwein*?" he asked, referring to the huge roast pork hocks the restaurant was famous for, together with a large pitcher of the strong apple cider to wash it all down.

"Yes, that's fine Jakob" she replied, also remembering other times they had visited the restaurant.

Jake ordered, then waited for the waiter to get out of range before asking "Have you heard from your father? I got a rather cryptic message from him in Vancouver, just after we both got out of L.A.. He had me stumped for a while . . . he said I should talk to my old hiking partner."

"That was my idea, father is so naive some times, he won't believe that people will tap your phones, spy on you."

"But why?" Jake asked. "Why is all this going on? Who are these people and why are they looking for your father, and why did I have a couple of thugs trailing me as soon as I got off the plane?"

"Slowly Jakob," she smiled, "First . . . why they are after him, he will tell you himself, tomorrow. The only reason I can think of for them to follow you is that they know you can lead them to father."

"Plus a matter of a few samples and some data." Jake added.

Jake continued, explaining the events of the past week, describing her father's suspicious behaviour in Los Angeles, and how he never did find out what his latest research project involved.

"That too, will be explained," Christa added, "Father couldn't stay around here, but he couldn't go home as well. They have our house bugged and watched 24 hours day."

"Bugged? How do you know that?" he asked, "And how do you know they are watching your home?"

"I know, that's my job. I work with security systems all day . . . that's Steinbock's specialty, sort of an adjunct to the financial empire of the parent company." She paused a moment, then added "You should remember the firm, we supplied much of the surveillance equipment you used when you were with Foreign Affairs and Counter Intelligence."

Then he remembered the name of the company, *"Sicherheit Steinbock* . . .of course!" he blurted out, "Steinbock Security! It just hadn't dawned on me before."

Christa nodded, starting to laugh. "Yes, father calls them the 'S.S.', from *Sicherheit Steinbock,* he says the company gives him the creeps. In any case, I discovered some bugs during my last trip home, before all this mess . . . one of our models, actually. Earlier this week, I drove down there to pick up something, that's when I found they were watching the house. That's where father did a lot of his work, so they're expecting him to return to pick up some papers or something."

"Jesus! This is getting more complicated all the time!" Jake exclaimed. "So where is your father, where can I see him?"

She glanced around quickly before answering. "Remember the old inn we stayed at years ago in Sommerhausen?"

"Yes, that's only a couple of hours drive from here, just south of Würzburg."

"That's where you'll find him, still working on some theoretical parts of the process, some unexpected problems . . . he figures he's very close to the answer. You can use my car, otherwise they'll find you if you rent one." She stopped, looking into Jake's eyes. "Please be careful Jakob, these people are serious. They will try anything to follow you and find father." Her eyes dropped as she added "It's wonderful to see you again. It's been a long time, and we must get together again soon, so I don't want anything to happen to you."

Her words struck Jake as foreboding, almost prophetic, adding yet another piece to the puzzle.

The arrival of their dinner interrupted their discussion. The ambience and meal replenished their bodies and lifted their spirits as they devoured the food and wine, laughing over old memories and private jokes. The rest of the evening was a dream for Jake, combining faded memories from the past with new promises for the future.

Chapter 16

Erik Weigel stormed into the room, flinging a newspaper down on the polished surface of the long black walnut table. The two men closest to the end of the table started to stand up, cringing as the paper bounced toward them. Their eyes blinked nervously at every sudden move, as they followed the angry man moving quickly around the table. A meeting called on a Sunday was almost unheard of, so they both knew they were in trouble. Rage and undisguised scorn clouded the man's face as he turned on the two men.

"*Setz dich!* . . . Sit down!" he hissed, continuing past them. Halfway around the table he stopped and turned towards a third man who had calmly remained seated, a thin smile crossing his face as he watched the other two.

"*Können Sie mir sagen, was* . . . Can you tell me, what the hell is going on over there?" he began quietly addressing the third man, then turning to include the others, his piercing eyes sheltered by dark, bushy eyebrows that contrasted with his slicked back, well groomed silver hair and beard. He paused briefly to light a cigarette, sucking the heavy smoke deep into his lungs. Squinting through barely open eyes, his cold stare burned through their defences, melting any resolve or resistance they had left. Exhaling loudly, he continued his reprimand as clouds of smoke enveloped his audience.

"Well, don't you have anything to say?" he continued, glaring at all of them. "We knew this could happen, but I thought we had agreed on a plan of how to cover our collective asses, redirect the attention" he spat out. "Kurt, you were supposed to have our people in place . . . ready to cover and control the information. How did this get out?" he said, stabbing at the newspaper.

The first two men sat still, faces burning, obviously not even aware of what their leader was talking about. Before the third man, Kurt, could offer anything, he was cut off.

"*Idiot!* I'm surrounded by idiots!" He turned and moved further up the table, finally easing his body down in a large, throne-like chair at the end of the table. He shook his head, then wiped an already soggy handkerchief across his sweaty brow. The short man, Helmut Schmidt, flipped open the paper, hoping the topic of the reproach would be apparent. He wasn't disappointed, as the article about the LA disaster almost jumped off the page. His boss had circled the offending sentence in red. "*Local test laboratory may have isolated poison! An interview with Ed Seymour of Seymour Labs today indicated . . .*" he stopped reading, lowering the paper.

Helmut's balding head now glistened with sweat, releasing a few beads that trickled down his forehead. "But, Herr Weigel, I thought . . ."

"You thought? . . . you thought?" Erik Weigel hissed. "*Mist!* . . . Rubbish! You two wouldn't know how to think! If either of you worked in one of our labs, you probably would have killed yourself by now!" He paused, then turned again to the third man.

"And you Kurt, with all your security expertise and contacts, I expected more from you!"

Kurt Landau steeled himself as the veins at his temples bulged, his jaw set firmly. Barely controlling his smouldering hate for this man, he decided to at least try to defend himself.

"We had our man in place in Los Angeles, you know him, an expert . . . he was to keep track of Schiller, control the counter groups, as well as the press and propaganda."

"Well, it didn't work did it? The idiot couldn't even keep track of Schiller . . . then he let this Prescott slip away as well, with both physical samples and data. Now this Seymour has moved in, taken more samples and is holding press conferences!" Shaking his head, he rose from the table and walked to the large picture window looking out over the Main River. "If we are not careful, this whole thing could get out . . . then where would we be?"

Werner Klein, the tall man, fidgeted as he listened to the last comment, the consequences too terrible to contemplate. He moved his bad leg around, trying for a more comfortable position, almost impossible for his lanky body and long legs. He tried to shrink as Weigel turned to him.

"*Und Herr Klein . . .* " he murmured quietly to Werner, a cloud of smoke following the words from his mouth, "Would you be so kind . . . where is this Canadian, Prescott now? The last we heard, he was on his way to Germany to meet with Schiller. What's happening?"

It was Klein's turn to sweat, and he could feel his head getting hot and something run down under his armpits. Bad Luck, maybe he could just plead bad luck. He looked up at his boss, immediately knowing that approach would get him crucified!

"Well, uh . . . " he stammered, "We don't know, we lost him."

"Lost him, what do you mean, you lost him?" He drove the words home as he viciously ground his cigarette into the pile of butts in the large crystal ashtray. His voice much louder now, eyes rivetted on the trembling man. "Are you telling me that an *auslander*, a foreigner comes to Frankfurt for a visit, and you lose him? How many people did you have?"

"Just two . . . " he replied, glancing nervously at his partner. "But this one's different, he knows the city, he . . ."

"*Unglaubich!* Unbelievable!" Weigel cut him off. He paced some more, this time a little faster, his hands alternately wringing together and then stroking his beard. Lighting another cigarette, he puffed more clouds of smoke to the already hazy room. Finally he stopped and turned to his reluctant audience. "*Können Sie mir Bitte sagen . . .* Could you please tell me, what is your plan . . . or do you even have one? What are you doing to catch up with Schiller, or Prescott . . . what about Schiller's daughter?"

Kurt Landau answered first, deciding he needed more personal control of this fiasco, almost ashamed of listening to the other two.

"Considering the situation Herr Weigel, and where she works, I'll take over responsibility for activities here in Frankfurt. We'll watch the girl much closer, as we know now that she's the key to finding both of them. She had dinner with Prescott last night, but . . ."

"Last night! What's this? . . . nobody mentioned this" he spat out. "So you know where Prescott is now? Why . . .?"

"I'm afraid not, Herr Weigel, we didn't know until it was too late . . . when we played back the tapes on her phone at work."

"I want a man on her phone tap around the clock, one who knows both German and English! We can't wait until later when the tapes are played back . . . this is stupid! What do you know of the meeting?"

"Only that they had dinner at a place they used to go to years ago. They used some sort of code, so we don't know where they met."

Erik Wiegel slowly shook his head, scarcely believing what he was hearing from his subordinates. "Kurt, I'm depending on you to straighten this out! Watch the girl, she's your only hope now, you idiots! You should be able to keep track of her, after all, you of all people have the advantage." He paused, staring out the window. Turning again to Kurt Landau, he continued "It appears that this Prescott is no fool, and seems to have no trouble staying one step ahead of us. Maybe you'd better find out a little more about him, use your contacts in America . . . maybe he isn't exactly what he appears."

"*Ja, mein Herr*, I'll make some calls immediately!"

Weigel continued "As for Los Angeles, I want some action, I want some results! Use a few sacrificial lambs if necessary, but get their attention off those test results and back on the radical groups, I don't care which one!"

"Yes sir," they echoed, realizing the meeting was over. Kurt Landau was the last to leave. Holding back until the others left the room, he planned on saying something further, his head twitching slightly from side to side, then decided at the last minute remain quiet and followed the others out.

Erik waited until he was alone in the room, then went to the liquor cabinet in the corner and poured himself a large glass of scotch. As he sipped the amber nectar, he stared out the window, looking down on the city below, his city. Located in his opulent offices high above the financial centre of Frankfurt, he gazed over the complex network of streets, buildings and bridges across the Main River. "Where are you, *auslander*?" he mumbled, trying to figure out where a foreigner would hide in the city. He tossed back the last of his drink and picked up the phone.

"Monique, get me Klaus Müller in Washington."

Frank Haywood was surprised at the knock on his door. Nobody should have known where he was staying, as he had flown out of L.A. in a hurry, catching the afternoon flight to Washington. He fumbled in the darkness for the light on the little night table. The knocking came again as he found the light switch.

"Hang on, for Christ' sake, I'm coming!" he swung his feet out of the bed, picking up his watch from the night table. "Two o'clock? Jeez, this better be good!"

He shuffled to the door. "Who is it?" he called, as he squinted through the little peek-hole in the door. Two uniformed men stood outside the door.

"Frank Haywood? This is the police, please open the door."

Frank quickly unlocked the safety chain, opening the door to two large police officers. Before he had a chance to say anything, one officer crossed over to the bed, then checked the bathroom, looking for someone else. “I’m alone, if that’s what you’re looking for” he offered. “Can I ask what this is about?”

“Mr. Haywood, we’d like you to come with us down to the station, we’d like to ask you a few questions.”

“Questions? About what?” he asked.

“Please get dressed sir, we can explain everything to you at the station.”

“Come on . . . can’t you say something, tell me something?” he asked as he pulled on his pants. He slipped into the bathroom to splash some water on his face and quickly brush his teeth. “Am I being charged?” he called out.

“No sir, not yet . . .”

“Not yet?” he rushed out of the bathroom. “What does that mean, am I under suspicion for something?”

“Sir you are being held for questioning on the Los Angeles poison gas attacks.”

“I think I should call my lawyer.”

“In due time, Frank. You’ll get your call.”

Frank stopped asking questions, the entire scene just too ludicrous to consider. Once dressed, he picked up his brief case and followed the two men down to their car.

The next two hours faded from memory as he was led from office to office, questioned by first one man, then another, each one it seemed was from a different government organization, including the FBI, NSO and Homeland Security and others. The questions involved events and organizations he had never heard of, from his own WASTE group to fanatic renegade cults known for their radical behaviour. Not satisfied with his answers, they tried vaguely disguised threats, suggesting they might have to bring out damning details of his past, referring to the old Millwood case.

“But that’s all past, finished,” he mumbled, half asleep. “You can’t bring that back.”

“Nothing’s finished Frank, until we say it is!”

"I want to talk to my lawyer . . . now!"

He had little recollection of the next steps, only that he woke up the next morning in a cell with a heavy head and a murder charge over his head!

Chapter 17

THE EASY DRIVE TO SOMMERHAUSEN was a welcome break in the hectic pace of the past week. After a good night's sleep and a substantial breakfast at the little hotel on Neue Kräme Street, Jake settled his bill and headed out, initially on foot. After a circuitous route around the market and a few tourist areas, he found Christa's car at the place they had pre-arranged the night before. Without any delay, he headed across one of the car bridges towards Sachsenhausen, continuing south-east to the A-3 Autobahn just south of Offenbach. This highway took him straight east towards Würzburg, through pleasant countryside scenery, wooded areas and the occasional village along the way. As he neared Würzburg, the highway bypassed just south of the city, where Jake eventually turned off on a smaller road heading almost due south to the village of Sommerhausen.

Sommerhausen was an idyllic little example of a typical old German village, situated on the banks of the Main River, in the middle of the thriving Franken wine growing area. The surrounding sides of the valley that sloped down to the river were covered with vineyards, broken occasionally with another village or small farm settlement. As Jake approached the north end of the village, he could see the little hamlet of Winterhausen, located directly across the river from Sommerhausen. He knew the names came from "Summer house" and "Winter house", but Jake never found out the original story behind the names. He did remember the plaque that Christa and he had found one day, in the centre of the village, mounted on a stone wall in a small courtyard. The plaque had been installed in honour of Franz Pastorious, a man born in Sommerhausen, the first German settler in America and the founder of Germantown, Pennsylvania.

After passing under the arched stone gateway in the old medieval wall surrounding the village, he continued along the *"Hauptstraße"*, or main street, a cobblestoned route that cut the town in half. Near the centre of the village, he turned off and pulled into a small courtyard beside an old "*Gästhaus*", or guest house. Old memories returned as Jake got out of the car, surrounded by the smells and history of the wine culture. Stefan had known the proprietor's family for many years, and often stayed there during trips to Frankfurt or abroad.

For a person from North America, the interior of the inn was a cross between a museum and a movie set. The hand hewn wooden beams, glowed with generations of dusting and polishing. The stone thresholds of the doorways and flagstones on the floor were worn down by thousands of footsteps. For Jake, coming from a place where something was really old if it was over a hundred years, these numbers always amazed him. Here, some structures were Roman, up to two thousand years old. Even the buildings still in use dated back to the fourteen or fifteen hundreds, some claiming to be dated back in the twelve hundreds! The sheer age and permanency of things, even the people were so foreign to him. In this case, the same family had run the guest house for almost 400 years!

Stefan welcomed him in tears, climaxing his anticipation of the meeting. The tension of the past week had taken its toll, stamping his features with new and deeper creases. Jake was shocked by the pathetic combination of a pallid, stubble covered face with dark, sagging circles under bloody eyes.

"*Mein Gott, Stefan! Was machst du* . . . My God, Stefan, what are you doing . . . what have you . . .?" He couldn't believe the change in his old friend since he last saw him, barely a week ago! The room was a mess, soiled clothes piled on the bed, reference books open everywhere, the entire room permeated with the musty odour of an unwashed body and the sour stench of overripe food. The large work table was covered with papers, some weighted down with empty wine bottles, pieces of dried bread and bits of sausage and cheese. "When was the last time you had a real meal?" he asked.

"Oh, come Jakob, don't you start . . . you sound like my Christa . . . we have too much to talk about."

"I have a million questions too, Stefan, but they can wait! Maybe you don't want to eat, but I'm starved." Jake moved across the room, opening the window wide to clear out the foulness. "You get in there and clean up, I'll go down and order us some lunch."

Stefan reluctantly surrendered, shuffling off to the shower. Jake went down to the dining room and ordered a large meal for the both of them. Before long, a slightly more presentable Stefan showed up, a weak smile already transforming his appearance. At Jake's insistence, they first gulped down a pint of beer each, "for old times sake" Jake said, knowing it would help Stefan relax. For their meal, he ordered a bottle of *Ernst Gebhardt's Müller-Thurgau*, one of Stefan's favourite Franconian wines, bottled right there in Sommerhausen. Before long, they were well into both the wine and the food, recharging their energy for the ordeal ahead. Jake waited until Stefan had finally pushed away his plate, surprised at how much he had eaten.

"See, I told you! You can't think or work properly when the engine doesn't have any fuel!" He laughed as he added "A very wise old man told me that years ago, when I was struggling with my thesis paper." Jake paused, repeating Stefan's favourite old German poem that Stefan had taught him years before. "Remember Stefan . . . this little gem . . . the one you reminded me of last week in L.A.?"

"Frankenwein ist Krankenwein
Heissts im Lande auf und ab
Auf Wein gestelle Frankenbeine
Gehen nicht so schnell ins Grab."

"Franconia wine is for when you're sick
So they say throughout the country
Legs that stand on Franconian wine
don't step so early into the grave."

Stefan chuckled, also remembering the time he had to force Jake to slow down and take better care of himself, or "the machinery will break down" he used to tell him.

"Stefan, old friend, I think it's time we talked. Let's go for a walk, the fresh air will do you good!"

They left the guest house and headed down a little side street towards the river. The sun was hot and bright, warming their bodies and lifting their spirits. Stefan was quiet, saying nothing until they neared the river. White swans drifted gracefully along the shoreline, followed by their little cygnets, trailing behind.

"How would you like me to tell you?" Stefan asked, his face once again lined with concern.

"Just start at the beginning, what is this all about, what do you have to do with the Los Angeles problem, why are these men after you . . .?"

"O.K., O.K., *Langsam,* slowly Jakob, all in good time!" holding up his hands in self defence. He paused briefly, gathering his thoughts, then continued. "It was I who killed all those people!"

"Wha . . . what are you saying, Stefan?" Jake cried, "How do you figure that . . . why don't you start at the beginning?"

"It's true . . . but . . . you are right, I should start at the beginning." They continued walking along the bank of the river, pausing occasionally to skip stones as Stefan related the events leading up to their present situation.

"About eight years ago, I was working on some fuel research in Munich, part of a long term emissions study we were involved in. Most of the research involved the use of catalysts, my specialty. Just when we were on the brink of trying something new, a slightly different twist you might say, in the field of fossil fuel emissions, the research money dried up. For almost a year, I travelled around, trying to get somebody to sponsor additional work. The research cost was high at that point, because I needed more test equipment, engines, fuel and enough manpower to pull it all off." He paused, his face hardened by the memories. "Finally, during a conference in Washington, I met someone from the U.S. Government, Department of Energy, or something like that. When they heard my ideas, that there were both energy savings and environmental benefits, they were definitely interested. After a few meetings, we arrived at an agreement. I still don't know which group finally financed it, I think they set up some kind of consortium, even interested some private firms to help, but eventually, a special fund was set up to cover all of our costs. Luckily, one of the companies allowed us to use their main research facility near Munich."

"Which one?" Jake asked, "And which company owned it?"

Stefan shook his head slowly, almost embarrassed at the question. "Jakob, I honestly don't know . . . we just called it the *T.U.Z., Technischer Umvelt Zentrum*, or Technical Environmental Centre."

Jake smiled, knowing Stefan's naive nature wouldn't worry about any of the details of the agreement, only whether he had enough money to complete his research.

Stefan continued "The next three or four years are a blur, we covered hundreds of tests, tried all kinds of combinations, finally picking what we thought was the ideal combination." He stopped a moment, turning to Jake. "Jakob, you're familiar with the use of lead in the automobile gasoline?"

"Of course . . . it's outlawed now in most jurisdictions, but it was used for years as an additive to help combustion, prevent knocking in the car engines."

"That's correct . . . and it was that property of improving the combustion that we were trying to copy, only better. Several years ago, a professor in Canada developed a similar process using iron as the additive. By adding minute quantities of a special iron solution to the fuel, the combustion of gasoline or fuel oils was enhanced considerably, reducing fuel consumption only slightly, but significantly cutting both NOx and particulate emissions in the exhaust. Several attempts to market this technology were tried, but the idea really never took off, mainly because the fuel savings were small, barely offsetting the cost of the additive."

"Yes, I remember that, I was working on my new techniques at the time and was frustrated by the local government's total lack of action or even interest in environmental benefits."

They both paused as a long river barge chugged past them, its large bow wave surging over the anchor chained to the vessel's stem. The Main River was a major shipping route for the transport of goods through Germany, from the North Sea via the Rhine, down to Austria and Hungary through the canal connecting the Main to the Danube further south. To Jake, the barges were beautiful examples of an ideal nautical life. Most of the ships were immaculately kept by the family that owned them and lived on board, often a small car strapped on the cabin roof for use in whatever port they stop at along the way.

As the long vessel continued up the river, Stefan continued with his account. "We tried several metals, both in solutions or solid. Colloidal suspensions were big for a while, but always we came back to solutions. Each material had to be tested under every condition, using various types of engines under different loads, each time running a blind or control run to compare our results. Each time we thought we had a good one, something would come up to disappoint us . . . like the time we had fantastic results, but the engine burnt up after only a few hours of running!" He chuckled as he mulled over his memories, preparing for the next step.

"It was then, just over a year ago, I finally came up with what I thought was the right combination. We had tried it before, but not in the right additive medium. After months of tests, we finally decided this was our best combination."

He stopped talking, still deep in thought. They continued to walk, Jake waiting for the other shoe to drop. Finally, he couldn't wait any longer.

"Well, what was it . . . what did you decide?" he asked.

"Nickel" Stefan replied. "We used a very precise solution of nickel compounds to add to the fuel."

The word hit Jake like a slap in the face. His thoughts all jammed up in his mouth as he tried to confirm the statement.

"Nickel . . ." he repeated, "Like in nickel carbonyl?" he asked.

Chapter 18

Stefan's face grew sombre, his jaw clenched tightly. Tears filled his eyes as he shook his head, covering his face with his hands.

"*Nein, Nein . . . Oh Mein Gott!* My God, I didn't mean to kill all those people, it wasn't supposed to happen! They were supposed to stop it!"

Jake put his hand on the older man's shoulder, trying to console him. "Stefan, please, don't blame your self . . . what do you mean, it wasn't supposed to happen, who was supposed to stop it?"

Stefan dried his eyes, finally controlling his trembling. "No, I must tell you everything . . . where was I . . .?" he mumbled.

"You finally decided on nickel as your main component." Jake coached.

"Right! Ah yes, after a few tests with our new formulation, we knew we had it. It was very tricky, the mixture had to be prepared carefully, just the right proportions . . . but the results . . . they were fantastic from the beginning!"

"In what way, Stefan, what did you find?"

"Of course we still had months of tests to do, results to document. We couldn't leave anything to chance, the outcome was too important." The old man paused, gathering his thoughts as he scanned the pastoral landscape around them. The summer sun glinted off the water, silhouetting a couple of swans coasting along the shoreline. "The first thing we noticed was the increased performance of the engines, while at the same time, the fuel consumption decreased dramatically."

"How much Stefan, do you remember any of the numbers?"

"Remember? I'll never forget! Engine power output increased from five to ten percent, depending on the type of fuel used. At the same time, fuel consumption dropped by a similar amount, five to ten percent. Under certain conditions, it was even better!"

"My God," Jake gasped, "That's incredible . . . are you sure?"

"Of course my boy! This was my life for almost eight years, I cannot forget a single detail."

"But, with ten percent savings . . . Jesus, Stefan, that would mean millions of dollars, maybe even hundreds of millions in fuel savings alone! That's incredible . . ."

"Not just millions Jakob, billions! Think of the millions of barrels of oil used every day around the world, think of what we could achieve if we could cut that use by almost ten percent! Think of the beneficial effect on the greenhouse gas problem, *mein Gott,* how do you say in English . . . it bogs my mind!"

"It boggles the mind." Jake corrected.

"*Genau!* Exactly! Boggles the mind! We knew we had a 'hot one', as you put it, so we tried to keep it secret within our own group as long as possible, before announcing the results to our sponsors. We needed to be sure, document the numbers."

"Of course."

"The more we tested, the better the numbers became. We were elated, but we had another surprise . . . the emission numbers! Of course with less fuel, etc., one would expect some drop in the numbers, but nothing like what we experienced. As you can imagine, because of the better combustion, the carbon monoxide dropped slightly, but only at first . . . that's the one that caught us later. The NOx, the Oxides of Nitrogen, dropped significantly, less than half of normal emission levels!"

"Less than half? But how . . . wha . . ."

"Depending on fuel again, gasoline or diesel fuel, the NOx levels dropped between forty-five to fifty-five percent."

"Do you realize what that could mean Stefan? My God, it would be the biggest breakthrough in recent history for both the environmental and the energy industries!"

"I know Jakob, I know . . . that's what we thought as well. Don't forget, we had been working on this for a few years, so we had done all of the arithmetic, we knew what the numbers meant." His face became troubled, angry.

"What is it Stefan, what's wrong?"

"That's when the word leaked out."

"So? You had results, you could really show them what they had spent their money on."

"*Ja, richtig!* Yes, that's right! but as soon as they heard the results, they wanted to start immediately to market the product, do mass field tests, etc. We weren't ready for that, there were too many unanswered questions."

"Couldn't you just hold the results, tell them?"

"No, there were too many people involved, they had spies within the T.U.Z., our own group, scientists who had close ties to the 'mother' company, the people who supplied the money. These scientists knew the process, almost as much as I did."

"So what did you do?"

"Nothing. Oh, I tried . . . meetings, pleading, trying to prove to them that we needed more tests . . . nothing. As soon as the . . . what do you call them . . . 'the number crunchers' got our test figures, they worked out what the process was worth on the world market. That's when things became ugly!"

"What happened?" Jake was thoroughly captivated by the older man's account, the entire picture now starting to clear up.

"We had a visit, from our sponsor in Washington, this guy from the U.S. Government, Klaus Müller."

"Sounds like one of your countrymen, Stefan."

"He was, not far from our village actually. After finishing university in Munich, he moved to the U.S. to study politics. He's the right type, cold, hard . . . a good talker. He did well for himself, landed a good job in Washington . . . well the rest is history. In any case, we had been working with Klaus for a few years, he was our liaison man in Washington for the funding consortium, so he had to come over to congratulate us. Actually, what he wanted was to take the results back to his boss to get all the credit. I didn't give a damn about who got the credit, I just wanted to do more testing!"

"So what happened, did they give you any more time?"

"Yes and no. They took the results, said they wanted to do some additional tests themselves, but we could continue with our testing."

Stefan continued his account, describing in detail the additional tests they performed. The sun was dropping low over the trees on the far side of the river, stretching out their shadows as they left the river bank and walked slowly back towards the village.

"I was worried about the CO levels, the carbon monoxide. The numbers seemed to change with every test. It wasn't until much later we noticed that the levels fluctuated with the surrounding temperature, the temperature of the combustion air. That proved to be one weak part of the program, but not serious. It was much later that we found the real problem."

"The real problem?" questioned Jake. "How so?"

"You must realize, up to this point, all of our tests were done in lab conditions, sort of ideal, clean, controllable conditions. I was worried about the CO problem, so I suggested we had to vary some of the other conditions as well. That's when we got some real car engines, exhaust systems, the entire system, and mounted them in our environmental test chamber. At first, things went well, the systems performed as expected, plus or minus . . ."

"Plus or minus?" Jake asked.

"No, really, they were good. It was later, much later, we started increasing the ambient temperature of the chamber, you know, simulating a hot summer day. At the same time, we also started recirculating some of the exhaust within the chamber, simulating a smoggy day, or cars sucking in other exhausts . . . that's when it happened."

"What . . . what happened?"

"The numbers quite suddenly went all weird . . . CO, NOx . . . almost like something had happened to the analyzers. That's when one of the technicians went into the chamber to do a quick check on our connections, make sure the analyzers were O.K." Stefan stopped walking, his face grimacing with anguish. "He never came out."

"My God! The nickel carbonyl . . . is that what happened?" Jake whispered.

"Yes, nickel carbonyl . . . of course we didn't know it then, we had no idea what the problem was, it reacted so fast! In fact, we almost lost another technician, going in after the first! Luckily, we realized what was happening and we stopped them in time. Unfortunately it was too late for the first man."

"So what was it, could you figure it out, what happened?"

"Yes, but it took weeks of work, different kinds of tests, this time very carefully controlled . . . with a few more safety measures installed." He turned to Jake and asked "Do you know how nickel carbonyl is made Jakob?"

"From what we could find out, it had something to do with the nickel refining process, by passing carbon monoxide over finely powdered nickel."

"Something like that. In this case, a whole series of events and chemical reactions lead up to the final reaction." He waved a finger at Jake, squinting his eyes in a conspiratory manner. "It just proves, Jakob, don't take anything for granted, everything can affect the reaction, no matter how insignificant. You see, the one thing we didn't have during the first tests were the *Katalysator*, the catalytic converters they use on cars now."

"Of course, they cut down the NOx levels, convert back to nitrogen, water, etc." Jake offered.

"*Genau!* Unfortunately, we didn't realize what our nickel additive was doing to the converter. Later tests showed that the inside of the converter was coated with a very fine layer of nickel residue, an interesting compound or alloy that acted as a very powerful catalyst, pushing our reaction along. As you know, an effective catalyst doesn't have to be present in very large quantities."

"I know, Stefan" Jake agreed. "Do you know what the reaction was? You have standard exhaust gases to work with . . . don't you? Did you ever figure out anything specific about the reaction?"

"No, not exactly, that's where things fell apart. With elevated temperatures, plus the re-circulation of the exhaust, the system worked as designed up to a critical point, then a catalytic chain reaction started, a reaction somehow using the nickel-doctored converter, together with additional nickel additive in the fuel, reacting with the excess CO in the exhaust! The result . . . large quantities of nickel carbonyl, which as you know by now, is deadly!"

"But Stefan, that doesn't make sense! Have you worked out the formulas . . . what's actually happening?"

"I don't know Jakob, but believe me, it happens . . . and we now have almost seventy people dead to prove it!" He paused again, curbing his emotions. "Even though it is my specialty, we really understand very little about catalytic reactions, how they really work. From our studies, we estimate that when the additive material coats the inside of the converter, it transforms somehow into a very powerful catalyst, one we cannot control, but we must learn how to stop!"

"You said earlier that it wasn't supposed to happen. What did you mean by that?"

"Greed! That's all that drives them!"

"Drives who? Who are you talking about?"

"Those *Schwein* in Washington! When we started to report these problems, they sent their people in, a blanket of security was thrown over the entire project . . . we weren't allowed to discuss any of this with anyone. We wanted them to stop their tests, but they would not listen, they had already gone too far. Unknown to us, they were planning a massive field test in the U.S., in Los Angeles as it turned out. They managed to produce enough of the additive to doctor all of the fuel supplies in the north end of L.A. . . . they actually delivered some additive to every gasoline filling station in the area. Only an organization with government clout can handle a project of that size. They figured that if they could influence even part of the city, the results should show up on the monitoring network. That's why they picked a slightly separate part of the city, because the commuters would be more likely to use those stations and the emissions would tend to be concentrated more in that area."

"That explains the extra analyzers . . . " Jake mumbled.

"What's that? Oh, the analyzers, right, they wanted them in place to confirm some of the numbers, then they could announce the results. The formal announcement was planned for the closing day of the W.A.W.A. conference, but as you know, the results were not quite what was expected, so all publication and press releases were cancelled."

"So . . . is that why you were there?"

"Yes and no. Klaus Müller asked me to be there for the press releases, to answer questions. I think that NSO man, Paul Butler, was watching me, to make sure I didn't let anything else loose, you know . . . talk about the problems. Unfortunately, after the first incident, all press contact was forbidden, they wanted to keep me quiet . . . that's when I took off."

"But who are 'they', who are we talking about here Stefan?"

"At first, I thought it was the U.S. Government, the consortium." He stopped, confused. "But it's more than just that. Someone, some other organization is behind the government, probably the company that owns the T.U.Z., the major financier of the project . . . I still don't know who . . . that's who is driving this thing."

"So why are they still chasing you, why are they chasing me?"

"Of course they want me to continue the research for them, work out these problems. As for you, I think they feel you are a threat to the project . . . without even knowing what was going on, you managed to outfox them, analyze the gas, and figure out a large portion of the puzzle. This bothers them, to have someone coming even close to the answer, that's why they are using that smoke-screen of environmental terrorists or fanatical cults. After all, there are billions at stake, and they do not want to be implicated." He turned to Jake, concern in his face. "Be careful Jakob, do not underestimate these people! They will go to any lengths to push this through, and if anyone gets in their way, they will be run over."

Chapter 19

FRANK HAYWOOD BREATHED A SIGH of relief as soon as he and his lawyer hit the street. They released him later that afternoon shortly after his lawyer appeared on the scene. George Barnes was efficient and thorough, and the Washington police had enough experience with him not to argue the finer points of law. Ed Seymour's press conference in Los Angeles the day before had helped George's plea, but still had not totally convinced the authorities that Frank was not responsible. The findings of the analytical work in L.A. had determined the cause of the deaths, but had still not resolved the problem of where the gas had come from and who was responsible. Frank was as puzzled as anyone about the poisonings, but even more puzzled by what his lawyer told him after his release.

"I don't usually work on a Sunday, Frank. This is going to cost you dearly!" George's New England twang flavoured his comments and his broad smile belied their meaning as they left the building together. He steered Frank down the street to a popular coffee bar, something obviously on his mind.

"Frank," he began slowly, "We've been through a lot over the years, so I've got to tell you . . . something stinks here!" he blurted out the words between sips of coffee.

"What do you mean George?" he asked, thinking his old friend was just concerned about his overnight stay in jail. "I figure these Washington cops got wind that I was back in town and got a little over-zealous . . . figured it would be good if they caught the terrorist responsible for the L.A. attacks."

"No, Frank, it isn't that at all," he said as he lit up yet another cigarette. Clouds of blue smoke engulfed his head as he continued to explain his findings to Frank. "First, how did they know you were in town, and where you were staying? You said yourself, you only decided to fly to Washington at the last minute. You have to have some influence or clout with the authorities to pick up that kind of information."

"Christ, I don't know George . . . what are you saying?"

"Let me finish . . . second, why wait until you got here . . . if they suspected you, why didn't they arrest you in Los Angeles? Third, as they didn't have a single reason or a shred of evidence, I should sue their asses for wrongful arrest, harassment at least . . . to say nothing of preventing you from calling me until this morning!"

Frank stared, almost afraid to see where this was going.

George continued "It sounds like some kind of scare tactic and I don't like it! It reminds me too much of the last time . . . you remember Millwood?"

"Millwood . . . yes . . . they even mentioned that last night . . ."

"Last night . . . what do you mean, Frank, after they arrested you?"

"Yeah, later . . . after they had questioned me for a long time, suggested I cooperate or they might drag some of that old stuff up again."

"The old bastard! After all this time . . . I thought he had better things to do!"

"Who George? Who the hell . . .?" He stopped abruptly, his eyes wide, unbelieving. "Oh, my God . . . not again! Dick Pelly? Do you really think he has a hand in this George . . . after all these years?"

"It sure sounds like it Frank . . . our old nemesis, Senator Richard Pelly has both the clout and the motive. I'm sure he still hates your guts after the Millwood fiasco!"

"The feeling is mutual! For four years I've tried to forget it . . . too many people got hurt real bad in that blood-bath!" Memories of the stress and anguish of months of hearings returned, almost choking him. "What the hell is he doing now, why is he dogging me again after me after all this time?"

"That's what I'd like to know! I have a few scores to settle with Big Dick myself!" said George, using a nick-name that nobody dared to use in the Senator's presence. The overweight, southern 'gentleman' had made a lot of enemies during his years in Washington, but always seemed to have enough clout and support to survive in office. His self-appointed goal in life seemed to be to crush all forms of environmental reform. To the joy of industrial leaders from his own state, he voted against all environmental bills, pushing for growth, expansion and unlimited development. In his mind, it was the 'American Way', and the God-given right of every industry to go all-out in pursuit of the almighty buck!

"I'm going to ask around town . . . see if I can find out what's happening, what he's up to." He paused a moment, looking at his client closely. "Are you all right Frank?" he asked.

The question brought Frank back to the present, leaving the bitter memories of past years behind. "Yeah, I'm fine George, thanks."

"I talked to this Ed Seymour in L.A. this morning . . . had a helluva time tracing down his home number. Seems like there's a lot more to this thing than what has hit the press so far."

"Wha . . . what are you talking about?" Frank asked.

"Do you know a Jake Prescott . . . some Canadian that runs a hi-tech environmental operation up in Vancouver somewhere?"

"Jake Prescott . . . of course . . . I met him again at the WAWA conference, but I don't think he even remembered me. He was in L.A. when the shit hit the fan!"

"I know, that's what Ed Seymour told me. But that's not all . . . in the middle of all that confusion the first day, they actually got samples from the cadavers from the first attack, plus data from the L.A. monitoring network."

"So . . .? I would imagine all the government agencies had their share of work to do in that disaster!"

"That's what I thought, but no Frank, nobody else got any samples . . . in fact, nobody else was even sampling! Someone had controlled the entire operation, prevented anything from being done, anything from leaking out. I've checked with a few other sources, and it's the same thing. Someone orchestrated the entire show, everyone thought that someone else was doing it!"

Frank's mouth hung open, scarcely believing what he was hearing.

"Not only that, but they came to Seymour's lab and confiscated their samples, then went to the South Coast District and deleted all their data files . . . no mean feat, believe me, when you understand how they protect and back up all their data! That way, they could now control all the results, what was released to the press, etc."

"But that's crazy! What in hell would they have to gain by that . . . why would they want to do that?"

"I'm not sure . . .I'm almost afraid to speculate . . . that's another reason why I want to ask a few questions around town, find out who has the clout to handle something like that."

Frank's attention was total, concentrating on every word that George told him. "Wait . . . you said that Jake Prescott got some samples the first day? What happened to them, how come he was allowed?"

"He wasn't. He and his friends in L.A. did it on the sly, then Jake took off with extra samples and duplicates of the data . . . and has been on the run ever since!" He related much of the story that Ed Seymour had told him over the phone, filling in as many of the gaps as possible.

"Christ, George . . . I don't like the way this is going!"

"You're telling me! In any case, I want you to do something for me, while I'm snooping around Washington."

"What's that George?" Frank asked, glad to offer anything he could to solve this mystery.

"Call your friend . . . this Jake Prescott . . . see if you can find out what he knows, go up to see him if necessary. You speak *lingua environmentus*, that environmental language, so you'll know what he's saying more than I would. Call me as soon as you find something. In any case, we'll meet again on Wednesday . . . we should have something by then."

George dropped Frank off at his hotel before heading to his own office to prepare for the coming week. These new events gave him energy and interest he had been missing lately . . . driven by an underlying desire to see Senator Dick Pelly's hide nailed to the wall!

Frank Haywood was tired, having lost most of his sleep the night before. He phoned Jake Prescott's lab in Vancouver, hoping that someone would be there. Unfortunately, he was forced to leave a message with a hi-tech voice-mail system before crashing for a few hours sleep.

Kurt Landau's temper still burned from his meeting with Weigel. When he left the building, he headed directly to the communications centre securely located below ground in the old office building where he worked. Only one worker was in the office as a result of a manpower problem he had been fighting for years with Weigel. With the go-ahead to get people on the phones around the clock, he quickly made a few calls, tracing down a few people he could trust.

He then entered a closed communications booth, secure from prying eyes and ears. After looking up some numbers in a small book from his pocket, he used a special scrambler telephone to make two long calls to a couple of interesting and diverse locations thousands of miles away. Once complete, he was satisfied that he had started events in motion.

Chapter 20

JAKE STAYED OVER SUNDAY NIGHT at the little *Gästhaus* in Sommerhausen with Stefan, enjoying an entire evening of reminiscing about years past. Long conversations in German gave him excellent practice. By the time the evening was over, he was back up to speed, any remains of an accent indistinguishable from one of the many regional dialects. His love for the hearty German food and wine added to his enjoyment, but he started to wish that Christa was with them, like the old days. No, not like the old days, much better. Thinking back to the previous night in the restaurant, he remembered his first sight of her, radiant and beautiful! He realized how much she had changed and how much he had missed, a mistake he was hoping to rectify!

Later Sunday evening he called Christa at home in Frankfurt. Suspecting her telephone would be tapped, they used a prearranged code to plan another meeting the following day. They both had to suppress their desire to talk, to ask and answer questions, but they realized they would have to wait. He also desperately wanted to call both Los Angeles and his office first thing Monday morning, but being almost a day ahead of them, he would have to wait until Monday afternoon, Frankfurt time.

The following morning he enjoyed breakfast with Stefan before returning to Frankfurt. He tried to gather as much information as possible about what Stefan knew about his backers, his contacts in Washington. As a successful businessman himself, Jake was amazed at Stefan's ignorance and innocence in business matters, for years always trusting someone else to look after the details. He only hoped he would have enough information to continue his investigation of this riddle.

Avoiding the commuter rush the following morning, he left Sommerhausen shortly after breakfast, arriving at the outskirts of the city almost three hours later, turning Christa's little car north to cross the bridge into the downtown area just before noon. Rather than risk a well known, chain hotel where he might be traced, he returned to his favourite little Neue Kräme Hotel after parking the little car a few blocks away. Christa didn't disappoint him. As planned, Christa had taken the day off and they met in the Kleinmarkthalle, the large public market building where Jake had lost his two pursuers a few days previous. Their meeting was even more emotional than the first, Christa now worried about both her father and now Jake. Jake knew it was more than concern, on both sides. Seeing her again, his heart-rate quickened.

Their embrace was more than that of a couple of old friends. When the prolonged kiss started to attract earthy remarks, they pushed each other apart, faces flushed and pulses racing.

Jake changed the subject by telling Christa about her father, at first skipping over the details of the research and potential dangers. He tried unsuccessfully to assure her it was only some private funded research that had gone wrong. Unconvinced, she kept prodding, digging with little questions until he finally was forced to tell her everything. At worst, she at least knew what to expect. Who knows, he thought, this was her territory and she might be able to help.

They continued walking, heading up Hassen Gasse after they had left the Kleinmarkthalle. They turned left along the Zeil, now packed with summer tourists, and headed west towards the Hauptwache. Jake felt more comfortable mixing in with the crowds, but continued to watch over his shoulder. He was sure that nobody would be following them now, but he remained cautious nevertheless. They picked a little weinstube restaurant to have lunch and plan their next move.

"I've missed you Jakob" Christa murmured after they were seated, clasping his hands tightly. "More than you know" she added. Jake watched her face as she talked, drawn by her flashing blue eyes and full, inviting lips. She told him how she had missed him for years, how her teenage crush had continued long after he had left to return to Canada. Later, when she heard that he had got married, she felt shunned, totally rejected. Her eyes misted over as she described her anger towards him and Lori, his wife, and how she had secretly wished all kinds of bad luck upon them. She quietly sobbed as old feelings of guilt and anguish caught up with her.

Jake reached across the table, trying to comfort her. He had dealt with his grief years ago, Lori's memory fading over the years. It was almost as if Christa had not come to terms with the event.

"No," she said, quickly drawing her hand away. "I must get this out, I have to tell you." She continued her 'confession' as she called it, explaining to Jake how guilty she had felt when Lori died, how she felt she was responsible for her death, because of all the wishes and bad luck she had called upon them.

"But that's crazy, Christa! You were not responsible for Lori's death . . . you can't continue to feel guilty just because of your feelings at the time!" He tried to reassure and comfort her. Christa's teenage infatuation had grown over the years to a deep love for Jakob. Unfortunately, her jealousy and rage had turned inward, in a form of adult guilt and remorse, yet with no valid reason.

Once she had poured it all out, Christa felt much better, leaving Jake dazed and confused, not sure what he should do or say. Luckily, they were rescued once more by the waiter bringing their lunch. An excellent Rhine wine completed the meal, smoothing their nerves as well.

As he settled their bill, a little flattery, negotiation and a rather obscene tip provided them with the temporary use of the manager's office for a few phone calls. Jake assured the manager he would cover all costs and then some. As he picked up the phone, he glanced quickly around the office, noticing a fax machine. He motioned to Christa to negotiate for the use of it as well.

Shannon Hall answered the telephone, almost choking on her morning coffee when she found out is was Jake.

"Jake! God, am I glad to hear your voice! I suppose you've already heard about the latest L.A. thing? Brent called Friday . . . talked to Alan."

"Yes Shannon, I heard the next morning and called Alan early Saturday morning. Anything more since then?"

"Not much, I haven't talked to Alan this morning yet. Ed and Linda Seymour held a press conference late Friday and released the results of their tests for the downtown attack. It seems to have done the trick, the N.S.O. guy and the others have backed off, they're not bothering them now, and we haven't heard anything more from C.S.I.S. or the R.C.M.P.. There was an important message for you though . . . ah, our phones are still acting up . . . can I fax it to you?"

"Right Shannon," knowing she was referring to the phone tap. Glad that he didn't have to use the pre-arranged code with the book, Jake knew the fax was almost as secure. "Here's the number, 011 49 69 . . ." he finished with the number off the fax machine beside him, knowing anyone listening wouldn't be able to trace the number and act on it before they were gone. He continued "Please send it right now, as I'll only be here for a few more minutes."

He hung up, hoping Shannon wouldn't waste time sending the message. He didn't have to wait long, as the fax machine started to ring a few minutes later, and the hand written note from Shannon crept out of the machine.

> *"Please call Frank Haywood in Washington at this number. Imperative you talk to him . . . something's wrong, apparently they arrested him on suspicion of being involved in the L.A. thing. He spent the night in jail.*

He's been released, but he wants your help. Also, call Ed Seymour again, a Scott Anderson from WBC interviewed them on Saturday and he is very anxious to talk to you as well. Alan and Peter have some interesting information for you, but it can wait. Keep in touch, Shannon."

Before they left the office, Jake returned a fax with a quick summary of some of his findings, only that he had found the source of the gas, how it was formed, etc., but was still trying to track down the people responsible. He then made several more calls, first to Brent Willis in Los Angeles.

"Jake, you've heard?"

"Yeah, Brent . . . I got it all from Alan on Saturday. You'd better be more careful Brent . . . that stuff is deadly!"

"Tell me about it! Ed and I were wandering around among all those poor bastards . . . gives me the creeps to think about it!"

"Brent, listen . . ." Jake continued, filling in Brent on the cause of the disasters, the source of the nickel carbonyl. "You've got to talk to your boss . . . get the authorities in on this, because you're going to need a lot of help. Ask Ed or Linda to come up with another story to back you up . . . about tracing the source of the problem to the gasoline . . . just keep me out of it for now. Then, they'll have to come up with a quick field test for the nickel compounds in the gasoline . . . you'll have to go around the north end of town . . . find out which gas-stations are still selling gas with this additive. Once the problem showed up, they probably stopped any further shipments or adding the stuff, and it might already be diluted enough not to matter, but we can't take the chance! Maybe just another load of clean gasoline will do the job. We don't know how effective this catalyst is . . . or how long the catalytic reaction will continue once the additive is removed."

"Right Jake. Thanks for the call . . . it's really going to hit the fan around here when this gets out!"

"Ah, Brent . . . maybe you'd better try to keep a lid on this. Talk to someone in your department . . . I don't think this should get out . . . at least until the problem is solved. Besides, we're still trying to find out who's behind it." He thought for a moment, something nagging at his subconscious. "Has Paul Butler been around lately?"

"No, I don't think so . . . in fact, I haven't seen him since the first event. I think Ed and Linda's press release took the wind out of everybody's sails."

"And nobody's been back to confiscate your data?"

"No . . . but then I did the same thing as Ed . . . I made back-up copies. Right after the incident, I down-loaded the data and made a copy . . . which is hidden away. Actually, I don't think they are interested in us any more, once the word was out about the actual cause, they are most likely running around trying to find out who did it . . ."

"Or trying to decide who they will blame it on." Jake interjected.

"Well, like I said, they're really putting pressure on all of the environmental groups."

"Yeah, I heard they just arrested Frank Haywood in Washington, they thought he was in on it. Knowing Frank's background, are they ever wrong! Just out of curiosity Brent, if you see Butler around, or even hear about him in the area, call my office and let me know. I'll talk to you again soon.

Chapter 21

Jake didn't need the inquisitive glances of the restaurant manager to remind him he had overstayed his welcome. Settling his account, with another large tip, they quickly left the building and continued down the Zeil towards the Hauptwache. The mid-summer sun had enticed tourists from their hotels and sprinkled them along the streets, scurrying like ants to the nearest tourist attraction. Jake and Christa picked their way through the crowds, not heading anywhere in particular, but just putting distance between themselves and the restaurant.

"I have to make some more calls." Jake finally announced as they arrived at the Hauptwache. They headed underground into the large complex, stopping at a kiosk where Jake bought a special *Telefonkarte* for use in the special telephone booths scattered throughout the city.

He called Frank Haywood first, hoping he would be in his room. He glanced at his watch, quickly calculating the time difference. It was almost noon in Washington, an unlikely time to catch a man as busy as Frank.

"Hello?" Frank's voice answered after the first ring.

"Frank? . . . Jake Prescott . . . I'm glad I caught you . . . didn't think you'd still be at the hotel."

"Jake . . . Thank God you called!" he almost yelled, relief in his voice. "I've been making phone calls all morning trying . . . where are you?"

"Frankfurt . . . Germany. What's up Frank? Shannon, my secretary, said you had been arrested . . . something to do with the L.A. thing?"

"The witch-hunt is on Jake . . . remember . . . just like the old days . . . they're out to find a patsy . . . someone to blame!"

"Wha . . . what are you talking about Frank?" Jake asked, confused with Frank's references.

"I'm saying they're out to find a scapegoat . . . someone they can crucify . . . unfortunately I just happen to be a likely candidate. I though you might like to hear who's pulling the strings on this one!"

"I'm sorry Frank, you're leaving me behind. Can you go over it again in simple terms . . . what the hell are you talking about?"

Frank recounted the happenings of the past few days since he had arrived in Washington, covering his arrest in the middle of the night, to his release on Sunday. "Do you remember Millwood?"

A chill went up the back of Jack's head. "Of course, Frank . . . who wouldn't? What's that got to do with this?"

Do you remember a Senator Richard Pelly?"

"Big Dick!" Jake spat out the name. "Yes, I remember him . . . that sonuvabitch almost single-handedly put the environmental industry on the rocks!"

"Right! You got it!" Franks paused a moment, then continued. "I had a talk with my lawyer yesterday, George Barnes, and he figures Dick Pelly is involved with this thing. We now know for sure he had a hand in 'arranging' my arrest."

"But why Frank? What the hell reason does Dick Pelly have for . . ."

Frank cut him off. "He still holds a grudge for the Millwood screwup. He couldn't lay the blame on me then, so he figures he could get me me for this one!"

"Christ, Frank . . . that's a pretty serious accusation . . . but wha . . ."

"No Jake, don't get me wrong . . . that's not the important part! We figure Pelly's involved with this Los Angeles thing . . . the one you're into."

Jake stared at the telephone, his mouth sagging open, waiting for some orders from his brain. He knew whoever was involved would have to have a lot of clout, enough power not only to finance this thing, but to be able to arrange all the gasoline deliveries to appear to be their regular cons, consignments, all happening during the normal working days in Los Angeles.

"Are you sure of this Frank?" he finally asked.

"No . . . not absolutely sure . . . yet! We're still digging, but we've already dug up some interesting material . . . stuff you should see. Once your friend, Ed Seymour released all that information over the week-end, the F.B.I. Have been pushing pretty hard to find out who's behind it. Is there any way we can meet and discuss this Jake . . . when are you coming back?"

"For this, I can fly over there right away. I've got a few things you should know as well." Jake continued, briefly filling Frank Haywood in on some of his findings.

"That's incredible!" Frank announced as he heard of Jake's discoveries.

"There are over seventy people dead over this Frank, maybe more by now . . . that makes it very credible!" Be very careful . . . don't underestimate these people . . . a few more won't make much difference!"

They arranged to meet in Washington on Wednesday evening, when Frank and George had planned their meeting.

"Book me a room out near the airport . . . we can meet there. Then I won't have to come into town . . . I'll just stay over-night and head home."

Frank told him the name of the hotel. "If they're full, I'll leave a message with your secretary."

"One more thing Frank . . ." Jake added, thinking how he could save time and an extra call. "My secretary said that Scott Anderson from WBC has been looking for me. I think he's doing a story on this. Could you call my office and get his number? I think he's still in L.A. This looks like it could be a good meeting, so maybe we should invite him!"

Jake explained the call to Christa as they headed out of the shopping area and south towards the river. They discussed what they knew of the problem, both very worried, not only for Christa's father, but all of them involved in this crazy game. As he just told Frank Haywood, there was too much at stake to let anyone screw it up!

From the area just south of the Hauptwache, a few blocks south of the Main River, the city quickly changed from a modern steel and glass financial nerve-center to the old, stone and brick structures, many dating back hundreds of years. They continued to stroll along, picking the smaller, quiet streets that basically followed the river, trying to work off the worry and concern. The walk gave them both a chance to get to know each other again, time to discuss their likes and dislikes, as well as their desires, hopes and fears.

The summer sun was dipping low when they finally turned around, stopping at a small *Bierstube* for a snack and a cold beer. Picking a place that overlooked the Main River, they watched the barge traffic move up and down the river, almost wishing they were on board, heading for some distant port. Darkness had enveloped the area by the time they had finished, the lights on the far shore reflecting across the water, shattered periodically by yet another barge.

They continued back along the river, the city lights silhouetting the *Eisener Steg,*the old iron footbridge, in the distance. As they neared the bridge, they turned up towards Jake's hotel, poking around the little shops on Neue Kräme Street. The closer they got to the hotel, the more often their glances met, unasked questions answered. Finally, Jake bought a chilled bottle good Rhine Wine in a small shop, grabbed Christa's hand and headed purposefully up the street.

As they entered the little room, he could feel her hand trembling, her eyes sparkling with tears. He didn't turn on any lights as the room was already glowing from the shops and street lights of the busy pedestrian area below. He turned to her, slowly embracing, their lips meeting in a tentative, almost gentle introduction, like a first kiss. His arms enclosed her, pulling them together, intensifying the kiss. A quick flicker of her tongue sparked an explosion, as they both seized each other, wanting more. Hands flew over each other's body, tentatively exploring, touching, probing. Their s grew in intensity, the kisses more passionate as they tore at their clothes, quickly removing outer garments, giggling and cursing as they clawed at the buttons and zippers that slowed their progress. The last garment discarded, they faced each other, bodies glowing in anticipation, pulses throbbing. Jake could scarcely control himself as his eyes explored her body. Her long blonde hair draped around white shoulders, almost reaching her full, inviting breasts. His hands reached out, cupping each breast tenderly, then following the curves downward, dipping in at her tiny waist, over her hips to her long legs. Christa responded in turn, exploring Jake's body with equal tenderness, their passion growing with each new discovery, each new touch. Kisses followed, touching, nibbling each new find, setting each spot aflame with desire. The silence of the room was broken only by ecstatic groans and gasps of pleasure. Pulses racing, they finally collapsed on the bed, fusing together in a fiery consummation of passion and love.

Chapter 22

Senator Richard Pelly settled his huge bulk into the over-stuffed, over-patterned arm-chair that dominated one corner of his over-decorated office. Trying to recreate his private microcosm of the deep south, the gentleman senator had succeeded only in producing a seedy version of a movie set left over from "Gone with the Wind". He had scarcely relaxed when the intercom on his desk buzzed.

"Senator . . . Mr. Müller just 'phoned . . . he's on his way, but he'll be about five minutes late."

"Thank you, my dear" he called out from the corner. Pulling himself upright again, he shuffled over to the adjacent corner and opened an old, elaborately carved mahogany armoir, exposing a well stocked liquor cabinet. A large fan flicked around in the centre of the ceiling, trying vainly to refresh the air in the oppressive room. Sweat already beaded his brow and soaked his armpits as the senator fretted over the reasons for Klaus Müller's visit . . . he did not sound happy when he called for a meeting. Pulling out a large handkerchief, he mopped his brow and glistening head, careful not to mess up the arrangement of the little hair he had left. After filling a large whiskey glass with his favourite bourbon, he slowly prepared a long, black cigar from a box that was a generous gift from one of his many 'admirers', as he preferred to call them. The air was already thick with cigar smoke by the time Klaus Müller was shown in.

"God, Richard, if your whiskey doesn't get you, this smoke surely will!" he laughed, with a cough more genuine than feigned. He crossed the room to the thick floral drapes covering the windows. "Do you mind?" he asked as he proceeded to pull the drapes and open a window. Sunlight invaded the room, illuminating the ceiling fan's feeble attempts of churning the smoke.

The senator did mind, but remained quiet, his mind occupied with the subject ahead as he set up a defensive position behind his huge oak desk. Richard Pelly hated Germans, and Klaus Müller was no exception, but the senator was too much of a politician to pass up an opportunity, especially when there was this much money at stake. He watched the slim, well dressed man walk across the room, almost envious of his poise and demeanour. A few years older than the senator, Klaus Müller was slightly taller but at least a hundred pounds lighter, his stylish clothes reflecting his European heritage. The senator smiled weakly and offered his visitor a seat, suggesting they get down to the business at hand.

"I've been meaning to call you since Saturday, Richard," Klaus started, his face taut, "I don't know how much your man has kept you informed, but this Los Angeles thing has got out of control."

"I agree! Now we have George Barnes poking around . . . asking a lot of questions."

"Wait a minute, one at a time!" He grimaced slightly as his ulcer took another bite out of his stomach. Fishing an antacid tablet from his pocket, he popped it in his mouth and continued. "First Los Angeles. You told me everything was . . . how did you put it . . . cool? You assured me this N.S.O. guy . . . Butler was taking care of everything."

Richard Pelly shifted uncomfortably in the chair, his clothes soaked with sweat. "I . . . I thought it was . . . until those smart-asses in L.A. got those samples and went public! Everything would have gone just fine . . . we had the environmental groups lined up . . . we just had to pick one!"

"It was your man Butler that let them get those samples, idiot! What the hell was he up to . . . he should have been controlling things, God knows he had enough people in the area."

"Back off Klaus! Watch who you're calling an idiot!" The senator's temper flared, his southern manner shaken by this kraut upstart! God, he hated dealing with this guy! He took a slow, deep breath, then calmly continued. "I might remind you, sir . . . it was you who said nobody would get hurt . . . all you wanted to do was to test this 'wonder drug for cars' . . . this material . . . in a typical field situation. O.K., I went along with it . . . after all, what's the harm? We supplied the situation . . . arranged the deliveries, the manpower . . . and a field agent to oversee the operation. All I see from your end, sir, is a defective shipment . . . one which has cost the American public dearly! I'm beginning to think your countrymen just can't get out of the poison gas mode!" He immediately regretted the words as they glibly rolled off his tongue.

Klaus Müller's face tightened suddenly, his eyes smouldering beneath dark brows. His voice was clear and controlled as he spat out the words in the senator's face. "Don't give me that crap about the American public Richard! As long as you're making money, you don't . . . what do y'all say in the south . . . you don't give a pinch of coon-shit for the American public!"

"I beg your . . ."

Klaus cut him off again. "Look, Richard, quit acting like an offended saint. I've a pretty good idea what you've made from some of your deals in the past! Don't try to deny it, for Christ' sake, why the hell do you think we approached you for this project in the first place? I've told you before, we have a file on you that makes terrific reading! Besides, the money that's being dumped into your Swiss account is enough for any man to be happy with for the rest of his life . . . that's the reason you're in this . . . not the American public!"

They glared at each other, both realizing this was not solving their problem.

"Let's get back to the problem . . . it's time for a little damage control." Klaus continued as he walked across the room, head down, hands clasped behind his back. "What can we do about L.A.?" he said, popping another antacid and turning back towards the senator.

At first, the senator was silent, weighing his options, not wanting to say the wrong thing again. "Nothing!" he said at last. "At least nothing about the disaster. The cat's out of the bag . . . the reason for the disaster is already out . . . we can't change that. We could still try to implicate some environmental group, but I've almost given up on that." He paused a moment, his face twisting in a rueful smile as he thought about Frank Haywood. "I thought I could drop it on an old adversary of mine, a reminder of a past disaster . . . but that press conference in L.A. spoiled my plans!"

"So . . . what do you suggest?"

"Back off . . . retreat . . . at least for now, until things die down. We've got to get Butler out of there . . . there's F.B.I. agents crawling all over the place! That black sonofabitch, Jackson I think his name is . . . the same one that was snooping around here a few weeks ago has been asking a lot of questions." His southern upbringing burned into his consciousness, the senator cringed as he thought about some black, son of a slave F.B.I. agent questioning him . . . him, Richard J. Pelly, a white senator of the United States of America!

"Just how much does this Butler know? Is it traceable back to us?"

Senator Pelly stopped talking as he puffed heavily on his cigar, then cautiously answered the question. "Unfortunately, Paul knows almost everything about the operation . . . except . . . well, maybe with his contacts he even knows where it all came from. All he's concerned with is how much he gets paid. Don't worry, Paul's dependable, and can keep his mouth shut." He watched across his desk for a reaction. He then paused a moment, recalling some of the original plans of the project. "We're O.K. as far as the delivery firms are concerned . . . nothing can be traced there . . . all payments were cash . . . all orders through a double blind setup. Nobody knows who ordered it, or where the stuff came from." Unhappily, he added "The only one that holds all the cards is Butler." As he thought more, he added "I think it's time we pulled him out of there, maybe he should go on vacation or something, as long as he gets out of the country . . . at least until this blows over!"

Klaus Müller' face was impassive, unreadable, as he weighed the senator's words. He dropped his head again and continued to pace the room, turning quickly each time he was blocked by a wall. " . . . 'Don't worry' . . . Christ, Richard, I get paid to worry! Maybe you should try a little of it, you might think things through a little more next time." He stopped pacing, and turned to the Senator. "In any case, I have to agree with you on one point . . . I think Mr. Butler is our problem now, but I'm not sure getting him out of the country is enough. Do you really think this is ever going to 'blow over' as you call it?" He stopped pacing, turning to face the Senator. "If we're really going to control this thing, we must cut off all ties back to Washington! It won't take the F.B.I. long to trace everything and figure it out once they get to Butler, and believe me, they will. We have to make sure that does not happen!"

Standing directly in front of the senator, he leaned over, hands on the desk, glaring directly into the man's glazed eyes to make sure he had his attention before he continued in a low voice. "What I'm saying Richard, is that if you know what's good for you, these ties must be severed completely, do you understand? . . . completely!"

"Paul's good, we've used him for years on several projects, I wouldn't want to lose . . ." Müller's meaning finally hit him. "What do you . . . are you suggesting . . .?"

"You know what has to be done, Richard!" he hissed, "Don't act the innocent with me . . . you've done it before!"

"I must protest sir . . . you can't . . ."

"I don't think you understand Richard . . . I'm not asking you!" His index finger stabbed repeatedly down on the polished surface of the senator's desk. "Your Mr. Butler is no longer an asset, but a liability . . . the only one that can provide a direct link back to this office! He must disappear . . . quickly and completely! If you can get him out of the country without any trace, good! If not, you know what has to be done. Richard, if you place any value on that Swiss account, you'll act fast. If you don't, you might not live long enough to enjoy it."

Richard Pelly felt sick to his stomach. He reached forward, savagely butting out his cigar in the large crystal ashtray on his desk . . . suddenly, it didn't taste very good. The whiskey turned sour in his mouth. What sickened him the most was not that Klaus had suggested it, but that he, Senator Richard Pelly agreed . . . actually looked forward to eliminating the source of trouble.

"Don't worry . . . I'll handle it." he said finally. "Which brings me to the other matter I mentioned earlier . . . about George Barnes snooping around."

"Who the hell is George Barnes?"

"Another ghost from the past . . . Frank Haywood's lawyer. When we had Frank arrested the other night, George Barnes was there the next morning to bail him out. He then proceeded to take action against the Washington Police Department, and then started poking around, asking a lot of sensitive questions. I think he suspected somebody behind it . . . maybe even me, the way some of his questions are coming out."

Müller's agitation was now very visible, his pacing more rapid, occasionally clutching his abdomen. "God, Richard, I warned you to be more subtle with that whole issue. You've got some legal experience, you should have known you'd have to have at least had some cause, some evidence against the W.A.S.T.E. organization before you made your move."

"But I wanted . . ."

"I know . . . you just wanted to get even with Frank Haywood for some screw-up from years ago! You imbecile! This is too big for that, there's too much at stake here for you to get wrapped up settling old scores!

"How was I to know . . .? he whined, then continued as he thought of another problem. "Now there's some whiz-kid reporter from W.B.C.."

Klaus' frustration had reached the limit. All he wanted to do was to get out of this oppressive room, away from this pitiful excuse for a man!

"Let me handle Barnes . . . I'll throw a few curves, a few red herrings, maybe he'll lose interest. Maybe I can make a few calls . . . something to get this reporter off our case. Let me know what happens in Los Angeles. Call me as soon as things are under control!"

He had barely got out of his chair before Klaus Müller had stormed out of his office. Glaring at the door, he wished he had more back-bone when dealing with this German upstart that had the nerve to call himself an American! He hated the man for it, but he realized that the kraut was right . . . Senator Richard Pelly was only in this for the money . . . more than enough to retire as a gentleman to his plantation in the deep south. He walked over to the mahogany cabinet and poured himself another whiskey . . . a double this time . . . maybe a double will taste better. He then settled down in his chair again, sipping at the amber liquid, reviewing his options.

It was two more drinks and almost thirty minutes later when Senator Richard Pelly decided that doubles did indeed taste better. He pulled a small book out of his desk, then reached over and picked up his telephone . . . his private line. His mind made up, he thumbed through the book, then dialled the number.

Chapter 23

Two puffs of smoke erupted from the tires of the huge jet as it touched down at Dulles International early the next day. Once at the gate, Jake wasted no time leaving the plane and headed out for a taxi. The uneventful trip had offered Jake little rest, his mind still whirling between the horror and confusion of the recent disasters and his discussions with Stefan, still trying to piece together the chain of events and who was behind it all.

Luckily, these grim thoughts were being rapidly displaced by the pleasant memories of the evening spent with Christa the night before. Memories of her touch, her voice, her kisses had replayed continuously throughout the flight, displacing any other mental efforts to work or even read. His normally relaxed composure and independent attitude towards women had been seriously shaken. He could scarcely believe how much Christa had impacted him, how powerful his emotions were reacting, and how much he missed her already. Before he left Frankfurt, they had planned to meet at her apartment a few days later when he returned from New York. Already he was looking forward to it.

It wasn't long before the cab pulled up in front of the hotel they had previously agreed upon. Grabbing his small bag and his cane, Jake paid the driver and limped into the hotel. As he checked in, the desk clerk handed him a message from Frank Haywood telling him where to meet. He headed directly there, not wanting to waste a minute.

Frank met him at the door, relief clearly visible on a face pulled and tormented by the strain of the events of the past week. His bloodshot eyes confirmed what the rest of his face betrayed.

"Thanks for coming Jake," pumping his hand vigorously and pulling him into the large room. "I hated to drag you back from Germany like that, but I think you'll enjoy this little meeting."

Frank introduced him to the others as they walked around the room. "You might remember George Barnes, my lawyer . . . George was very active during the Millwood case."

"Of course," Jake replied as the familiar face brought back memories of the unpleasant episode.

"And you probably recognize Scott Anderson, investigative reporter for WBC. Scott arrived a little late in Los Angeles, but has been catching up fast. He's already talked with the Seymours about your early findings and theories."

As Jake shook his hand, he felt at ease with the reporter, even though he could feel Scott's eyes scanning him, evaluating everything he said. His initial appearance was a middle-aged, pleasant looking businessman, but closer scrutiny revealed the lined face and sadness in his eyes that told of too many years of seeing misery and suffering that a man was not meant to see.

"Glad to meet you Jake," he said in a soft voice, "Ed and Linda Seymour told me a few things about you, but I'm looking forward to hearing your version of your story, especially your recent adventures in Germany." He paused a moment, not missing the quick look of concern crossing Jake's face. "Don't worry Jake, they played it very cute for awhile, until they realized I was on your side."

Jake smiled, knowing how cryptic his friends would be when questioned directly. "I'm looking forward to telling you Scott, as well as hearing the rest of the story from all of you."

Frank pointed across the room "There's sandwiches and coffee over there on the counter Jake. You might as well grab something to eat and relax until Jackson gets here."

"Jackson?"

"Bert Jackson, F.B.I." Frank explained. "He's a special agent from the Washington office, but was in L.A. right after the first problem." Frank continued, explaining some of agent Jackson's skills and track record.

"I think I've had enough of special agents for awhile." Jake offered, uncomfortable with the prospect of meeting with the F.B.I. after eluding them and other various agents for the past week.

"Don't worry Jake, ever since the Seymours' press conference about their analysis, nobody is interested in tracking you down, in fact, you've become a bit of a hero for finding it first. When Scott heard that both the N.S.O and the F.B.I. were involved in L.A. right from the first day, he invited Bert to join us today . . . on the condition that he share information."

Scott added "Actually, Jake, and you can confirm this with Bert Jackson, the only thing the Bureau wanted you for was to ask you about the samples you took . . . what you found. They were as interested as yourselves as to why all the evidence was destroyed."

"Great!" mumbled Jake, still not convinced. "Then why are they still trying to follow me in Germany? And how about that N.S.O. guy, Butler?"

They were interrupted by a knock on the door.

"That's probably Bert now" Frank said as he crossed to the door. A tall, black man stood in the hall, his sharply dressed appearance right out of a fashion magazine, hardly the standard image of an experienced special agent for the F.B.I.. In fact, Bert Jackson was one of the best, his tough investigative skills had broken some of the most puzzling crimes in the Washington area. His cases usually involved corruption, coverups and general political skulduggery. Jake still wasn't sure how the agent fitted into the present situation, and especially why he was involved at the beginning of this mess.

Before long, the introductions had been made and the five men settled down with their coffee. Frank Haywood acted as a meeting chairman.

"I think we all know the general outline of the events up to this point. Jake, maybe you could fill us in on your part of the story . . . we all have a lot of catching up to do."

"Where do you want me to start?"

"At the beginning . . . at least, the day of the first event, how you guys got the data and the first samples . . . you know."

Jake started slowly, recalling the happenings of a day that seemed so long ago, yet was only last week. As he continued, memories came faster, technical details became clearer. Starting on that hot afternoon in L.A., Jake recounted the events of the past week, finishing up with his discussions with Stefan in Germany.

Frank spoke first. "You're saying it was all caused by a gasoline additive . . . through some catalytic reaction?"

"We're pretty sure . . . that's the research that Stefan was working on." Jake paused, trying to simplify some of the terms for the laymen in the group. "You're all familiar with the lead additives that were used in gasoline for many years. This was designed to accomplish the same thing, better combustion, less engine noise and wear, etc.. Catalysts are funny things, we're not even sure how they work, but we do know that in many cases, it doesn't take a lot of material . . . sometimes only trace amounts . . . to make a huge difference in a reaction. In this case, it appears that the very small amounts of nickel, together with the other additives they were using, reacted with the material in the catalytic converters on the cars. This very thin coating then took over as the main catalytic agent, acting at least an order of magnitude more efficiently than anything else. Stefan's still trying to figure it out, trying to come up with a fix, or at least some way to control it . . . that's why these guys are trying to find him."

By the time he was finished, it was past noon. Frank ordered more sandwiches and another pot of coffee.

"Wow Jake!" exclaimed Scott, "That story would make great stuff for prime-time TV . . . just as you told it! God, I had no idea you had been through all this and had pieced together so much of the puzzle."

"Not enough, Scott," Jake replied, "We still don't know who's behind it all."

"Well, maybe not Jake, but I'm damn sure that Big Dick Pelly had something to do with it . . . but we don't have anything concrete." Frank continued, describing his arrest and night in jail.

George Barnes then explained his work behind the scenes that convinced him of Senator Richard Pelly's involvement. "I'm pretty sure it was Pelly that put the pressure on the WASTE group in L.A., had Frank watched, waiting for a good reason to pick him up. Pelly was using Paul Butler a lot during the Millwood hearings, he has enough clout with the N.S.O. to arrange all of that."

"That's another thing," interrupted Jake, "The N.S.O.! How come this Paul Butler was on my case so much, and where is he now?"

Bert Jackson was on his feet, crossing the room. "I think I might be able to help you there Jake." He paused a moment, then sat down, facing the group. "Maybe I should fill you in on some of the background . . . why I was involved before any of you." He was on his feet again, crossing to the counter for another coffee. "As you know, Frank, and you George, there were too many 'irregularities' during the Millwood case, too many witnesses bought, evidence tampered with. As you might suspect, the Bureau has kept files on all the participants since then. Most of this is confidential, so I can't get into too many details."

The rest of the group listened intently, waiting for each new piece of information.

"Following some leads from my investigations in Washington, I was in L.A., trying to explain some anomalies. As you mentioned George, Paul Butler and another N.S.O. agent did a lot of work for Pelly during Millwood, and now Paul was also in the Los Angeles thing. During my investigations in L.A., I found our paths crossing too many times, so we kept our eyes on him. We've occasionally butted heads with the N.S.O., but generally, we leave each other alone. It wasn't until after the first mass killing that I suspected that Butler's presence in L.A. was not as innocent as it first looked."

"Are you saying that Butler had something to do with this thing?" George Barnes asked.

"Originally, George, I didn't think so, I was following something else . . . but I didn't like the way things were going. In short, we were tracking some money . . . a lot of it . . . moving in and out of Washington from an offshore source. A lot of it was spent in California, obviously to get something done. Paul Butler's name kept coming up, he was always too close to the action to be an innocent." He paused, carefully choosing his words. "In any case, right after the first event, I couldn't catch up to Butler . . . " he laughed, looking at Jake. "I guess he was too busy trying to catch you Jake, and grabbing all that data and your samples. We learned he had confiscated all the other data and samples, that was the final clue that convinced me that he was definitely involved in this, more than we originally suspected."

"What happened Bert, when you finally talked with him?"

"We haven't talked with him . . . at least not much. You must remember, Paul is a very skilled and experienced N.S.O. agent, when he wants to disappear, he does just that."

"You mean he's gone, you haven't found him?" Jake asked.

"Yes and no, he found us. Paul called me early this morning, he wants to meet . . . and talk. He knows I've been dogging him, and would catch up sooner or later, but that's not what turned him. Whoever he's working with must be getting nervous, wants Paul out of the picture. Paul found a bomb rigged to his car, so he knows it's only a matter of time before they catch up with him. He wants to make a deal."

Kurt Landau crossed the room again, his mind calculating every move, every option. A man in his early forties, he was just under six feet tall, with a grudge against his parents and the world that he wasn't taller. He had a rounded face with a broad forehead with heavy, dark brows covering deep-set black eyes. His thinning hair was combed back, accentuating his forehead even more. As he became agitated, his head snapped from side to side, his eyes darting around, like a caged animal watching for its enemies.

Kurt's office reflected his own efficiency. His desk was unnaturally clear, the telephone placed just within reach, a small note-pad ready beside it. Even the books on the bookshelves were neatly organized according to size of book, rather than subject . . . Kurt preferred it that way. As he paced the room, he checked to make sure each volume was placed on the shelf so that the spines were all perfectly in a row, no book stuck out more than its neighbour. He stopped by a small window which overlooked one of the old sections near the river. Glancing up, he could see the tall building in the centre of Frankfurt that contained Weigel's opulent office, and he felt resentment rising out of envy. Some day, he thought.

Now that he was taking over the Frankfurt portion of the project, he knew he could clean up the mess that Klein and Schmidt had dumped them into. His only disappointment was Los Angeles, and the actions of his old student and associate Paul Butler. He thought he had taught him better, but then the student never should exceed the capabilities of the master.

His decision made, he picked up the phone, made two quick calls, then headed down to the communications room.

Chapter 24

Paul Butler was pleased with himself. Confident of his own abilities, backed by many years of experience, he knew something was going wrong with his relationship with his friends in Washington. Ever since the screw-up with the gasoline additive, they had expected him to handle some kind of damage control in an area much too big for him and his crew, a situation much too complicated for a "quick fix". Even before the event, he knew that Bert Jackson, an experienced FBI agent, was nosing around, asking too many questions. NSO headquarters had given the FBI the usual story about keeping their eyes on environmental extremists, but Paul didn't find out until too late that Jackson had been tracing some of the payments he had made and suspected something a little more involved.

The first disaster had shaken him. Although experienced in a few 'messy' jobs over the years, the mass killing of over 40 people did not fit into his job description, and he was quick to question their motives. They convinced him that it was a huge mistake, and that someone had tampered with the additive. His instructions were to destroy all the evidence, and try to shift the blame on to some militant environmental group. He thought he had done a pretty good job, but that damn Canadian had been one step ahead of him. Even Paul's attempts to shed some of the blame on Prescott had failed, as the man knew too much of the business and had moved too fast. Even so, he was still confident he could control the situation . . . until the second event happened.

It was too much, too many people had died, someone was going to take the blame, and Paul realized he was in the wrong place, on the wrong side. His "business partners" in Washington felt the same way, but they also realized Paul knew too much, not just about this situation, the Washington contacts, etc., but also the links to Germany, their contacts in Frankfurt and too many details on other projects over the years. Their asset had turned into a liability.

His suspicions were confirmed during a telephone conversation with Washington. Although they were telling him to cut and run, preferably out of the country, he had been in the business too many years to miss the overtones, the nuances in the voice . . . he knew he was in trouble and had to get out. It was bad enough trying to stay one step ahead of the FBI, but this added another dimension to the game. Expecting some kind of retaliation, he immediately went on guard, wary of every move he made. He had already planned his own escape, his complete disappearance from the scene. He thought he might have a few more days, but decided to move immediately. An alternate identity and offshore money could now be enjoyed, away from the threats of both the law and his associates. That was when he found the bomb.

Amazed that they had reacted so fast, he tried to analyze his moves for the past week. Someone must have been watching him, keeping track of his whereabouts. He was sure he had covered his tracks, melting into the busy L.A. scene, moving into a non-descript hotel in a busy area. Today, he had left his room and walked directly to the underground carpark area. Something triggered his awareness, a sixth sense told him something was out of place as he reached with his key to unlock the car. He froze, scanning the car for obvious signs of tampering. Dropping to the ground, he gently rolled under the car, looking for something that didn't belong. He had placed enough of the devices himself not to miss it; a small explosive device taped to the frame, near enough to the gas tank to cause a major explosion. Closer inspection revealed a clever little motion detector, a small steel ball in a pill bottle. From the size and position of the device, Paul figured it was set to trigger as soon as he sat in the car or slammed the door. Carefully, he disconnected the triggering device and gently removed the detonator from the small wad of Semtex explosive. That done, he ripped off the tape and threw the entire device into a nearby trash can.

Returning to his room, he paced the floor, balancing his instinct to escape with his need for revenge. Within minutes he had decided . . . he could do both. Those bastards in Washington . . . they didn't even give him the option of leaving town! He would show them! He quickly picked up the phone and dialled the local FBI number, identifying himself and asking for Bert Jackson. He knew the call would be traced, but he would be out of here in minutes. Within seconds, the called was patched through to Bert's car phone in Washington, on his way to the meeting near the airport. Bert answered the phone, surprised to hear who it was.

"Hello Paul, I must say I'm a little surprised at your call, you've given us a little run around lately."

"I know you're tracing this call, so don't waste my time! You want to know who's behind all this stuff in L.A., I'm willing to talk. I'll give you enough information to put the whole shebang away forever! I want to make a deal . . . amnesty for my story."

"Ah . . . great, Paul, who are you talking about? Can we meet and talk about this?"

"I'm not saying now, but the bastards can't do that to me and get away with it!"

"Paul! What are you talking about . . . do what to you?"

"I just found a bomb in my car, so I know they want to get rid of me, I know too much!"

Realizing things had turned around, Bert thought fast. "Can you get into the local FBI office right away? Better still, give them a call so they can send someone to pick you up, offer you protection. I'll fly out today and we can talk."

"No way . . . they probably have their spies in your office . . . most likely on their way now." Paul started to sweat, this wasn't going as smoothly as he had thought. "I'll take my chances . . . I'll come to Washington, maybe tomorrow . . . call you then.

Knowing Paul was an experienced field man, Bert realized there was no way he could convince him to stay put. "O.K. Paul, we won't set a place now, call me as soon as you get in, we can set something up then."

A brief confirmation ended the conversation as the line went dead. Bert stared at his phone, wishing he had gleaned more information from the man.

Paul felt better as he hung up the phone. At least he had the ball rolling, events that would tumble the little empire in Washington. Although something still nagged at him about their speed in finding him and setting the device, he felt he had to get moving. Grabbing his brief case and overnight bag, he headed down to his car.

As he approached the car, his feeling of satisfaction and confidence overshadowed his usual sixth sense and suspicious nature. He was smiling confidently when he turned the key. A last, split second thought raced through his mind as he realized he had just triggered a second bomb that blew him apart, the car erupting in a huge ball of flame.

Chapter 25

THEY WERE STILL COMPARING NOTES after lunch when Bert Jackson's phone rang. When he stepped aside to answer it, his loud exclamations betrayed the nature of the news. After a long conversation followed by a few terse comments, Bert slowly pocketed his phone and turned to the others, face grim.

"What's up Bert, that didn't exactly sound like good news."

"That was our L.A. office . . . Butler, Paul Butler . . . you don't have to worry about him any more Jake, someone just blew him up!"

"Wha . . .? Blew him up? I thought you were just talking to him before the meeting! What happened?"

"Our office had traced that call and were on the way to his hotel. There wasn't much left of him when they arrived. Forensics experts are still on site, they're taking what's left of the car back to the lab. It must have happened right after he talked to me . . . he was just leaving the building, probably on his way to come here." He hesitated, blaming himself for not handling the situation differently. "I guess he found the first bomb, but got a little careless and missed the second one."

The only sound in the room was the low whistle of someone exhaling. Several minutes passed before anyone spoke. Scott Anderson was the first to move, crossing the room to phone his office. He wanted to make sure WBC had a crew in L.A. to cover this story.

"Just get a crew there, I'll explain later." he said, almost shouting at the phone. "I don't know, check with the local FBI office, they should know!" He hung up, agitated at the lack of concern shown by someone in his office.

"Relax Scott," Jake offered, "We're all a little too close to this thing, not everyone feels the same sense of urgency we do."

"I know Jake, I guess I'm getting a little edgy. I've seen too much of this kind of thing, too many people 'neutralized' because of political ambitions or big business motives. Some of these guys in the studio should get out in the field more."

Bert Jackson interrupted. "Scott, I hate to tell you this, but I doubt if your crew will even get close . . . Butler was N.S.O., and they'll be pissed. They've probably already blacked out all news coverage on the explosion. Like the Bureau, they won't rest until they find out who did this." He then stood up, facing the rest of the group. "Guys, it's pretty obvious that things are getting out of control. As the only representative of the law here, I am obliged to warn all of you to step down and leave this matter to the authorities."

His warning was greeted with derisive laughter as they mumbled some rude comments about what he should do with his warning. Jake was the first to speak.

"It's unanimous Bert . . . I think you've just been told to screw yourself. I must add that it's because of the authorities that we are in this position now, and the only results we've seen so far is what we've done ourselves!

"I realize that Jake," Bert answered rather meekly, "But, officially, I at least had to say it. I just hope we can keep in touch, and share any further information we run across. Can I ask all of you what you plan to do now?"

George Barnes spoke first. "As you know Bert, Frank and I have been reviewing the records of the Millwood trial. Maybe with what you've found, we could try to find what common links there are between that and the L.A. thing."

"Sounds good to me George," Bert answered. "I have some men at the Bureau tracking some money transfers. We've asked Interpol for a little help in Europe, but everyone just clams up when you start asking about money transfers or private accounts over there." He paused a moment, as if debating with himself. "Actually, you might be interested in this little bit of information . . . might not be worth much now." He then launched into a long story about some of the detective work he had been involved in for the past few years, including specific details about Paul Butler. "We knew he had been making too much money for years . . . not even the N.S.O. pays that well. The fact that most of it was in offshore accounts sort of hinted at impropriety," he chuckled, "They're still putting it all together. A lot of money ended up in Los Angeles, where Butler was orchestrating most of the activity, anonymous payments for gasoline deliveries, etc., all under the guise of checking out possible terrorists, environmental nut-cases, etc. None of it was illegal of course, that's the problem, we didn't know about the additive in the gasoline at that point." He sipped some water, and cleared his throat. "What I can't tell you about just now are some other investigations involving other notables in the Washington scene." Turning to Jake he asked "What are your plans Jake?"

"I'm heading back to Germany tonight, meeting Christa tomorrow. We'll see what we can find there, maybe Stefan can tell us more about this mysterious research organization that is behind this." He stopped suddenly, remembering something. "Bert, I just remembered something Stefan told me. Have you ever run across a Klaus Müller? I think he works here in Washington, some kind of government job."

Bert's eyebrows went up, surprised at the question. "Klaus Müller? Why do you ask?"

"Oh no, Bert, don't play that game with me . . . I asked you first."

Bert smiled, caught at his own game. "No Jake, I was amazed again at what you've managed to dig up in such a short time, you should be working for us. To answer your question, Müller's some kind of high-up staff advisor with the feds, Department of Energy or something. He does travel a lot, many times to Germany. At one time he was chief liaison on some joint energy research projects between the U.S. and Germany. Most likely what you're looking for is yes, we have been watching him, mainly because his name keeps coming up in other matters . . . nothing specific, just too many coincidences." He stopped, watching Jake's response. "What did Stefan tell you, how does he know him?"

"In the research centre . . . probably the same joint project." He paused, thinking. "Can you find out who was involved in those projects . . . which companies . . . better still, names of people that were involved?"

"Sure, I can do that, we most likely have all that in the file now. What are you going to do with it?"

"Maybe I'll pay them a call . . . you know, maybe my firm can use the services of a good research lab."

Bert shook his head, always terrified at amateur investigators. "It won't wash Jake, even if you did happen to get lucky and walk into the right firm, you can bet they already know about you, and what you did. Best-case scenario, they'll already have a good cover story . . . worst-case, you'd probably disappear, or maybe find a present in your car like Butler did."

"You're right of course, but it would be valuable information to have. If you find anything, just fax it to my office." He handed out some business cards to all of them. "Here's my fax and phone numbers, as well as my e-mail address. Please fax or call my office if you have any information or want to track me down."

As if on cue, the telephone rang again. Frank answered, then motioned for Jake to come to the phone. "I think it's for you Jake", a smile on his face.

Puzzled at the expression, Jake took the call. The first words made his heart skip with delight as he recognized Christa's voice.

"*Wie gehts, Liebchen.*" he switched to German, mainly to tell the rest of the group to mind their own business. He didn't have a chance to say any more, as Christa's frantic voice cut through the greeting.

"Oh Jake, thank God I found you, your office told me you would be there. You must come, they've got Papa!"

"What do you mean . . . what are you saying Christa?"

Her voice broke as she sobbed out the news. "They must have tricked me . . . Papa called . . . or at least that was what they told me. I telephoned Sommerhausen, but he said he did not call me. They must have known I would call him there, and they found out where he was staying. I didn't realize this until later . . . I called the guest house and Herr Wankel said some men came to visit and they all left together." More sobbing ended her tale. "Oh Jake, what should I do?"

Jake's mind was spinning, quickly piecing the picture together. "Where did you phone from when you called your father, and where are you now, Christa".

"I got the message when I got back to my office, so I made the first call from there, then later, when I thought about it, I called from home. I'm there now."

"Get out of there Christa, right now! Just leave everything and get out! Don't even pack anything!"

"But why Jake? I can't just leave, Papa might call."

"No, Papa won't call, at least not voluntarily. If they've got him, they'll use you to force him to work for them! Don't you see? Your life is in danger too!" Jake's brain was working overtime, trying to put the pieces together. "You'll have to move fast Christa, it's obvious they have your work phone bugged, maybe your home phone is too. Remember our last night in Frankfurt . . . the hotel?"

"How could I forget? . . . Oh Jake!"

"Go there, and stay! Don't go out! I'll be there as soon as I can." He hung up the phone, already planning his next move.

Chapter 26

WITHIN SECONDS, JAKE HAD GRABBED his brief case and was putting on his coat.

"What's going on Jake, who the hell was that on the phone?" Frank asked, surprised at the move.

"Christa . . . Stefan Schiller's daughter. She thinks her father has been kidnapped!"

"Kidnapped? But who . . .why?"

"Like I told you, they've been trying to get hold of him ever since this screw-up began. Butler was supposed to be watching Stefan in L.A., but he managed to slip away when the shit hit the fan. They know Stefan has the answers they need, so they either want to get their hands on him or his notes, preferably both. From what I discussed with Stefan in Germany, he still hasn't got it all figured out yet, but they don't know that. Considering the amount of money that's at stake, they'll do anything to get those answers!" By this time Jake had his coat on and was heading toward the door.

"Hang on Jake" Bert called after him, "I'll drop you at the airport . . . I'm catching the next flight to L.A.. Has Christa called the local police?"

"She didn't say, but I'm sure she will once she's safely away from her place." Turning to the others he said "Well, gentlemen, I guess we're finished here?"

Frank answered first. “Sure, Jake. You guys keep in touch, let us know if you need help, information or whatever.”

Jake wished the fast Concord flights were still running, but remembered they did not even go to Frankfurt but from New York to Paris. He caught himself and decided to stick to his original plan. ‘Slow down’, he told himself; think, analyze, plan things through. The direct flight he had already booked from Washington to Frankfurt later that evening would get him into Frankfurt early the next morning, local time. The drive to the airport and time before their respective flights gave him a chance to talk further with Bert.

They pulled out of the hotel parking lot and headed towards the airport. “Thanks for the lift Bert, I’m glad we had a chance to talk today and compare notes.”

“My pleasure! As I mentioned earlier, you should be working for us.” He paused, watching Jake as if to decide whether he should continue. “I hope you don’t mind Jake, but I checked out your background a little . . . part of the Bureau’s check on anybody involved in this thing.”

“And . . . “ Jake waited for the other shoe to drop.

“And, like I said, you should be working for us. Your experience in languages and counter-intelligence would be a big asset. From where I stand, it’s already helped you a lot on this little fiasco.”

“Thanks Bert, but no thanks.” Jake answered, smiling. “I’ve already got enough on my plate, and besides, if you’ve checked far enough into my background, you should have learned that I am not a politician . . . I don’t work well in bureaucracies, I find it stifles initiative and creativity.”

“You’ve got a point there, that’s probably why you got away with what you did in L.A., you can decide fast and move even faster. If you worked for any government agency, every move would have to be cleared first.”

“Right, and that’s why nothing gets done most of the time! I like to decide what to do and when to do it.”

From the hotel nearby, the mid-week traffic on the Dulles access road was merciful and they were soon at the main terminal. Bert parked the car and they headed inside, each checking in at the appropriate airline.

"Let's grab a coffee and a bite, we've each got a couple of hours to kill." Jake suggested. "Besides, I wanted to ask you about some things you mentioned back at the hotel."

"What things, Jake?" Bert asked, knowing what was coming.

"First, some more about Paul Butler, and then you might expand on your comments about checking up on other Washington 'notables', I think you called them."

They found a quiet booth in one of the many airport restaurants and placed their orders. Bert was silent, wondering just how much he should tell Jake. Despite how much he liked and admired the man, he was still a foreigner, not a person he should be sharing F.B.I. investigative information with. Weighing the benefits with the cost, he decided in favour of Jake, realizing an ally of his calibre would be an asset.

"O.K. Jake, I'll try to give you a few more details on some of the stuff I was alluding to earlier," Bert started, "but only on a need-to-know basis, things you've already been involved in, or that directly affect you. Actually, a lot of it is in the public records anyway."

Bert then explained some of the background of his ongoing investigations . . . a project that had consumed him for several years, almost since the Millwood incident.

"As Frank was saying today, and as you all no doubt suspected, there were too many anomalies during that affair, too many little 'accidents' that derailed the progress of both the investigation and the trial."

"I was only a distant spectator during that trial Bert, can you refresh my memory?"

"Well, for instance, very early in the hearings, many of the witnesses who originally were at the forefront of the protests, suddenly had a change of heart and backed off, saying they really didn't want to get involved. If that wasn't bad enough, over the next several months, a few key witnesses had health problems or accidents."

"Accidents?"

"Yeah, two were involved in car accidents, one died, one crippled for life; one died from a stroke and one from a heart attack."

"Possible," said Jake, "But unlikely . . . is that what you're saying Bert?"

"That's it! We've had some experts go over the medical reports, but at the time, there were no autopsies done, and the bodies were cremated shortly after . . . didn't give us much to go on."

"So what's this got to do with Paul Butler?"

"Well, Paul and another agent were around during the entire series of hearings and later the trial. We couldn't figure why the N.S.O. was interested in this case, basically it should have involved only the local and state police, as well as the F.B.I. . . . God knows that should have been enough, we were almost tripping over each other. Paul convinced everyone the N.S.O. was sticking close, watching for international involvement, environmental terrorists, etc. At the time, everyone bought it, and it wasn't until later that we started to suspect that Paul had some other agenda, maybe even working for someone else."

"But what of N.S.O. headquarters, didn't someone question their motives, or ask why these guys were there?"

"Not at the time, but we did later. You've got to remember, Paul had a lot of time with the organization, and a lot of clout . . . he could pretty well do whatever he wanted and explain it away."

"God, that's kind of scary," Jake said, "I'm always amazed at the lack of controls or oversight some of your spook organizations have."

"Me too, sometimes." Bert agreed. "Anyway, what I started to say was that we had been keeping our eye on a few people ever since the trial, Paul being one of them. At the same time, our communications people in Washington started monitoring a lot of international traffic involving a few of these people . . . you know, faxes, telephone calls, etc. This is how we caught wind of some significant money transfers as well, probably some of the money Butler used in L.A."

"How's that . . . what money?" Jake asked.

"Well, a couple of months ago, Paul started travelling back and forth to Los Angeles a lot, eventually renting an apartment and staying there. At first, we couldn't figure out what he was up to . . . he was moving around, talking with petroleum companies, delivery firms, etc.. It didn't make any sense, he was acting more like a salesman than a special agent. In retrospect, it became very clear, he was secretly arranging all of the gasoline deliveries with this additive . . . cash basis . . . no records."

"It looks that way," Jake added, "So who put him away?"

"I don't know," Bert answered, "My first guess would be whoever he was working for, not the N.S.O., but his other boss."

"But why?" Jake asked. "If I have this right, there is a possibility that Paul has been involved in this kind of hanky-panky for a long time, sort of a private hit-man.

"O.K., very possible . . . so he knew too much, and they had to get rid of him."

"I don't buy it Bert! If he's been involved for that length of time, he's already proven himself! He's probably been paid very well, it looks like they can trust him to keep his mouth shut, and if he didn't, he'd be in more trouble than anyone else!"

"What are you saying Jake, do you think someone else is involved, someone else killed Paul?"

"I don't know Bert, there are too many pieces of this puzzle that just don't fit." He stopped suddenly, remembering something. "Did you say Paul was working with another agent at that time?"

"Yeah, but we don't have a name for him yet."

"So I suppose you don't know if he's still around?"

"No, but we're still looking."

Jake thought it over, thinking there were too many coincidences.

"Bert, if you find out anything more, like who he is, where he is, or who he is working for, let know right away. I've got a funny feeling we're going to hear more from him. Also, it might be interesting to see if Paul had any other accomplices, any friends or associates he likes to work with, even on an occasional basis." Recalling his own experience with the man, he added "I picture this Butler guy as real pro, not likely to fall for anything some local thug might try on him. I'll bet when you check out some of the details of his death, you're going to find some other 'anomalies' as you called them."

Bert Jackson nodded, his brow furrowed as he looked at Jake for a long time, mulling over what he had just said.

"I'll see what I can stir up." He paused again, shaking his head while he broke into a big grin. "Christ, Jake, you really know how to open up a can of worms!"

Chapter 27

THE BLOOD DRAINED FROM SENATOR Richard Pelly's face as he watched the news on WBC that evening. Eyes fixed on the screen, his jaw hanging slack, he appeared to be suffering some kind of attack.

"Oh dear! Are you feeling all right my love?" his wife asked, fearing the worst.

The senator recovered slightly. "No, I'm fine, honeysuckle," he smiled, "It's just the television these days . . . so much crime and violence!" He looked at his watch and said "I just remembered, I have to make a call."

His wife watched as he shuffled off to his study, not convinced by his reassurances.

Behind closed doors, Senator Pelly quickly dialled a number, anxiously waiting as the phone rang. When Klaus Müller answered, the senator didn't waste a second.

"Klaus, you sonovabitch! What the hell you doing, going around me like that! I told you Butler was a good man, I could deal with it!"

"Pelly! Hold on, what the hell you talking about?"

Butler . . . L.A. . . . haven't you seen the news? Someone planted a bomb in Paul Butler's car!"

"A bomb . . .?" The words hit Klaus like a hammer. The fact that Pelly was blaming him meant something was terribly wrong. He recovered quickly. "Richard! Not now, not on the phone! Let's meet . . . right away!" Thinking quickly, he suggested "How about that little coffee shop down the street from your office . . . I think it's open all night. Meet there in what . . . half an hour?"

—~—

The place was almost empty, the day customers from the government offices now replaced by a much smaller number of late workers, night school students and a few theatre goers. They picked a quiet booth in the back, ordered coffee and donuts to keep the waitress away for awhile.

Impatient to get some answers, Pelly started again "You sonovabitch!" He hissed in a loud whisper. "What . . .?"

Műller cut him off. "For Christ sake Richard, hold on . . . don't go off half cocked! I had nothing to do with this. I haven't seen the news, what the hell happened?"

The senator started, remembering some other details as he explained. "Actually, I've been trying to get hold of Butler all day. I talked to him yesterday, after our meeting, but I wanted to talk to him again today. All I got was his answering service. When I called the N.S.O., some of the guys I've talked to before . . . nothing! They were tight as hell with their answers, wouldn't tell me anything. This has happened before, so I didn't think much of it . . . at least until I saw that news item tonight on T.V. . . . apparently someone put a bomb in his car, blew him and the car all to hell!"

"Jesus!"

It finally dawned on the senator. "You mean you didn't arrange this Klaus? But I thought . . ."

Oh Pelly, for Christ sake, stop that!" he whispered. I don't go around blowing people up! The big question is . . . if I didn't do it, and you didn't . . . who did?"

The senator's face grew an even lighter shade of grey as sweat started running down his forehead and temples. Finally trickling down into the folds of his full jowls.

"I don't like this Klaus . . . don't like it a bit!" Richard Pelly shuddered as he thought of the news item. He didn't know what to do next, he always had someone else handling these kinds of problems, he was never directly involved. He looked across the table and suddenly felt a little better knowing Klaus was on his side. In spite of his personal prejudices, he knew Müller was a very capable man, a man with tremendous clout and connections. If anybody could make sense of this, he would. "What should we do?"

"Do?" Klaus repeated. "You do nothing! Someone has done us a favour, removed a problem. You weren't involved, so you have nothing to worry about! Just go back to work and forget about it." He glanced quickly at this watch, thinking it was almost morning in Germany. "I'll make a few calls, see what I can find out. I'll let you know what happens. In the mean-time, you see what details you can find out about the attack, maybe the N.S.O. can find out for us . . . I'm sure they're working on it as we speak."

A sickening feeling settled in the middle of Klaus' stomach. He fumbled quickly in his pocket, trying vainly to find his little roll of antacids. His stomach knotted again, part confusion, part fear, he wasn't sure which part was the larger. His entire life displayed a model of control, every step carefully planned and executed with precision. Unknowns just didn't happen, everything had to be calculated and allowed for. He came from a modest farm background in southern Bavaria, emigrated to America and over the past 30 years had worked his way into a senior staff advisory position in the U.S. Department of Energy. To facilitate this success, he had drawn on the resources of a well-heeled benefactor from his homeland, a wealthy company that considered it a good investment to have someone in the U.S, government sympathetic to their needs. It had worked for many years, but always on a much smaller scale; minor contracts, research projects and the like. Everyone involved new that this project was the big pay-off, the project that would make them all millionaires. Klaus had eagerly accepted the challenge, knowing that if it worked, he could be a hero on both sides of the Atlantic. This latest twist wasn't in the plan, it wasn't supposed to happen.

Eric Weigel picked up the phone quickly when his secretary announced who it was.

"Klaus? Wie geht's Was machst du . . . ? What's going on?"

Before he had a chance to continue, Klaus interrupted, quickly outlining the latest news reports about Paul Butler. Expecting a violent reaction, the utter silence surprised him. He waited for a reply, but nothing came.

"Eric? Did you hear . . .?"

"Yes, yes of course!" Eric answered quickly. "I'm sorry, I was just thinking."

"Well . . . what do you think? Do you have any ideas? Do you have any of your people over here, are you involved in this?"

"No, no, Klaus, nothing as simple as that. I just wish I did, at least we'd know what was going on!" He paused, leaving the line dead again for what seemed a long time to Klaus. Just before Klaus was going to say something again, Eric spoke.

"I was hoping this wouldn't happen, hoping they would leave us alone . . . but I suppose it was not to be."

"What, Eric . . . what are you saying, who are you talking about?"

I can't tell you now Klaus . . . not yet. You might be able to figure it out for yourself . . . just think, there are people in the world that would rather see this project fail right now, die before it lives! You know how much money is at stake here . . . just consider that whatever we have to gain, someone else stands to lose!"

As the meaning of the words sank in, Klaus' stomach wrenched again as his ulcer bled a little more, doubling him over.

Chapter 28

THE HUGE JET LUMBERED DOWN the runway, engines roaring at full power. As it finally lifted off, Jake stretched out and immediately fell asleep. For the second time within a twenty-four hour period, he was on his way across the Atlantic. A week of turmoil added to the last two days with only a couple of hours sleep had finally caught up with him. His sleep was not restful, his body and brain disagreeing about which time zone they were in. Beautiful, erotic dreams of Christa clashed with worries about Stefan's kidnapping, while horrifying visions of dead bodies and car bombs kept jerking him back to a semi-conscious state.

He woke a short time before landing, stiff and aching from his uncomfortable position. A splash of cold water on his face and a quick cup of coffee helped restore him as the plane started its descent over the German landscape.

As he sipped his coffee he mentally reviewed his discussions with Bert Jackson, trying vainly to put some of the pieces together. The Butler incident had put another slant on things, adding more confusion to the puzzle. For the present, he knew he must stay focussed and concentrate on working with Christa to find Stefan. Later, if Bert's investigations turned up anything in Washington, together with what Stefan could tell them, they might find out who was behind this. As he mulled over the problem, he was painfully aware that whoever was holding Stefan was behind it all, and getting him back was not going to be an easy task.

Erik Weigel slowly hung up the phone, his mind numbed by the implications of his conversation with Klaus. He slowly stroked his nicotine stained moustache, first in one direction, then the other, like a cat grooming itself. His confidence a little shaken, he lit another cigarette, ignoring the one smouldering away in the ashtray. Used to being in control, Erik Weigel ruled his little domain with precise, almost brutal policies and procedures. He did not tolerate loose ends, and abhorred any sort of interference from outside sources.

He reached over to the intercom. "Monique, is Kurt Landau still in the building?"

"Yes, Herr Weigel, he just went down to personnel for something, I can catch him there if you'd like."

"Please do, have him come in here immediately!"

Several minutes later, Kurt Landau was shown into the office, a worried look on his face. "You wanted to see me?" he asked, an uneasy feeling coming over him.

"Yes Kurt. First, I must congratulate you on your work in finding Schiller . . . a very clever ruse, using his daughter that way."

An almost audible sigh of relief relaxed Kurt. "Thank you sir, but unfortunately in the meantime, the daughter has disappeared."

"Again, it's that Prescott, he's made her go underground." He almost admired his opponent, wishing he had him on his team. "That reminds me Kurt, did you find out anything about this man?"

"Not much, but what we do have is important" he said as he pulled a small notebook from his pocket. Erik's head turned, waiting for the information.

Kurt flipped the pages over as he started "You were right, he's not exactly what he appears on the surface." Reaching the right spot, he started to read. "Apparently he has a couple of university degrees, is a recognized expert in environmental matters, has travelled most of the world and more significantly, he worked for the Canadian Foreign Affairs for a few years, speaks several languages, German among his fluent ones, and is trained in counter-espionage and counter-terrorism, besides his skills in martial arts."

Erik Weigel smiled to himself. "I knew it!" he exclaimed as he leapt to his feet. "He was just too damn good to be just another visiting scientist!"

"Good," Kurt agreed, "But not good enough! We'll get them both, and very soon!" he added. Kurt's own experience in espionage and counter-espionage during the cold war had hardened him, made him scornful of any amateurs or newcomers to the business. He admitted to himself that this Prescott had been very clever, outsmarting his old friend Paul Butler, but not clever enough to outsmart the master! If only Weigel had let him handle the project from the first instead of just assisting Paul from a distance. Just one more little score to settle, he thought as he smiled weakly to his boss.

Weigel continued, his face more serious. "I'm afraid I have bad news Kurt. Paul Butler is dead . . . a bomb in Los Angeles! The N.S.O and FBI are all over this thing!"

Kurt appeared shocked and hurt, asking for more details.

"We know nothing yet, but I'm afraid it could be what we feared, some oil producers trying to level the field!"

Kurt nodded seriously, again, appearing to be the concerned employee, agreeing with his boss. Once again, the situation represented all of the things he despised, an operation run by a layman, complicated by the incompetence of the people he had to depend on.

"By the way, I have an idea to get both Prescott and the Schiller girl, so call off your men and concentrate on making both the T.U.Z. and the lodge secure."

Although curious, Kurt remained quiet, agreeing with Weigel as he left the room.

Once alone, Erik flipped on his intercom. "Monique, could you come in here please, and bring your notes on Schiller?"

Monique Brehmer was an attractive, middle aged woman, always well coiffed and fashionably dressed. She inherited her intellect and determination from her German father, her beauty and impeccable sense of fashion from her French mother. As Erik Weigel's personal secretary, she certainly had a more than adequate salary to live on, and as his mistress, her expensive tastes could also be indulged. In Monique, Erik recognized the rare combination of beauty and brains that made her excel in whatever she did, a perfect partner for both business and pleasure. It was at times like this that he would draw on Monique's intellect and intuition.

He watched her enter the room, flushed from her brisk walk from her penthouse apartment nearby. She smiled, recognizing the hungry look in Erik's eyes.

"*Guten Morgen, mein Schatz.*" she said as she wrapped her arms around him and kissed him hungrily. Erik responded, almost losing himself to her desires. Pulling her hands from around his neck, Erik forced himself to concentrate on the problem.

"*Nein, Liebchen . . .bitte.*" He sat down, asking her to do the same. Once again under control, he explained the latest twists to their already complex problem. They discussed the situation in detail, Monique interrupting periodically to ask a question.

"Thanks to Kurt's little plan, we have Stefan Schiller, but he is useless to us unless he talks, or works on the problem. We don't know if he is just stalling, or if he really needs the notes he keeps talking about."

"What notes?" asked Monique.

"Some notes he made during the original experimentation in Bavaria . . . maybe his daughter knows where they are. As we discussed, he won't do anything for us unless we have something to force him . . . that's why we need his daughter, Christa."

Monique interrupted again. "We can't find her. She disappeared right after we grabbed Schiller in Sommerhausen. From the phone taps, we know she called Prescott, first in Canada and then in Washington, but they talked in riddles. All we know is that she is staying at a hotel, here in Frankfurt . . . by the time we find out which one, she'll be gone. Kurt has six men working on it now."

"No, I've just told Kurt to call them off, I want to handle this myself", punctuating his words by viciously butting his cigarette, then reaching for another. As the smoke once again engulfed him, he looked across at Monique, his fingers drumming nervously on the surface of the desk. "I've asked Kurt to handle security at the T.U.Z. and the lodge, I don't want anything to go wrong there. In the meantime, I think we have to change our approach. First, I want to call this Prescott myself."

"But he's in Washington, probably on his way back now."

"I know, but from what our informants tell us, he checks into his office quite regularly . . . I'll just leave him a message. I have some ideas on how we can catch him and our illusive Fräulein Schiller together." Sucking on his cigarette and inhaling deeply, Erik continued "In the meantime, for this evening, have Werner bring Schiller to . . . no, on second thought, have him call me . . . and the captain too . . . I have a job for them both."

He reached over, taking Monique's hand in his. "Patience, *Liebchen*, once this is over, we'll be able to retire in South America and live like royalty!"

She smiled up at him with a look akin to adoration.

Chapter 29

By the time the plane touched down in Frankfurt, Jake felt more refreshed and ready to meet the challenge ahead. Within a half hour, he had picked up his car and was heading back into the downtown core of Frankfurt. Once parked in a lot near the hotel, he pulled out his cell phone, checking his watch at the same time. Now that he knew the authorities weren't after him or tracing his phone calls, he could use his cell phone instead of phone booths. It was almost midnight in L.A. and Vancouver, so he knew it was unlikely to catch anyone at that time. He called Seymour Labs in Los Angeles and left a voice message to call him as soon as they could. He then called his office and left messages for both Alan and Peter to call him as soon as they got in the next morning. A spark of an idea was smouldering in his mind, something that eventually might shed some light on their problem. While he was on the line, he checked his own messages, jotting down notes from his secretary, Shannon.

The main message from Shannon was another scolding to stop using the voice mail, and look at his messages on his phone. "You've got a smart phone now Jake, so use it! I hate to see the phone smarter than you." Jake chuckled to himself as he heard the message, then looked at his phone. Sure enough, all the messages were there, just like Shannon said. Although he was used to hi tech equipment and problems, the smart phone technology had left him behind, and he was struggling to catch up.

The last voice mail message, however, did catch his attention. It was in German, and he replayed it, writing down the details. *"Guten Tag, Herr Prescott,"* the voice was firm and assertive. "Hello, Mr. Prescott, I hope you had an enjoyable flight from Washington." He couldn't believe it, he had just arrived, and they were already one step ahead of him. "If you or Fräulein Schiller are thinking of going to the police, I would reconsider. As you already know, we have Stefan, and although we do not want to harm him, we will do whatever is necessary to protect our investment. If the Fräulein expects to see her father alive again, make sure you bring her down to the river-bank, near the Eisener Steg, tomorrow night at nineteen hundred. I know you are very regular at checking your messages Mr. Prescott, but I'm giving you an extra day to pick up this one, don't disappoint me. Remember, the Eisener Steg, nineteen hundred. Look for Monique. *Auf Wiedersehen."*

"Monique?" he thought, as he wrote down the message. "How the hell am I going to find someone called Monique?" He then replayed the message, to see what time it was logged in. It was recorded shortly after his takeoff from Washington, which was after midnight Frankfurt time. That probably meant they had been looking for Christa all day and couldn't find her. The next best thing was to get both of them by contacting Jake, and stop them from going to the police at the same time. At least Christa is safe, Jake thought, feeling the satisfaction of being one step ahead of them . . . for now.

Scott Anderson had not been able to get Linda Seymour out of his mind all week, so he was looking forward to the opportunity to see her again. Once the meeting in Washington was wrapped up, a quick check with his office was all that was needed to send him off again, back to Los Angeles.

He red-eye flight from Washington had left him tired, but anxious to continue with his story. Just as Bert warned him, the WBC film crew had been turned away from the scene of Butler's bombing. N.S.O. forensic crews had been working around the clock, returning to the scene every few hours to look for something else. After twenty-four hours, they finally left the scene, taking down their 'crime scene' tape, leaving little for the film crew to record.

By the time Scott arrived from the airport by cab, the crew had covered the entire area, recording the burnt areas of the parking lot concrete floor, walls and roof. A large scorched area scarred the floor after the last pieces of the car were taken away. Very little evidence remained to indicate a man had died a violent death here the day before.

After a cursory inspection of the site, Scott flipped out his phone, dialling the number on the business card he held. The phone rang once before Linda Seymour answered.

"Linda . . . Scott Anderson, WBC. We met . . ."

"Of course Scott, I remember. What a surprise! I didn't expect to hear from you until your story came out on television, you know, another big exposé."

"We have to write the story first Linda," he explained, laughing. "there are still a few things we haven't learned yet. That's where you might be able to help me."

"We'd be glad to Scott, what do you have in mind?"

Scott explained the problem, and she agreed to meet him within the hour.

Linda Seymour smiled as she hung up the phone, her heart beating a little faster than normal. Quickly, she gathered the equipment she needed, left a message for Ed, and headed out the door.

"As you can see," Scott explained to Linda in the hotel parking lot, "there's not much left of either Butler's car, or any evidence of he explosive device. The guys from N.S.O. have done a pretty thorough job cleaning up, but I'd sure like to find out more about this thing."

Linda looked around at the marks on the floor, agreeing with Scott. "You might think they've cleaned it up, Scott, but there's still a lot of information left here. . . . you just have to know how to read it. She then walked around the full inside perimeter of the building, inspecting every corner and overhanging beam.

"Are you looking for anything in particular Linda?" asked Scott. "You seem to know what you are doing, how did you learn this?"

"My graduate thesis was on crime scene forensics, specializing in trace analysis of materials left at the scene."

"My God, I had no idea . . . I just thought you might be able to analyze some of the smoke residue, tell me what kind of explosive was used.'

Linda smiled at him, her eyes flashing with the challenge. "Oh, we'll do more than that Scott. Who knows? We might even find something the N.S.O, missed."

"I doubt it, those guys are pretty thorough."

"Well, just like criminals, they can slip up, overlook something . . . like this for example," pulling a plastic bag and some tweezers from her kit.

"What . . .?"

"Look, here . . . something driven into this crack in the wall." She looked around, examining the surface of the wall around an expansion joint. "See those marks? It looks like a fair amount of material hit the wall around here . . . and probably fell to the floor. N.S.O. most likely swept the entire area, picked up all the remnants." Reaching up with her tweezers, she extracted a tiny sliver of material from the crack, slipping it quickly into a plastic bag, jotting some notes on the label. Linda examined the fragment closely. "It looks like a piece of wire . . . square wire" she said.

Scott watched, captivated by this attractive woman. He felt himself drawn to her, a rare combination of beauty, intellect and sense of humour. He helped her take additional samples scraped from the walls and the floor, especially the area of the explosion. They moved her car into the place so they could climb up and take samples from the ceiling just above the explosion. Scott was impressed even further by her thoroughness and professional techniques.

"Let's head back to the lab, I'm anxious to see what we have." Linda said eventually. Scott agreed, eager to watch this woman at work again.

Jake's meeting with Christa was a mixture of distress and passion. Her worries over her father had consumed her for the past forty-eight hours, replacing her need for food and rest. Their welcoming embraces released some of the stresses that had occupied both of their minds, passionate kisses firing up deeper feelings and needs. As things started to heat up, Jake reluctantly pulled away, reminding himself again to stay focused.

"Come on," he said, prying her arms from around his neck, as much as I'd love to continue this, Christa, we must keep our mind on the problem at hand. I've got something important you've got to hear, but I think the first thing we should do is get something to eat, then we'll drive to Sommerhausen see what your father left in his room."

"Oh . . . right, I didn't even think of that. But Jake, I'm not even hungry."

"You will be, once you see and smell some food!" he answered. And right after that, we're going to get some sleep. When was the last time you slept?"

Putting their passions on hold, they left the little hotel and headed up to the Zeil where they had eaten before.

As they entered the restaurant, fragrant smells of the daily special drifted from the kitchen, teasing their appetite. Settled into a private booth, they ordered the lunch special and a carafe of coffee. Jake described the telephone message and their appointment for the meeting the next day. Christa nodded, tears surging up in her eyes. Expecting such a call ever since her father was taken, she was almost relieved.

"I don't think we have many options at this point," Jake offered."As long as your father is safe, we should go along with what they ask. I'd feel more comfortable with the police behind us, but whoever is holding your father might panic and do something stupid. We can't take that chance."

They agreed their only option was to go along with them and meet the following evening as requested. Jake had some things he wanted to do, but killing an entire day could be frustrating.

Once their lunch was served, Jake finally felt like he could ask some questions.

"O.K. Christa, let's go back to the beginning. Tell me what happened when I was in Washington, about your phone call . . . everything. And when you're finished that, I want you to tell me everything you know about your father's work, who he worked for, where, everything!"

Between mouthfuls, Christa recounted the events of the past two days, describing how she was tricked into talking to her father in Sommerhausen from her office. It was later she realized that the call had been monitored, revealing her father's location. Jake watched her brow wrinkle with frustration as her deep blue eyes filled with tears. He reached out, his hand on hers.

"Don't worry Christa, they won't hurt him, they need him too much. We'll have him back soon." He realized the words sounded empty as he had no idea how this was going to be achieved. She nodded and smiled, the reassurance was all she needed.

"Oh goodness, Jake!" She laughed, chewing on a chicken leg. "You were right, I was starved!" She sipped some coffee and continued with her story, describing her job, as well as some of the details on the company. Sicherheit Steinboch is a small, relatively new firm, about ten years old, a subsidiary of a much larger financial empire, the Steinboch Foundation. The foundation's head office is here in Frankfurt, up in one of those office towers somewhere. They control operations world-wide from here." A smile flicked across her face. "I mentioned before, Papa calls the firm I work for the S.S. for Sicherheit Steinboch. Their office, the one I work at is down near the river, close to the rail yards, not exactly a choice location."

"Yes, I have your business card your dad gave me. I wondered about that address."

"It's been a sore spot with my boss for years. He sits in his office and looks up at the head office, mumbling something about the 'fat cats' and a few other choice remarks."

She paused again to take another bite and some coffee, then continued. "As you already know, they specialize in security of all kinds, both personal and corporate. They can provide personal security services, alarms, surveillance devices, etc., all the equipment a person need for protection." She paused briefly, smiling at Jake. "Or everything required by the well equipped investigator."

"Or spy." Jake added, recalling her comments about her phone being tapped both at her office and at Stefan's home in Bavaria.

"Right! We supply many devices to various scientific research firms as well as government departments for high-tech surveillance, night photography and the like." "I don't understand," Jade interrupted, "If they are so involved in this stuff, how come someone can tap your phone at work . . . monitor your calls?"

"You're right! I don't know . . . all our phones are protected, secure lines, everything! The entire system is swept at least every week, it's part of our testing procedure." She paused, thinking. "Unless . . ."

"Unless . . . they are involved somehow?" Jake offered.

"Yes . . . but how . . . why? They have nothing to do with this."

"We don't know that yet, for sure . . . but . . ." Jake slowed down, trying vainly to put it together. He continued, anxious to glean as much information as possible. "Tell me about who your father worked for . . . when I talked with him he didn't even know the name of the parent company, only the lab where he worked, somewhere in southern Germany."

"I can tell you where it is, but not much more. Papa only referred to it as the *T.U,Z,* the *Technischer Umwelt Zentrum.*"

"The 'Technical Environmental Centre' . . . yes, I remember. Maybe we can trace things from that. Can you tell me any more?"

"Not really. For the past few years, I've been living and working in Frankfurt, and Papa's been wrapped up in his research in Bavaria. We only got together at Christmas and a few other occasions during the year. These were special times to spend together, as we tried not to talk much about our work."

To Jake, the situation was frustrating and almost unbelievable. With his own inquiring mind, he could not understand how someone can work for a company for several years and know so little about them. From what Christa told him, it sounded like both companies not only liked it that way, but provided only the basic information required, nothing more. It occurred to Jake that the similarity between the two companies was curious.

Chapter 30

AS SOON AS THEY ARRIVED back at the lab, Linda took charge, sending Scott to make some coffee while she worked with her lab technician, Jenny, to prepare the samples. They carefully divided some of the explosion residue from one of the plastic sample bags into separate, minuscule samples. She placed some samples on microscopic slides for visual inspection, while Jenny worked across the lab dissolving other samples in water and an assortment of solvents for further analysis. They then moved on to the next bag, each carefully logging the details of the sample location, conditions, etc.

Scott returned from their little lounge, the pleasant aroma of coffee replaced by the aseptic air of the lab. He watched Linda closely as she started the first samples in a Gas Chromatograph and Mass Spectrometer, her dark hair tossed recklessly about her shoulders. The white smock only hinted at the curves beneath as she bent over the dissecting microscope to examine the fragment of wire she had found.

Clearing his throat, he started "Linda . . ."

"Look at this," she interrupted, oblivious to his words, "that's weird . . . this wire is almost square . . . and it looks like it's been broken off at both ends, not cut, broken. See the irregular end?" she asked, moving away from the microscope. "It doesn't even look like electrical wire . . . maybe it's not even from the bomb."

Scott moved closer, a hint of fragrance from her perfume teasing him as he bent over the microscope. He squinted through the instrument at the little piece of wire, confirming her observations. Linda noticed his face tighten slightly as he turned to her.

"No . . . it's from the bomb all right, and you're right, it's not electrical wire. I've seen this before, Linda . . . while on a story a few years ago in Central America . . . not something you forget in a hurry. I think they were used in 'Nam as well. It's from a frag grenade."

"Frag grenade?" she asked, noticing the expression on Scott's face.

"Yeah, a fragmentation grenade, one of those devilish devices that the military dream up to kill each other." He paused, thinking. "I did a story on this stuff once . . . a little side-bar to a special magazine exposé on that military junta a few years ago in Central America." Scott suddenly appeared much older, the lines on his face deepened and the shadows under his eyes hinted at the pain they had witnessed. "It really started back hundreds of years ago in naval battles when they used to fill the ships' cannons with grape shot . . . chains, scrap metal, whatever." He turned toward the girls, his face grim. "You've heard the term 'shrapnel'? Until I researched for that story, I didn't know where it came from. Apparently a thing called the Shrapnel shell was invented sometime back in the late 1700's by a Lieutenant Henry Shrapnel . . . a shell that scattered shot and pieces of shell casings when it exploded." He paused again, painful images flashing through his mind. "Of course, over the years, the master-minds of war have improved their techniques, developed even better ways to kill each other. This one's a modern example of efficient killing . . . it's all encased in a thin steel can . . . then they pack in little coils of wire around the explosive, square steel wire like the kind you found, notched so that it breaks up into little pieces like the one you have under the microscope. When it explodes, these pieces are fired out in all directions like miniature bullets, but just as deadly . . . makes things pretty messy."

The thought horrified Linda, but she had read about such devices. "I've heard about this kind of thing used in anti-personnel land mines, but would a grenade like that do all that damage, Scott?"

He thought about Linda's comment, realizing she had a good point.

"No . . . you're right! From what we saw at the parking lot, I'd say there was a lot more to that explosion than just this grenade."

Linda moved back to her equipment. "It looks like we'll be here for a while, Scott, how's that coffee coming?" As she continued working, Jenny brought one of the first printouts spat out by the machine, along with a huge reference manual from the lab library. They studied the chart together, checking each of the little peaks drawn on the paper. Puzzled, Linda checked another book, again referring to the printout.

"Problems?" Scott asked as he returned with three coffees on a tray.

"No . . . I was just checking . . . we've got several peaks here . . ." She paused, confused. "It's almost as if . . ."

Scott waited, fascinated by her every move. "As if what?" he finally asked.

This time Jenny answered, "Almost as if we had at least two different bombs." She spread the printouts on the table, along with the open reference books.

"How come you have all this reference materials on explosives? Isn't this kind of work a little unusual?" Scott asked.

"No, not really . . . not as unusual as you might think," Linda replied, "we are asked quite often to provide some independent analysis of material from arson sites, explosions, etc. We do a lot of it for private investigators, security firms or even the police. Actually, most labs have this type of information, or at least some of it. Jenny's pretty good at this because she works with Ed most of the time . . . he's the expert on arson and explosives and usually handles most of those cases."

Scott nodded, feeling totally out of his element and intimidated by these two very capable women.

Linda continued "From what I can see, it looks like the most prevalent material is Semtex."

"Semtex?" asked Scott. "God, Linda, that's real bad stuff! It's not very common here is it?"

"No, not common, but we still see it from time to time. Semtex is sort of a European or specifically Czech version of the American C4 . . . hang on, I'll check what is says about it here." she said, flipping the pages of a large volume. "Here it is, Semtex . . . first made in Czechoslovakia . . . a mixture of RDX and PETN explosives."

"OK, that tells us a lot, what the hell is RDX and . . .what?"

"RDX is another name for Cyclonite, and PETN is Pentaerythrite Tetranitrate, both very powerful explosives in their own right" she continued, reading the information from the book. Looking up, she smiled at Scott, enjoying the confused look on his face. "This Semtex is really bad stuff, extremely powerful and very difficult to detect. For instance, they figure it was only about six ounces that brought down the Pan Am 747 over Lockerbie a few years back."

Scott shook his head, remembering some of the horrors of plastique explosive that he had witnessed.

Linda continued "There are also some other components I don't have a name for yet, probably from your grenade." She turned toward the analyzers. "There should be more data coming soon."

They continued working through the rest of the afternoon. While Linda and Jenny logged the results of each new analysis, Scott remained in the background, asking questions and offering a variety of theories on the bombing.

"I wish we knew more about this Butler guy . . . what he knew, where he was going." He paused, pulling a card from his pocket. "I'll bet the N.S.O. have that information," he said, "and I'll bet Bert Jackson has most of it!" He picked up the telephone, dialling the number of the local F.B.I. office, asking for Bert Jackson. He was told to leave his name and number. Within minutes, Bert called back.

"Bert . . . Scott Anderson . . . yeah, how about you?" He paused, winking at Linda. She winked back, smiling warmly, almost derailing his train of thought. " . . . Ah, Bert, what did you find out about Butler's bomb, anything new?"

He listened as Bert relayed some information, then started shaking his head at Linda with his thumb turned down, indicating that Bert was stalling, acting dumb.

"Come on Bert, don't give me that . . . you've probably been working with N.S.O. all day . . . no, I don't accept that! I thought we agreed in Washington to share information." He quietly listened again before playing his next card. "Bert . . . listen!" he said firmly, interrupting Bert's long winded excuses. "We already know about the Semtex and the frag grenade . . ." The triumphant look on his face and a thumbs-up told Linda he had scored some points. "We're still putting things together, but if I can't get any more information, I'll have to release what I have for a short item on the six o'clock news . . . I thought so . . . meet us at Seymour Labs, you know where it is."

Within the hour Bert Jackson had arrived . . . a little subdued, but now eager to share information. After some light hearted kidding, they finally settled down to discuss their findings. Bert's admiration for Linda's analytic skill was obvious.

"You were right, Linda, the explosive was mainly Semtex . . . must have been a huge chunk, maybe a few ounces, placed for maximum effect. We think the grenade was a bonus, sort of insurance to make sure Butler was finished off, not just thrown clear."

Scott was surprised at Bert's comments. "Are you telling us that N.S.O. actually volunteered that information, Bert?"

"Well, yes and no." Bert smiled. "With Paul out of the picture, they sent a new man out from Washington . . . actually I flew out with him last night. It seems like our man Paul has not been exactly the ideal model of an N.S.O. field agent. Apparently even before Paul's demise . . . probably due to some of the F.B.I.'s investigations, they were looking into some of his activities."

" And . . ." Scott could hardly wait.

"And they didn't like what they found. First, they had very little to go on . . . Paul was too good to incriminate himself very much. As I mentioned in Washington, he was senior enough, with enough clout that he could operate fairly independently . . . without much interference from his head office."

"My God!"

"Right! In any case, from what I learned last night, they had already planned to replace him when this happened . . . just a little too late." Bert paused, pulling out a little note-book from his jacket. "We met again today, over at their local temporary office. As you know, they had already swept the crime scene, all the material was handled locally by the F.B.I. lab . . . so they didn't have much choice but to share the information. In any case, like you guys already found out, it was a combination of Semtex explosive and that frag grenade." He smiled at Linda. "Actually Linda, they are still running the tests, but one of the reasons they were sure about the Semtex is the other bomb they found at the scene."

Everyone was silent, the only noise in the lab was the soft hum of equipment, punctuated by occasional traffic noises from the street. The impact of Bert's last statement finally sunk in.

"Other bomb . . . what other bomb?" they asked together.

"The first bomb . . . a much simpler device . . . most likely the one Paul found just before he phoned me. He must have disarmed it, pulled it off and chucked it into the nearest trash can! In any case, it was far enough away from the blast so that it wasn't detonated as well."

"Wow, that's pretty dangerous, having a chunk of Semtex kicking around in a trash can!", said Scott, "but what a stroke of luck . . . to have an unexploded device. You should be able to tell something from that."

"They're working on it now. Semtex is not that common here so they're still looking for tags, and the detonator used was common household variety. The rest of the stuff was all off-the-shelf pieces of wire, batteries, tape, etc., something anyone can pick up at any hardware store. They did find some prints on both the tape and the plastique, the Bureau's running them now . . . probably Paul's."

Scott asked "Did I just miss something Bert? What are tags?"

"Theoretically, explosive manufacturers are supposed to put some kind of chemical tag in the explosive during manufacture, so that the source can be traced later if necessary."

Nodding, Scott still wasn't satisfied. "But what of Paul's car, his gear . . . surely you've found more than that!"

Bert laughed. "Always the investigative reporter" he said, agreeing with Scott. "They're still working on it, so I can't tell you much. We'll probably never find out because it involves the contents of Paul's briefcase . . . sensitive N.S.O. documents, etc."

"But that might give us a clue on who's behind the mass killings, the freeway and parking lot disasters. He must have some references in there that could help."

"I've already thought of that Scott," Bert replied, "I'm hoping we'll have access to anything relating to that, but N.S.O. want to sift through it first. The . . . ah, most of the stuff is in pretty bad shape, some of it only pieces."

Scott's alarm bells went off again. After years as an investigative reporter, he had a feeling that Bert was not telling him everything. "Come on Bert, the deal was you tell us everything you know, and I'll keep the lid on until you've completed your case."

"Scott, you're asking me to reveal key details about an ongoing investigation, I'll catch hell if anyone finds out."

"Just think of it as part of your investigation," Scott offered, "sharing some information to gain more."

Bert smiled, caught at his own game. "O.K., but you really have to keep this under your hats! Two things . . . first, they found some references in Paul's brief case about who he has been dealing with . . . his contact man in Washington. This, plus what we've already pieced together from our previous investigations, we think he is the one who was running this whole thing!"

"Who?" both Linda and Scott asked simultaneously.

"You probably won't believe this, but it involves a United States Senator, Richard Pelly."

"Isn't that the guy Jake Prescott and that Haywood fellow were talking about, something about an old case, years ago?"

"That's right . . . and we've been checking him out for several years, along with another guy who I think is the link to Germany.

"Wow!" Scott exclaimed, calculating the implications of Bert's words. "You mentioned two things, what's the other thing?"

"In the explosion debris they found fragments of something they haven't recognized yet, along with something that might point to who planted the bomb."

They waited, expecting Bert to complete his comments.

"Well, what is it Bert?"

"Well . . . it's funny . . . at the airport last night, Jake said we might find something like this."

"What, for God's sake!"

"The first bomb . . the one I just told you about, was made here. Like I said . . . except for being Semtex, it was all common, local materials, the whole nine yards. It's almost as if they wanted it to be found, or at least didn't care if it was found." He paused, enjoying their anticipation. "But the main blast . . . different ball game. The N.S.O. feel that this bomb was definitely not local . . . but foreign made. All the time we were thinking it was just a local hit ordered by those nuts in Washington. From the debris, especially the detonator and the style of assembly, they're pretty sure it was middle east, probably some Arab country. If they find any tags, it could help us pin it down."

"Arab . . .? How the hell did they get involved?" asked Scott, unable to make a connection.

Linda answered "Maybe the A.F.C., the Arab Freedom Corps. Remember, they were at the WAWA Conference, protesting about something."

"No, that's too easy." Bert replied. "Those protestors were just local types, hired to make a noise about someone's cause. No, this is even more sinister, something related to that gasoline additive."

"Oh God!" said Bert, "I think I see the way you are going."

"Right! These guys are experts, probably trained mercenaries, maybe trained in some terrorist school in Libya or wherever. As to who is behind them . . . who knows? If oil is involved, then it could be someone from any one of almost a dozen OPEC countries, or a combination. You see, if what Jake told us is true, that the additive can cut fuel consumption by that much, then billions of dollars are at stake. Two things can happen. One, whoever stands to make that money will go to any lengths to make sure it does happen. And two, whoever is in the gasoline business stands to lose that much, so will also go to any lengths to make sure it DOESN'T happen!"

Chapter 31

THE LACK OF SLEEP AND tensions of the past few days finally caught up with her. A good lunch helped, and as soon as they were on the autobahn heading towards Sommerhausen, Christa finally gave in and fell asleep for the entire trip. Pleased that she would now get some much needed rest, Jake drove the distance in quiet, reviewing the puzzle and calculating options.

When they arrived at the little guest house, Herr Wankle greeted them enthusiastically, but very concerned that Stefan had not slept in his room for two nights. "Some gentlemen came to visit him, and they left a short time later with Stefan. I thought they might be going out for dinner, but they never returned."

"Can you describe any of these 'gentlemen'?" asked Jake. He listened as Herr Wankle described briefly what he could remember. The main features of the three men were that one was short and stocky, and the other was tall and had a limp. The third man was quite average, not participating much, but seemingly directing the other two.

Not believing much in coincidence, Jake recognized the first two as probably the same ones that followed him when he first arrived in Frankfurt. The third man was a mystery.

They went up to his room, not surprised by what greeted them. The room was tidy and clean, a contrast to the first time Jake had seen the room. He had made arrangements for them to keep the room clean and make sure Stefan ate his meals. All of Stefan's clothes still hung in the closet, underwear and socks still in the drawers. The only things missing were his notes and his laptop computer.

"It looks like they took everything that had anything to do with the project." observed Jake. Christa nodded, her eyes brimming with tears.

"I'll pack Papa's clothes, Jake. When we find him, he'll need a change. Christa quickly moved around the room, packing the clothes and the few items left of her father's.

Jake continued to look around, hoping that Stefan had left a message, some clue about his plight. Recalling details of his visit to the same room less that a week earlier, it became obvious to Jake that Stefan thought he was safe and had not expected his captors to appear in Sommerhausen. After settling with Herr Wankle, they left the guest house and headed back to Frankfurt.

After returning to the hotel, they checked Christa's message service, then phoned his office in Vancouver. Shannon answered, surprised at his call.

"Jake! We were just about to call you . . . got your message from last night."

Shannon continued, a sense of urgency in her voice. "Both Alan and Peter want to talk to you, but first, your messages. Frank Haywood wants you to call him . . . he's still in Washington, so try him there. Bert Jackson wants to talk to you, urgently! Here's his L.A. number." She repeated the number the F.B.I, agent had given her . . . "And Brent Willis in L.A., not important . . . just wants to know what's going on."

"That's it?" Jake asked as he wrote down the messages.

"Not quite, Jake." Shannon was enjoying herself. "If you'd just check your phone once in awhile, you'd see all these messages there! And lastly, a guy from the R.C.M.P. came by, wants to talk to you.

"R.C.M.P.? What does he want, doesn't he realize I'm over here?" The last group he wanted to deal with now was a bunch of Canadian cops.

"We told them that, but apparently Ottawa's been working with Interpol and they are the ones who want to talk to you on this.."

"Interpol? When did they get into this?" He thought a moment, then added "And since when did Interpol work with laymen like me?"

"Well Jake, maybe they checked into your background and found out you're not quite the 'layman' you think you are!" Shannon was laughing now, "and besides, I don't know why they would want to talk to you . . . you can't even read your own messages on your phone."

"No Shannon, I can do that," slightly embarrassed, "but I just like to call to hear your sweet voice once in awhile."

"Anyway," continued Shannon, they've been involved longer than you might realize . . . something to do with Paul Butler and his work with a German firm. They think you might have some of the answers they need."

"That's crazy, Paul worked for the N.S.O. . . . oh!" Jake stopped, realizing the potential of what Shannon was telling him, and the reason they wanted to talk to him. "What did he say, did he give you any details?"

"No, that's all . . . you have to call a Jacques Manet at their headquarters in France." Shannon read off the number Jake was to call. "They'll tell you who to contact in Germany, in Wiesbaden, I think."

Jake wrote down the information, then talked with both Peter and Alan. They had additional technical information for him, information that was interesting, but useless for the present predicament. He gave them both additional instructions, requests for information he needed about some chemical companies.

"Alan, you dealt with a lot of European firms when you worked in the U.K., plus you"ve been in the business far longer than I have. I want you to dig out details on companies in Germany doing research on energy related projects . . . especially joint projects with the U.S.. Contact Frank Haywood and George Barnes in Washington, they already have some information, maybe you can work with them. I'll be talking with Bert Jackson later . . . maybe he can help as well. I want to know who and where this research facility is that Stefan worked for." With scarcely a pause, he continued his instructions to Peter. "Peter, you're the computer expert . . . you know what to do to help Alan with his search, maybe you can hack into some files or whatever you guys do. There's something else . . . a message on my voice mail, I want you to record it, then pull it apart. Its in German, so you'll have fun figuring it out, but the content is not important. I just want a record of that voice and want you to find out whatever you can about it, if possible."

After his call, he related the information to Christa, then called Bert Jackson on his cell phone in L.A. A sleepy voice answered on the second ring.

"Good morning Bert, Jake Prescott here."

"God Jake, you're an early riser . . . are you still in Germany?"

"That's right Bert, and it's mid-afternoon here . . . but the message said it was urgent."

"Hang on, I'll get my briefcase." Jake waited, the sound of papers rustling came over the phone. "You were right, Jake . . .about someone else setting that bomb."

Jake's satisfaction with his correct assessment turned into apprehension as Bert related the details of his day with the N.S.O. and with Linda Seymour and Scott Anderson, and the results of the lab analysis. "We're not sure who yet, but we know there's another player in the game." They continued to compare notes, omitting any reference to his planned meeting later.

"I have to call Interpol first . . . some guy wants to talk to me, a Jacques Manet. You should be able to find out what their involvement is through your office. I'll talk to you later and let you know."

Jake decided to call Frank Haywood later because he wanted to talk to Interpol first. He tried to remember details of Interpol from his early training. Formed in 1914, the 'International Criminal Police Organization' or Interpol, is a worldwide organization to fight crime. Currently based in Lyon, France, the organization had a turbulent past, but now boasts at least 176 member countries, with an efficient and sophisticated communication sharing system.

He was connected quickly to Jacques Manet. After Jake introduced himself, Jacques quickly picked up the conversation. "Jake, I'm glad you called . . . Jake . . . Jacques, do we share the same name, or is Jake short for something else?" he asked.

"Actually, my given name is Jakob, but I always use Jake." The man was very pleasant, his heavy British accent catching Jake off guard. "You speak English very well Jacques."

"I should, I was born and raised just outside London. A French name from my father, but very, very English, I'm afraid. In case you're wondering Jake, Interpol has over 80 police officers stationed here from 40 countries, so it's quite an international soup."

Jake filed the information, impressed by the size and diversity of the organization. "My office said you wanted to talk to me," he said, something about Paul Butler and the N.S.O."

"Quite right . . . actually two things, about two cases that converged this week in Los Angeles."

"How's that?" Jake asked, not sure what he was driving at.

"I don't know how to start, much of this is still confidential."

"Let's cut the crap, Jacques!" His patience with official secrecy was very thin. "Ever since this damn thing started, I've been harassed, threatened and chased by you so-called law enforcement organizations, but we still managed to find out more than you guys have. Remember, you called me! If you want some information, or have a request, please continue! In the meantime, Stefan Schiller has been kidnapped . . ." He immediately regretted letting that out.

"What's this, when did this happen, we haven't heard anything from Frankfurt police."

To pacify the man, Jake told him that everything was under control and he would apprise his local office. "Please continue with why you called me."

Uncomfortable with Jake's criticism, Jacques continued, telling more than he had originally planned. "I'm dreadfully sorry about your recent experience Jake, but don't sell us short. A lot of the mess you've been dumped into this last week or so, we've been tracking and keeping tabs on for months, in some cases years." The comment surprised Jake, calming his frustrations. Jacques continued. "One of our jobs here is to try to keep track of certain mercenaries and terrorists . . . where they travel, what their next job is, and who is paying them. One such group we have been tracking is a small group of mercenaries from an un-named Mediterranean country, very likely skilled in their trade. Their paths crossed with Paul Butler this week in Los Angeles . . . and Butler lost."

"Wha . . . what are you saying? Is this group responsible for killing Paul?"

"We think so, but are not positive. All indications point that way, so unless it's a deliberate attempt to mislead us, we are continuing on that assumption." He stopped, the rustling of papers the only sound over the phone. "The interesting thing about all this . . . which brings me to the reason why we contacted you . . . one being the fact that we were also watching Paul Butler."

"I don't suppose the fact he worked for the N.S.O. had anything to do with it?" Jake asked.

"Actually, no. Paul had a very complicated life, with a very complicated background. Invariably, when a chap leads this kind of life, things tend to get out of control. In Paul's case, he led a double, possibly triple life . . . the life of an N.S.O. agent was the one you saw. We also know him as a loyal employee of a small firm in Germany, a firm which has links to a much larger enterprise."

Jake interrupted "Like Sicherheit Steinbock?" he asked.

"Ah . . . yes . . . I didn't realize you were aware of that." Jacques paused, surprised. "I'm sorry Jake, I had no idea you were so well informed." Jake could almost feel the curiosity seep from the phone. "How long have you been involved in this Jake?" he asked.

"Almost two weeks, and you guys . . . pardon me . . . the authorities, have not made it easy for us!"

"Bravo Jake! I must say, I'm bloody amazed. You've most likely found out more in two weeks than we have in as many months."

"O.K., then tell me more." Jake asked, not diverted by the flattery.

Jacques continued, not sure how far to go with his disclosure. "First about Paul . . . suffice it to say, when his activities started involving the transfers of large sums of money, both to and from offshore accounts, we began to watch him more closely."

Jake absorbed the information, oddly not surprised. He waited. Manet offered nothing further. "Well . . . that's it? That's all you have?"

"All I can tell you now Jake about that. The main reason I wanted to talk to you is this. The people I just told you about, these mercenaries . . . some of the group are now in Europe. Half went to the eastern U.S. and the local police and F.B.I. are trying to round them up now. We fear they are in Washington for another job."

"How about the other half . . . the ones in Europe . . . where did they go?"

"From what we know, they took a flight from L.A. to London, then to Berlin. We have reason to believe they are on their way to Frankfurt."

"What's this got to do with me, why should I be interested?" Jake asked.

"For the same reason Paul was blown up, and probably the same reason Schiller was kidnapped. Jake, these chaps are bloody dangerous, eliminating people by whatever means possible is their job, their passion and are bloody good at it. For you, even with your limited experience and training in that area, you are still an amateur, and you could get yourself killed. You are what we call a 'loose cannon', an unknown factor rolling around in the middle of this, so we don't know which way things might go. We don't know what you're up to Jake, or who you are talking to, but you had better be very careful. You see Jake, we're not sure, but we think this group has been hired by one of the OPEC countries, or at least someone with large oil interests, someone who does not want Schiller's work to succeed!"

Chapter 32

JAKE AWOKE EARLY TO THE cathedral bells once again, only a block from the hotel. Christa remained sleeping, a hint of a smile on her pouting lips. Her golden hair was spread recklessly across the bed, while a full breast peeked provocatively out from under the duvet. Jake felt his body start to respond as he recalled the wondrous love-making of the night before. Knowing she would sleep for at least a few more hours, Jake quietly left the room, purposely leaving his jacket behind.

He stopped at the little *Frühstück Zimmer*, or breakfast room, where the hotel served a wonderful German breakfast. He loaded up with some crusty multi-grain rolls, a variety of sliced meats and cheeses. A little fruit and yoghurt with some strong coffee finished it off as he planned his actions for the day. When he thought some of the stores would be open, he left the hotel on his mission.

Although he didn't think anyone was watching or following him, he left nothing to chance. Heading up the street, he returned to the stores along the Zeil, eventually finding a general purpose clothing store that was open. Minutes later he left the store, now clothed in a new windbreaker and a baseball cap made for the German tourist industry. A small news and souvenir kiosk provided him with a disposable camera, which he slung around his neck. Thus outfitted, he headed south again toward the Main River, almost undistinguishable from hundreds of other tourists on the street. He only wished that he did not have to use his cane so much, a fault which made it difficult to blend into the crowd.

The hazy cloud cover trapped the summer morning air over the city, promising a thunder storm before the day ended. With his meteorological background, Jake kept a close eye on the weather, calculating when the storm would begin. Arriving at the Mainkai, the street that follows the north shore of the Main River, he strolled slowly along the sidewalk, stopping occasionally to take pictures of the river barges or other tourist attractions. Their riverside appointment was not due until that evening, but Jake wanted to check out the location, possibly gain some advantage, or at least try to make sense of his instructions.

Using every technique he learned in his surveillance training, he could not detect anyone following or watching him. For the next two hours, he toured the waterfront streets, searching for a clue that might give him some advantage later. Concentrating on the location around the old Eiserner Steg iron bridge where they were to meet later, he walked up and down the river, covering five of the busiest bridges and several of the popular tourist areas on the river-front.

It was just close to noon when he finally gave up and returned to the hotel. The cloud cover had thickened, the air even thicker. Without the relief of a river breeze, Jake's clothes clung to him in the heavy humid air.

Christa had been up for some time and was fresh from the shower when Jake returned to the room. The idea appealed to him, so he headed into the shower himself.

"Remind me, I have to call Frank Haywood in Washington later this afternoon, maybe Bert as well." he told Christa as he dried himself and got dressed. They left the hotel again, heading down to the Römerburg, choosing a nice restaurant for lunch. Christa was quiet, a frown hardening her face. Worried about her father, she both dreaded and looked forward to their meeting later that day.

"Christa," Jake pleaded, taking her hand across the table, "You must relax, try to think of something else . . . you'll be a basket-case by the time we have to go down there." Jake explained to her what he had been doing for the few hours that morning.

"I can't see anything down there called Monique, no bars, stores or anything. She must be the one that will meet us, maybe take us somewhere." He tried to act casual and confident, but in truth, he was also worried, unsure of what to expect. He knew he should listen to Interpol as Jacques Manet's warnings still rattled in his ears . . . he was playing with forces beyond his scope. He suddenly remembered he was supposed to call the local Interpol agent in Frankfurt. Remembering the warning about talking to the police in the message, he decided to postpone that call until the next day.

A brief shower had passed during lunch, wetting down the hot cobblestones of the square, adding to the muggy closeness of the afternoon. Although the rain had stopped, the clouds still threatened, and Jake knew there would be more rain soon as large thunder-heads built over the city. They walked down to the river, trying to catch a cool breeze off the water. Checking his watch, Jake finally decided it was late enough to call Washington.

"Frank . . . Jake Prescott . . . yeah, still in Germany. No, nothing yet, but tonight we should know." Not wanting to give away too much about their plans, Jake switched the conversation back to Frank. "You called me Frank, what have you got?"

Frank's voice raised a tone, obviously excited about his news. "We finally traced some of the connections." he said quickly.

"What connections Frank? What are you talking about?"

"The money transfers, the phone calls, the faxes . . . all the communications between Paul Butler and his overseas connections. Bert just called, the Bureau took some of the stuff that George and I had dug out, and used their sources to trace all this stuff. Apparently a lot of the calls that Paul used to make from L.A., some were to a couple of numbers here in Washington, but most of them to Germany."

"Do you know who, or where in Germany?" Jake asked.

"Most of them to a little research facility in the south of Germany, something called the "Technischer . . . " he paused as he tried to read the German.

Jake completed the sentence for him. "*Technischer Umwelt Zentrum*?"

"Yeah . . . how did you know?" surprise was obvious.

"That's the place that Stefan worked at, where he developed the nickel additive. What we don't know, is who owns it, who runs it or is behind it."

"Oh, that's easy," Frank offered, "Your men in Vancouver, Alan and Peter helped me with this one. It's owned by another firm which, in turn is owned by another, etc., until it is all owned by a large corporation called the Steinbock Foundation."

The name hit Jake like a lead pipe. All this time, both Stefan and Christa were working for the same firm. Suddenly things became clear, "No wonder the security was compromised and they knew every move she made," he mumbled to himself.

"Jake, Jake . . . you still with me?" Frank was asking, thinking he was talking to a dead line.

"Sorry Frank, yes, go ahead, what else do you have."

"The best part!" he said, enjoying himself. "The other calls, the ones to Washington . . . you'll never guess who they were to."

"Senator Richard Pelly" Jake guessed.

"Yeah . . ." his enthusiasm dampened, "How the hell did you know Jake?"

"I've been working on the puzzle, and your first bit of information sort of tied a few pieces together. Have you found out anything about Klaus Müller yet?"

"Not yet, but I think Bert's working on it. He just called me, he's finished in L.A. and is on his way back here today. We should have some more details for you tomorrow."

"Good, keep in touch."

He watched the look of surprise on Christa's face when he told her the news. They discussed the revelation, and how it explained many of the puzzling things during the past two weeks.

"I would imagine the F.B.I. will be paying a few visits to people in Washington before long, as well as the Interpol over here" Jake said as he tried to put the pieces together. "There are still a lot of pieces missing," he said to Christa, "too many questions unanswered."

A few more telephone calls and it was soon time to head back towards the Eiserner Steg, the little iron bridge over the river between the Römerburg section of Frankfurt and old Sachsenhausen. They watched as a Dutch river barge chugged by them, heading down the river, probably to a port in Holland. As they watched, another barge headed up the river towards them, passing under one of the low traffic bridges further down the river.

As the time moved closer to nineteen hundred, or seven o'clock, they walked along the bank, scanning the people for some recognition, some indication of their rendezvous. Tourists and residents passed them by, some heading into the old town, some walking up over the bridge. The chugging of a river barge became louder, finally becoming visible under the bridge as it came closer to the edge, where a docking area was available for tour boats and ships travelling on the river.

It wasn't until the crew jumped off to tie up the vessel that both Christa and Jake noticed the name, written across the stern in bold letters . . . "MONIQUE"

Chapter 33

Senator Richard Pelly was sweating. Not his usual greasy sweat of an overweight couch potato, but the acrid sweat of fear, oozing uncontrollably from every pore of his body. Leaning heavily on his liquor cabinet, his hands shook visibly as he poured a double shot of his favourite sour mash whiskey. Thus armed, he lit another black cigar, adding even more smoke to the already polluted room. The senator was worried, things were out of control, and there was nothing he could do about it. He started wishing he had an alternate plan, an escape. Paul Butler had always been his front line, Paul always handled these things for him. Klaus kept him informed about the overseas situation, and Paul took care of the details locally.

Not any more. It was almost as if he were cut off from the world. Paul was dead, Klaus was acting strange, keeping a definite distance between them. "Big Dick" Pelly knew the F.B.I. were getting close. Between the snooping around done before the accident, and all of the pressure since, he knew it was only a matter of time. That wasn't the real worry, the senator had always figured he could handle the law . . . after all, he had done it before. What really worried him was whoever killed Paul. It was different this time, he had no idea who was behind the bombing. If someone could get Paul, what chance did the senator have? He had to think of a way out, how he could disappear and enjoy some of the money he had "earned".

His intercom buzzed. "Courier delivery, Senator." his secretary announced.

"Fine dear, please bring it in."

His secretary entered the room, dropping a small package on his desk and retreating as quickly from the foul smelling room.

Over the years, the senator had received more than his share of gifts, little items of appreciation, usually from grateful corporations benefiting from his opposition to environmental groups and legislation. As it was inappropriate for a senator to receive gifts from corporations, only small token gifts were ever delivered to the office. The senator usually counted the real gifts in terms of four or five figures.

The arrival of the package momentarily distracted the senator from his worries, and he attacked the present eagerly. Pulling the courier envelope open, he pulled out a wooden box wrapped lightly in tissue paper. He saw immediately in was a cigar box, a beautifully crafted one, its deep grained wood glowing richly in the dim light. He drew a quick breath as he recognized the brand, a favourite Cuban variety, highly prized among cigar aficionados.

He sat down, gulping half a glass of whiskey, anticipating the enjoyment of a first class cigar. Putting down his drink, he broke the seal on the box, slowly opening the lid, ready to select one of the dark, rich cylinders that lay before him.

The device was cleverly designed, allowing Richard Pelly about two seconds of initial anticipation, then the horror of realization as he quickly tried to close the lid. A few ounces of Semtex erupted from the centre of the box, tearing off his arms and blowing cigars mixed with a thousand wooden splinters through the senator's head and body.

Later that day, as the news of Richard Pelly's demise spread through Washington, Klaus Müller's stomach felt like it was on fire. He threw some papers in his brief case and quickly left his office, briefly explaining to his secretary that he wasn't feeling well, and would be in touch later. After leaving the building, he headed for his apartment, a little brownstone flat in a respectable area within walking distance of his office. On the way, he stopped at the bank, withdrawing some money and a small package from his safety deposit box. Once home, he quickly packed his bag and called a cab. He then phoned the airport, checking for any available flight to Germany. He had no idea who was responsible for these bombings, and did not know how far they would go, but he wasn't going to take any chances. If he returned to Germany, at least he would have some hope, as well as the support of the Foundation. Booked on a flight later that afternoon to Munich via Zürich, he immediately left his apartment and headed for the airport.

Pain stabbed him again as they arrived at the terminal, almost doubling him over. Popping another antacid, he paused, waiting for the remedy to ease the pain. With two hours to kill, he had a lot of time to worry, his stomach pains increasing. With the next antacid, he took a couple of tranquillizers, thinking it would help calm his stomach. Within a half hour, it was feeling better, so he took two more tranquillizers, then spent the last hour in the bar, washing the pills down with some double schnapps.

By flight time, Klaus was feeling much better, but very sleepy. Once settled in his seat, he asked for an extra pillow and curled up in the corner by the window and was soon fast asleep.

Once the flight attendants had made him comfortable, they ignored him, a quiet passenger oblivious to the world and enjoying a good sleep. Other than a slightly paling skin over the next five hours, there was no indication that this was Klaus Müller's last flight as his perforated ulcer slowly bled the life out of him into his own abdominal cavity.

About the same time as Klaus Müller's plane was taking off for Germany, Bert Jackson's flight from Los Angeles was touching down. He had been notified during the flight about Richard Pelly's bomb, and the F.B.I. were already on the scene, trying to piece together the events leading up to the explosion. A Bureau car picked him up, whisking him away from the airport and back into the middle of town to the senator's office. The forensic crew were still on site, working on the gruesome task of trying to separate the pieces of the bomb from the pieces of the senator, now indiscriminately spread around the room. Bert felt sick as he walked into the room, the stench of death overpowered the sour smell of the senator's cigar smoke.

"Maybe you should stay outside for now, Bert." one of the men suggested. "We'll let you know as soon as we find something."

Bert left gladly, but not before telling the man about their findings on the Los Angeles bomb. "Just in case you find something similar." he added.

As he waited outside, he talked with the agent who had questioned Pelly's secretary. Far enough away in the outer office, she had missed the direct force of the blast. She was taken to the hospital but released some time later with only minor injuries. He made notes about the method of delivery, the packaging and the courier used, knowing it would tell them nothing.

Bert was worried. Picking off an N.S.O. agent was one thing, but attacking a U.S. senator in his own office was quite another. Crowds of the press were lined up outside the office, screaming for information, held back by police and fire department barricades. Bert knew this was all related to the experiment gone wrong in Los Angeles, and felt that only the people directly involved were being targeted. The Bureau could not take that chance, and started action with the Secret Service to step up security and offer at least a little more protection to other senators and public officials. As he thought about the people involved, Klaus Müller's name came up.

Walking swiftly, he left the building and headed over to Müller's office, within a block. When his secretary told him that Klaus was not feeling well and had left suddenly earlier that afternoon, Bert knew immediately he was gone.

Quickly, he dialled his cell phone. "Get me some help on this," he yelled to someone in his office. "Check the airports, see if Müller has left on any flight this afternoon . . . I don't know, try Germany, or maybe even Rio!" He had no idea what plans Müller might have, or in which direction he would move. He walked back to Pelly's office, trying to figure out his next move.

The answer came back within the hour. Klaus Müller had boarded a Swissair flight that afternoon for Zürich, with a connecting flight to Munich.

"Good!" said Bert, "at least we know where he's going. Have Interpol pick him up in Zürich." He thought a moment, then added "And try to get a message to Jake Prescott . . . tell that guy at Interpol and then try Frankfurt police . . . and leave it at his office as well . . . have him call me as soon as possible!" He just hoped he could get the message to Jake on time.

Chapter 34

THE "MONIQUE" WAS A BEAUTY, that rare combination of a sailor's dream and a rich man's toy. The European river barges were always a delight, both to the eye and the brain. Their sheer size is intimidating as they navigate up rivers, through narrow locks and tight corners, many times in heavy traffic with other barges and ferries. The MONIQUE was spotless and obviously well maintained. The telescopic metal covers over her huge holds appeared freshly painted, while the decks were clear and well organized. Like most of the barges, the bridge and main living quarters were situated in the stern, aft of the cargo holds, occupying less than ten percent of the boat's length. The white paint gleamed in contrast to the varnished dark wood trim, while fancy lace curtains were barely visible as they peaked through tinted windows. A small luxury sports car crouched on the roof of the main cabin, ready for use.

Before they had a chance to appreciate any further details, a stocky man in a business suit stepped off the vessel onto the dock and strongly suggesting they follow him aboard.

"*Kommen Sie mit . . .*" as he pointed and helped them step over the low rail to the main deck. The heavy clouds grew darker, the sun now almost set. The man looked up as occasional rumbles of thunder threatened again. He then pointed aft, towards a side entrance in the long main cabin. Jake immediately recognized the man as the second one who had followed him when he first arrived in Frankfurt, over a week ago. Christa and Jake entered first, stepping over the raised sill, the man following directly behind them.

They were scarcely prepared for the sight that greeted them. The large room was a little dark at first, the lightly tinted windows dimming most of the early evening light. As their eyes became accustomed, the rich details became apparent. Tiny brass wall lamps mounted on the panelled walls cast a warm glow over the richly grained wood. Deeply piled Persian carpets in rich reds and golds covered the floor, muffling the sound of their walking. Well stuffed chairs and sofas strategically placed around the room gave the occupants an excellent view of the river. A large table and chairs occupied a central open space towards the rear of the room. The table was set for four, with classic settings of fine china and silver with crystal wine glasses stuffed with folded, lace-trimmed napkins. To one side of the dining area was a companionway stairwell to other living quarters below. Tantalizing aromas drifted from another door forward, open to the galley or small kitchen where a second man appeared, a tray of drinks in his hand.

"Please, Fräulein Schiller, have a seat . . . and you, Herr Prescott." Jake did not recognize the voice, so he knew it was not the man who had left the message. The impact of the situation still sinking in, they responded mechanically by nodding and sitting down, then taking a drink from the man's tray. Jake felt the engines change pitch while something moved at the window. He looked up, noticing the barge had left the dock and was heading up the river. They looked at each other, wondering what was next as they tried a sip from their drinks. They didn't have to wait long.

"*Guten Abend* . . . Good evening. I hope Carl has made you comfortable" a voice announced behind them. Jake recognized the voice this time as the man in the telephone message, the man they had come to see. They turned to face him. A portly but very distinguished man approached them, waving them back into their seats. Dressed in a dark business suit, he appeared to have stepped out of a board meeting to talk to them. His long white hair was combed straight back, contrasting with his dark brows and moustache. He held a cigarette tightly between his index and middle finger, his hand flicking nervously back and forth to his mouth as he puffed constantly. Beside him was an attractive, middle aged woman, her hand linked with his.

"Where is my father?" Christa yelled at him, breaking the artificially cordial atmosphere. "I want to see my father!"

The man started nervously, but continued to ignore her questions as he puffed again on his cigarette and turned to the woman, making sure she was comfortably seated before seating himself. Carl hovered patiently, eventually handing them each a drink.

Eager for answers, Jake stood up and began to approach the man.

"Mr . . . whatever your name is, you'd better start talking . . . just who the hell are you, and what have you done with Stefan?

The man smiled at Jake, waving him back to his seat. With his right hand, he gently stroked his moustache, while the left was occupied with the lit cigarette.

"Always to the point, Herr Prescott . . . but impatient! I was told you were like that. But of course, how rude of me! My name is Erik Weigel, President of the Steinbock Foundation. I . . . ."

Christa responded first. "Oh my God! Steinbock . . . you mean . . . you . . ."

Weigel continued, once more ignoring Christa's outburst. " . . . as I said, my name is Erik Weigel, and this is my secretary, Monique Brehmer."

"Monique . . .?" Jake started.

"Yes, the same Monique. This vessel belongs to Monique, a little anniversary gift we invested in several years ago. It provides our travel and entertainment throughout Europe, yet continues to make money at the same time . . . good idea, don't you think?" He smiled at Monique, obviously his weakness. "But I must continue . . . you have met Carl . . . my butler you might call him. Outside, it was Helmut Schmidt that escorted you on board, but, Herr Prescott, I think you have already met him" he smiled. "In case you are wondering, his partner, the tall one, whom you have also met, is Werner Klein . . . he is now with Stefan."

"But . . ." started Christa.

"Yes, Fräulein Schiller, to answer your question; yes, we are the same company that owns Sicherheit Steinbock, and also owns the T.U.Z., the lab where your father worked. I must apologize, I thought you knew that . . . but then again, I suppose we don't really advertise that information."

"I guess not!" Jake added. "We just found out yesterday, and were wondering how it all linked together. To get back to Christa's original question . . . where is Stefan? I thought he was going to be here."

"Oh he's fine, don't worry. No, Herr Prescott, he's not here. I suppose I stretched the truth a little if I let you believe that, but I'm not that naive . . . I couldn't really trust you not to go to the police, so Stefan is safely out of the way for now." Enveloped in a cloud of tobacco smoke, he sipped his drink before continuing. "You will have a chance to see him . . . after all, that's why you are here, but in the meantime, we can get to know each other a little. We have some things to discuss, Herr Prescott, and then maybe later you can help the young lady's father with his problem. You see, that is exactly where we are going at this moment. I hope you don't mind being our guests for a few days . . . maybe a week."

"A week?"

"Maybe longer . . . however long it takes for you and Stefan to solve the problem!"

With few choices available, Jake accepted their situation, for now. "So, what's your next move, now that you've added two more kidnappings to your already long list of crimes?"

"Please, Jake . . . if I may call you Jake. I am not the demon you think I am. I am a simple businessman. I have invested a lot of time and money into this project, and I plan to reap the benefits." His face grew hard, belying the image he was trying to portray as he hissed "But I will not let some meddling amateurs get in my way!"

A businessman perhaps, Jake thought, but anything but simple. "So a lot of people have to die in the meantime?" he asked.

"That was not my doing . . . that was not in the plan!" He suddenly became contrite, almost apologetic. "According to Stefan, we had a viable product . . . right up until the accident in the lab in Bavaria. We put a hold on things, but too many steps had already been taken and your American friends got greedy . . . wanted to go ahead without any further tests. They figured the problems wouldn't show up in real life."

"Who . . . what American friends . . . who are you talking about?" Jake asked.

"That senator, Pelly. He had the first shipment of material before we could stop it. He felt he could continue with the plan, push it all through right away . . . they wanted the material being used for a long enough time that the results would be visible and start showing up on the monitoring stations. This would give them maximum exposure and publicity while your air quality conference was on."

The name Pelly surprised Jake, the fact that he was so involved. "So the senator managed to do all this by himself?" Jake asked mockingly.

"No, of course not. He had help . . . another greedy American . . . Paul Butler. He had the contacts, the clout . . . all driven of course by our money."

"But what does Müller have to do with this . . . Klaus Müller?"

"Officially, Müller works for the U.S. Government . . . sort of a liaison or coordinator between American and German investments in this project. There's nothing wrong with that, it's all in the records."

"And unofficially?" asked Jake.

Weigel's dark eyes blinked nervously as he stroked his moustache again. Taking a slow, long drag from his cigarette deep into his lungs, he exhaled loudly as he continued his account.

"Müller works for us . . . he's been an employee of Steinbock for many years. It has . . . how do you say . . . helped grease the wheels of progress."

"Having an inside man in Washington . . . I'm sure it did grease the wheels . . . and line your pockets too!" He could scarcely believe what he was hearing, yet, it was starting to make more sense.

Carl entered the room again, this time carrying a large tray of food. He placed it on the table and returned to the kitchen for more.

"Please," Erik announced, getting up and moving to the table, "Come, join us for dinner. I'm sure you'll find our fare quite superb."

Christa and Jake joined the other couple at the table, both uncomfortable with the situation yet resigned to it. Besides, thought Jake, it was getting late and they were both hungry. Darkness had closed around the vessel as it continued its journey up the river, passing the sparkling lights of towns and villages on either side. The engines slowed as footsteps thumped along the deck beside the cabin, fading toward the forward end of the barge. Then the engines almost stopped, the evening suddenly quiet.

Jake looked up, trying to figure out where they were, and what was happening outside. Erik Weigel answered his unspoken question. "We're going through one of the locks," he explained, "It only takes a few minutes. The Main River has many canal locks we must travel through to gain the elevation. There are almost fifty locks between Mainz and Nüremberg, and we should travel through almost twenty on this portion of our trip up to Würzburg."

"Würzburg? Is that where you are taking us?" Jake asked.

Weigel smiled, caught by his own slip of information. "You are fast, Herr Prescott. Würzburg is our first stop."

The meal was served and for the next hour or more, they enjoyed the food and wine of their host, offering only small talk as the circumstance required. Occasional thunder claps rumbled above them, punctuated by periodic lightning flashes. Jake had hoped to keep track of their progress, but soon lost track of the number of locks they had passed through. They were both soon wrapped up in the discussion with Weigel and had no idea where they were. It was well after midnight when the subject material returned to their present problems.

Weigel continued, talking again about the problems in the U.S.. "Klaus has been a good man, very conscientious, very dependable. I'm afraid it was your senator from the south that started the problems . . . " He paused, reaching for a bottle of wine. "Please try this . . . it's a wonderful little *Frankenwein* from our own vineyard, not far from here." He poured their wine, hoping to lighten the conversation, but then turned serious as he continued his comments about the senator. "Yes, he was a problem . . . but no longer, from what I see on tonight's television."

"What are you talking about?" they both asked, not liking the implication.

Weigel enjoyed being one up on them, but was so concerned about the story that he could not appreciate it. "Senator Richard Pelly was killed today in his office . . . from a package or a letter bomb, from what the TV reports say."

Christa gasped at the news. Jake nodded, analyzing the data and how it related to their situation. He wished he could talk to Bert right now and get the real story. He knew his suggestions to Bert at the airport were coming true . . . someone else was involved . . . seriously involved. He watched Monique closely as Weigel was talking. Her nervous glances towards her boss told Jake this subject had been discussed between them before. Weigel lit up another cigarette. The man was nervous . . . out of his element. Maybe he was right, he was just a businessman, a tough one, but still a businessman, trying to make a buck when something went wrong. It didn't quite fit, Jake had the feeling that Weigel had been through a few shady deals before, where things were not quite above board. Something else was bothering him, and Jake had a good idea what it was. He would take a chance.

"Herr Weigel," he started, "Why did you have him eliminated, did he know too much?"

Weigel twitched visibly. "No, you don't understand . . . you have no idea what forces are involved, what kind of money is at stake!"

"Oh, I have a pretty good idea." Taking a chance again, Jake added, "Monique, do you know who is involved? Is that what's worrying you now . . . is someone else in the game, and they're getting close?" A lightning bolt punctuated his question, startling them all.

Just then the door was flung open and Carl lurched in, staggering across the room towards Weigel, trying to say something as blood bubbled from his lips. As he collapsed in Weigel's arms, Jake noticed two small dark red blotches on the man's back. Jake looked around quickly, grabbing Christa and pushing her down off the sofa to floor level, shoving her towards the companionway stairs just as the room exploded with automatic weapon fire and shattering glass.

Chapter 35

A SECOND VOLLEY OF BULLETS raked the room, erupting indiscriminately across the table, blasting china and crystal into fragments. Clay flower-pots exploded on the side-board, showering soil, bits of geraniums and shards of terra-cotta into the air. Just outside the broken window, two louder shots commanded attention, halting the rain of fire.

Monique's screams filled the cabin as the gunfire died away. Her arms raised to protect her head and face, she fell to the floor, trying to crawl over to her lover. The rain of glass stopped, followed immediately by wind and rain pelting through the open windows. The ear-splitting clamour was immediately replaced by sounds of running on deck, punctuated with sporadic gunfire. Weigel dropped as well, pushing Carl's body out of the way as he reached for Monique. They scrambled quickly on their hands and knees across the glass covered carpet, following Jake and Christa down the companionway. Christa choked back her screams as Jake motioned desperately for her to be quiet.

At the bottom of the stairs, they paused, not knowing which way to go. "Oh Jakob, what's happening?" Christa sobbed. "I'm so scared!"

"So am I" Jake replied honestly, "But we'll be O.K., just keep your head down." He didn't really know what was happening either, or indeed if they would be O.K.. Unlike Christa, at least he had experienced simulations like this in his anti-terrorist training. Unfortunately, this was not a simulation, it was a little too real, he thought.

Jake turned to Weigel. "Do you have another way out of here?"

"This way, follow me first!" Weigel said, moving quickly across the stateroom to a tall wooden gun cabinet. Weigel opened its double doors and pulled out some drawers, exposing a selection of weapons. A half dozen hunting rifles were mounted on the rear of the cabinet, with an equal number of handguns laying in the drawers below, each with extra clips and ammunition.

"Christ!" exclaimed Jake as he looked over the selection, "You're really prepared for a war here!"

Weigel said nothing, quickly picking an old Walther P38 and a full ammunition clip from the top drawer, obviously his favourite. He quickly racked the weapon, readying it for action, motioning for Jake to do the same.

Feelings of terror ran through Jake's mind as he realized what he was doing! Brief visions of his early military training flashed back to him as he looked over the weapons, each drawer a classic. In addition to Weigel's P38, the next drawer held a mint condition second world war Luger, the next a little Walther PPK, then a beautifully engraved and inlaid pearl-handled Baretta. He quickly recognized a Sig Sauer P226, a 9mm semi-automatic pistol, a favourite of policemen around the world. It was a weapon he had practiced with many times at the range at home, so he felt confident with it. He slipped one clip of shells into his pocket and another into the handle, racking a round into the chamber. The familiar weapon felt cool and comfortable in his hand.

Both girls clutched each other as they huddled in the corner, terrified of the gunfire above. Jake went to Christa, trying to comfort her and convince her to stay put. Weigel's voice cracked slightly as he started to say something then changed his mind, picking up the telephone by the bed. He talked briefly, then listened for a longer time. He finally hung up the phone and turned to the others.

"The captain's locked himself in the pilothouse . . . but we're still underway. He said they slipped aboard just as we left the last lock. They must have timed it so the lock operator wouldn't have even seen them."

"You said the captain's in the pilothouse, isn't that where they will go first, take over the ship?"

"No, he's OK. The pilothouse is secure once the captain locked himself in, bulletproof glass, no way to get in. He'll keep the ship moving, hopefully arrive at the next lock to attract attention. There's at least three, maybe four of them, well armed. The captain spotted the one that jumped on the bow, that's what gave them away. When the others came down on the main cabin, Helmut and Carl cut them off . . . one is already dead, but it cost Carl his life. Helmut still has them up on the roof now, but not for long . . . the captain says the guy that was on the bow is working his way aft. We've got to help him."

"Hold on Weigel . . . who are we talking about?" Jake yelled, "and what are they after?"

"I don't know . . . " Weigel mumbled, "we're not sure who . . . maybe OPEC . . . someone who doesn't want Stefan's discovery to work!" He paused, waving his weapon in front of his face as he stroked his moustache nervously. His brow furrowed as he thought of the events of the past week. "From what they've done in Los Angeles and Washington, I think they are systematically eliminating everyone involved . . . probably looking for Stefan."

Jake looked around, then stared at the weapon in his hand, not believing what they were doing. "Can't you call the cops?"

Weigel looked at Jake, a mixture of scorn and disbelief on his face. "Under the circumstances, Mr. Prescott, I don't think so. Actually, I don't know who would be easier to deal with at this point. I think we'll handle it this way" as he raised his P38 in front of him.

The shots were now spread out, the rattle of automatic fire punctuated by single shots, probably from Helmut's pistol.

"It sounds like Helmut's still got them pinned down." Jake said, wondering how long he could hold. Leaving his cane behind, he moved carefully to the rear of the cabin and started up a small stairway to the main deck. As he stepped outside on the small aft deck area, cool night air and rain blew through his hair, contrasting with the warm dryness of below. He could smell the sporadic puffs of diesel smoke as the wind swirled around the exhaust stack above the cabin. Another lightning bolt flashed, lighting up the sky. Something moved above him. Jake looked up, gaping at the dark, ski-masked face of one of the gunmen on the roof a few feet from where he stood, equally surprised at seeing Jake. Before either of them could react, a burst of bullets from one of the others stitched up the deck towards him. He dove around the corner of the cabin as the slugs zipped past him.

The small overhang of the cabin roof provided a little protection as long as he stuck closely to the wall. Inching forward along the wall, he tried to see in all directions at once. He froze as he spotted something move on the deck ahead. Perfectly still, he watched, trying to confirm what he saw. Another movement. The man was crawling down the main deck between the telescopic hatch covers and the low gunwales, an automatic rifle preceding him. Jake lifted his gun, aiming carefully at the man as he inched closer. This is crazy, he thought, I'm not a killer. I can't just kill this guy in cold blood! Before he could react, the decision was made for him. As another flash lit up the scene, he watched in horror as the man stood up, letting loose a spray of bullets towards the cabin. Two shots exploded near Jake's head and he could see the man jerk twice, his gun still firing wildly as he pirouetted over the side into the river. Still in shock, Jake heard the thump of a man landing behind him on the deck. He spun around, staring into the barrel of another pistol. He brought up his Sig 9mm, ready to fire.

"*Nicht Schießen!* Don't shoot!" Helmut hissed at him.

"Jeez! you scared the shit out of me!" he exclaimed as he lowered his gun.

"There's at least two more!" Helmut whispered, "One still up near the car . . . I don't know where the others are, so watch your back. You go around the front. I'll go aft . . . just make sure you don't shoot me when we meet."

Jake turned and continued his tour, glued to the cabin wall. As he crossed the front of the cabin, he looked up, hoping to see the captain, but the overhang that protected him also obstructed his own vision. He had to get away from the cabin so he could see something. He looked around, trying to figure out what options he had. Remembering the man crawling down the deck, Jake quickly dropped to the wooden planks, turning on his back. By sliding up the space between the hatches and gunwales, he was protected on both sides, as long as he didn't jump up to expose himself. Slowly, carefully, he pushed with his feet on the deck, shoving his body forward, head first. Looking aft, he could see the outline of the main cabin form in the inky darkness. He held his pistol in front, above his body, pointing aft towards the cabin as he tried vainly to see their attackers. In the distance off the bow, the lights of another village came towards them, offering sporadic glimpses of the scene around them. Jake strained his eyes as something moved on the cabin top. The rain eased slightly and the village lights offered a dull glow to the cabin roof. Jake could now see Helmut, creeping around the cabin, watching for Jake, while the man above lowered his rifle towards Helmut.

Another flash brilliantly lit up the ship, startling both Helmut and his attacker. The man cut loose with a torrent of automatic fire, ripping off the corner of the cabin as he swung his weapon towards Helmut. Just as the firing started, Jake had the man sighted and squeezed his Sig Sauer semi-automatic. The 9mm parabellum shell kicked the pistol up, catching the man in the shoulder, spinning him around. With his two handed grip, Jake pulled the gun down quickly for another shot, this one centred in the man's chest. He folded up, his rifle spinning around firing wildly before both fell to the deck below. Helmut ducked back, ready to fire again, not knowing where Jake was.

Jake lay quiet, his heart pounding and his stomach churning. The downpour returned, stinging his eyes as he lay on his back. He wanted to throw up, but couldn't take his eyes off the scene before him. The rain drained off the forward section and streamed down the deck, swirling over and around him as he lay there. By staring at the pilot house, he could occasionally make out the captain, silhouetted in the window against the village lights as they passed. He wanted desperately to talk to Helmut, find out where the other attacker was. He inched forward some more, hoping to catch a better view of the rear cabin.

Helmut disappeared around the rear of the cabin, out of his line of vision. Everything fell quiet, only the chug-a-chug of the big diesels and the constant swish of the river broke the silence. Not knowing what was happening, Jake grew impatient.

A sudden burst of automatic gunfire in the cabin lit up the windows. His first thoughts were for Christa. Leaping to his feet, he had just started down the deck towards the side door when something snagged him from behind, spinning him around. He grabbed his arm, realizing a bullet had clipped his jacket, digging a small furrow along his upper arm.

Helmut yelled "Get down!"

More gunfire in the cabin, this time with screams.

He knew he had to get inside, but he suddenly remembered what he told himself moments before, you'll be alright as long as you don't jump up and expose yourself.

He had almost reached the corner of the cabin when another slug caught him directly in the other shoulder, slamming him against the corner of the cabin and along the deck. He staggered drunkenly, his bad leg collapsing under him. He tried desperately to regain his balance as the deck started to tilt. He grabbed for a handrail and missed, his feet tripping on a mooring cleat, the momentum flinging his body clear over the rail.

He drifted downward in slow motion toward the water, feeling powerless in his efforts to help Christa, his only regret was that he did not tell her how much he loved her. Then everything went black as the cold water closed over him.

Chapter 36

Scott Anderson concluded his visit to Los Angeles a very happy man. After a couple of days of footwork and detail follow-up, he was ready for a change of pace. The day he spent in Linda Seymour's world offered that change. He found both Linda and her work fascinating and informative. With the data collected on their little field trip and subsequent work in the lab, together with Bert Jackson's F.B.I. and N.S.O. disclosures, he thought he was slowly getting a clearer picture of what had happened.

When Bert threw in his little comment about possible O.P.E.C. or mercenary involvement, it threw him almost back at square one. Frustrated, he felt the closer he got to his story, the more it eluded him, and yet he also knew there was more to the story than he originally thought.

Although he knew he should have kept moving and digging deeper, he was experiencing a new sensation for him . . . personal enjoyment. He justified taking off all of Friday as part of his research, spending the time with Linda while she played tour guide for him. Scott's past visits to the City of Angels had given him only brief glimpses of the airport, quick rides on the freeways and equally dull views of city or corporate offices. Linda gave him his first chance to see Los Angeles as a fascinating centre of history, industry, commerce and modern tourist attractions and entertainment.

After Bert Jackson left them late Thursday afternoon, Linda invited Scott out for dinner, a request he had been trying to make to Linda all day. Working with Linda, Scott felt they were growing close, and he finally violating his first rule of investigative reporting by accepting her invitation to go out with someone involved in a story. They spent the evening driving around the city, viewing the lights and glitter of Hollywood, restaurant row and the downtown core. Later, they walked Olvera Street, soaking up the atmosphere of Old Mexico as they shopped at street vendors and viewed the brightly coloured wares in a variety of shops. A romantic dinner complete with strumming guitars and Mariachi music topped off the evening. Their admiration for each other continued to grow, eventually blossoming into a relationship neither of them expected.

Friday was even more enjoyable, as Linda drove around L.A., visiting some of the tourist attractions. Before they left the downtown area, she drove the length of freeway where the first group of people had died, then they stopped by the parking garage where the others had died and Ed and Brent had collected their samples. The experience was sobering for Scott, reminding him of the job he was supposed to be doing. Later in the day, they headed south to Long Beach, touring the seaport village attraction near the convention centre. It was late evening and they were enjoying dinner in a tavern overlooking the water when Scott noticed the story on a television in the corner. The announcer was just explaining how Senator Pelly had been killed, and the mysterious circumstances surrounding the event.

Guilt suddenly replaced the pleasure of the past two days. Berating himself for being distracted, he tried making excuses to Linda to leave immediately.

"Don't be in such a hurry," she scolded him, "We've hardly started dinner, and I'm not wasting it because of some Senator in Washington! Besides Scott," she said quietly, her eyes pleading with him, "I don't want to see you go."

"But . . ."

"No buts! Let's finish dinner, then we'll check the airlines to see what flights are available in the morning."

"There's a red-eye out tonight at . . ."

She placed her hand on his, her eyes rimmed with tears. "Actually, I had other plans for tonight" she whispered.

Reality slowly dawned on him, his feelings for Linda overpowering the habits of his job. Grasping her hands tightly, he smiled at her and relaxed.

"Old habits die hard" he said softly, "Forget I even suggested it." He picked up his wine glass, motioning a toast. "Here's to us, who knows where it will go?"

"To us" she replied, savouring the wine as she watched the look in his eyes. "I think . . ."

"Linda, no, please let me say something first . . ." he interrupted. "For the first time . . . well, for as long as I can remember, I've never felt this way. You've made me feel . . . well . . . special. I only hope . . . I mean . . ."

Linda laughed and a fleeting look of pain crossed Scott's face.

"Oh no!" she said quickly, "I'm not laughing at that . . . I love what you are saying. I was just thinking how funny it was that one of the greatest journalists of the century can't find the right words . . . I think it's sweet."

More relaxed, they enjoyed their meal, together with another bottle of wine. Later, Linda drove them both to her apartment where they discussed their feelings in more intimate detail.

The next morning found him on an early flight to Washington, spending the time on his laptop summarizing his findings so far. He hoped to glean further information in Washington about the bombers or who was behind it all.

As soon as he arrived, he contacted Bert Jackson at the F.B.I. to try for some of the 'behind the scenes' information, but Bert's hands were tied and he couldn't divulge any information about the bombing other than what had already been released to the press. That left him with not much more than what he already had.

A quick phone call to Frank Haywood brought better results, but it was only after contacting Jake's office in Vancouver that things really started to get interesting.

"We're worried, Scott." Shannon Hall told him after he had talked with Alan and Peter. "Jake usually checks in regularly . . . especially on this trip . . . you know, too many things are going wrong."

"Right, I agree!" Scott replied. "When did you last hear from him?"

"Friday morning . . . almost two days ago! He called as usual, we passed on his messages, he already had most of them, in fact he left a recorded message in the system for Peter to record and study . . . maybe find out who it is. He passed it on to Interpol and they were trying as well."

"Interpol?" Scott asked quickly.

"Yes . . . a Jacques Manet . . . here's his number, maybe you can find out something." She gave Scott the number, then added "He had an appointment with someone late that evening, so we expected a call either late last night or this morning. It's not like Jake to forget."

Scott learned as much as he could from Shannon, then placed a call to Interpol. It was a waste of time, as it was very late Saturday night in France and "M. Manet was not in his office". I'm not surprised, Scott thought, anyone in their right mind should be home. His thoughts briefly rested on Linda, their wonderful night together and how difficult it was to leave her this morning. Only the many years of habit and self-discipline prevailed.

He called Jake's office again, thinking about his failure at the Interpol office and wondering why Jake's staff were working on a Saturday.

"Shannon," he said quickly when she answered the phone, "I'm heading out for Germany tonight . . . I can be there by early morning, so I'll call Manet from there and I'll let you know what's happening later in the day."

"Oh Scott, I'm glad you called back . . . I thought about something else. Manet will probably tell you, but in case you don't connect . . . he told Jake about the mercenaries . . ."

"Mercenaries? What mercenaries?" Scott interrupted, recalling Bert Jackson's comments.

"The mercenaries they've been tracking since Los Angeles . . . the ones that killed Butler and most likely Senator Pelly. Manet was trying to reach Jake again last night to tell him."

"For God's sake Shannon . . . tell him what?"

"The one group they've been tracking to Berlin is now on their way to Frankfurt. He suspects they are systematically eliminating anyone involved in the L.A. disaster, or more likely, anyone involved in the research or production of this gasoline additive."

"My God . . . that means . . ."

"Yes, that means Stefan, Jake and probably anyone else that gets in the way!"

"And Jake doesn't know this yet?"

"No . . . unless Manet finally reached him . . . but neither of them has called."

"That does it! I'm on my way, I'll call you tomorrow."

As he sat in his office waiting for news that the head of Steinbock had been assassinated, Kurt Landau received a call from Weigel, the planned victim. He barely covered his surprise at the voice, disguising it as incredulity about the attack as he listened to the news of the failed attempt on the river barge.

"*Scheiss*! It's that damned *Auslander* again!" Kurt Landau thought, "I should have dealt with him myself!" He was getting angrier as one by one, his plans were being thwarted by an amateur. As a seasoned professional, he was not used to dealing with inexperienced opponents. He could feel the frustration grow as each step of his plans since Los Angeles had turned sour.

He continued to listen to Weigel as he told of the events that night, sadly reporting that Prescott had been shot and had fallen overboard.

"He was a good man, he would have been valuable as a bargaining tool in our work with Schiller."

A sense of relief washed over Landau, yet disappointment as well as he had been cheated of the satisfaction of disposing of the problem himself.

As he hung up the phone, he turned to the man beside him. "Have you heard from your crew?" he asked.

"Not yet, they are due to check in at noon . . . if they're still alive. From that call, there might be some doubt."

"From what Erik said, some of them did get away. Idiots! How could they miss? These were trained specialists against a boat-load of tourists!"

"Sometimes you just get lucky." the other man added.

"O.K., here's the plan. Weigel and his whore, Brehmer, along with Schiller and his daughter are on their way to Brehmer's lodge. As soon as your men contact you, let's all meet and head down there to finish the job. I'm getting tired of all these screw-ups!"

Chapter 37

Vague forms shifted in the haze, refusing to come into focus. His chest heaved painfully with a hacking cough, sucking in antiseptic smelling air. He tried to rub his eyes clear, but a sharp pain seized his shoulder. He tried again, only to find his arm immobilized. As he brought his other hand up to his eyes, another twinge tightened his upper arm.

The haze began to clear, the form sharpened into a man standing near his feet. Announcements in German droned in the distance . . . he was in a hospital. Confusion, pain, memories . . . the mercenary attack . . . the battle . . . he was shot . . . falling in the river . . . Christa!

He sat up, waves of pains reminding him of his condition. "Where am I . . . where's Christa?" He stared blankly at the stranger at the foot of his bed.

"Welcome back, Jake."

"Where am I, and who are you?" Jake mumbled, his head slowly clearing.

The man came around the bed to his side, holding out his hand. "Jacques Manet, Interpol. We talked on the phone the other day."

Jake looked at the man with renewed interest, a face he could place with a name. His stocky build filled out his dark, pin-stripe suit, accented by a precisely placed school tie. Probably early fifties, Jake estimated, but with sad eyes that had seen more than his years should have allowed. A dark, well trimmed moustache contrasted with the bald head and streaks of grey around the ears. He couldn't help smiling at this typical British gentleman with such a French name. Jake reached stiffly for his outstretched hand, encouraged by the firm handshake.

"Jacques . . . Interpol, right!" he mumbled, remembering their conversation. "But you're head office, aren't you . . . what are you doing here?" He stopped talking and looked around the room, realizing he didn't know where 'here' was. "Where the hell is this anyway?" he asked.

"You're in a hospital in Wertheim, a town between Frankfurt and Würzburg. Some youngsters found you on a river bank near Mondfeld, a little village on the river a few kilometres west of here."

"Mondfeld? I don't know it." Jake replied. "You don't have a map on you by any chance?"

"Yes, I just bought it in Frankfurt, I didn't have a clue where to go when I arrived here." He reached into his jacket pocket and pulled out one of the well-known travel maps of the area. "Look, see, right on the Main River . . . Wertheim. A few kilometres downstream is Monfeld, here . . ." as he put his finger on the map.

Jake took the map, studying it intently. "We must have been attacked somewhere here . . . pointing to a section of the river downstream from Wertheim. "See, that's the last lock between Miltenburg and Monfield. If I went off the barge during the attack, it had to be within that section. It's unlikely I would drift downstream through a lock, and impossible to drift upstream."

Jacques studied the map, making a few notes in his notebook. He then looked up to Jake and continued his account. "When the boys found you, they called an ambulance, but when the medics arrived, they saw your gun and called the *Polizei*. When the police saw your Canadian passport, they contacted our NCB at Wiesbaden. They . . ."

"Excuse me Jacques . . . NCB?"

"Oh, sorry old chap, I forget. NCB is the acronym for 'National Central Bureau', or the representative Interpol office for the particular country. Wiesbaden is the NCB for Germany, like Ottawa in Canada, or Washington in the U.S.."

"Thanks, but why? What made them contact Interpol, why wasn't I considered to be just another tourist that fell off a tour-boat?"

"Well, that gun rang a lot of bells for one thing, plus we had a special notice out for you."

"Right, I learned about your 'red notices' in my training."

"This wasn't a red notice, we reserve that for wanted criminals. It was just a request to keep an eye open for you."

"Are you saying I still had this gun, even after I had been shot, dumped overboard and washed up on the shore somewhere?"

"Yes Jake, I have seen much stranger things happen to a man under pressure. You were still clutching the gun in your hand, so I don't know how you swam ashore. The medics had a hard time prying it loose."

Jake shook his head, not remembering any of the events after he was shot and fell into the river.

Jacques had paused, trying to gather his thoughts again. "I must say Jake, you've been a bit of a pain . . . we had a jolly-good time trying to find you! Like I told you before, you're a loose cannon."

"What's happened to the boat . . . where's Christa?"

"We were hoping you'd be able to tell us what happened. First . . . who's Christa?"

"Oh God!" Jake cried as he remembered the last moments before falling overboard, the shots, the screams. A thought suddenly occurred to him. "What time is it, how long have I been out?"

"It's almost ten . . . in the morning. Today's Monday . . . you were found yesterday morning, so you've been out of it since then . . . over twenty-four hours."

"Monday? Oh my God!" he said, calculating back. "We went on board on Friday night, so we were attacked sometime that night . . . I would say well after midnight, maybe early morning sometime. That means . . ."

"That means you were in the river, or on the bank for over a day before you were found! It's a good thing it's still summer, you're lucky to be alive!" He paused, pulling out a small notebook. "O.K., start from the beginning . . . from your rendez-vous with Monique."

"Monique." Jake mumbled, smiling. "You know about that."

"Yes, we know about your planned meeting, and we just learned yesterday that Monique was a river barge. We found her docked in Würzburg, riddled with bullet holes. You chaps must have had quite a show!"

Würzburg! His hopes flamed, then died as he realized Jacques would have said something if Christa had been found.

"How far are we from Würzburg?" Jake asked, just in case.

"Not far, about an hour by car" he answered, then realized what Jake was asking, "but probably about a half a day by river barge" he added, "so if they carried on after you went overboard, they travelled quite a piece."

"Was the car on board?" Jake asked.

"No, there was no car." Jacques quickly took out a note-book again. "What kind of car was it, what colour?"

"A little sports job . . . Mercedes I think. It was dusk when we first arrived on board and saw it, so I would say it was a gold or silver grey colour, like thousands of other Mercedes in Germany . . . it's hard to say in that light, and besides, we were just getting on board and had other things to think about."

"Quite!" Jacques replied, making notes in his book. "I'll have them check the registration, put out a notice on it, maybe we can get lucky."

Confused, Jake faced the reality of his current situation and recounted the happenings of the time since their telephone conversation . . . at least as far as he could remember, while Jacques continued to take notes. Events of that night were foggy, especially after the attack, but he related as much as he could. When he was finished, he turned to the Interpol officer.

"Now it's your turn Jacques . . . tell me what's happened, how you found me, what you know about Christa and Weigel."

Jacques' ears perked up at the last name. "Weigel . . . yes . . . Erik Weigel."

"You know him?"

"Quite . . . his name has been showing up fairly often these days. But to answer some of your questions, I'll start at the beginning." He settled down at the foot of the bed, flipping pages back on his notebook. "After we talked last week, I contacted our people in Wiesbaden as well as the Frankfurt police, you know, just to keep an eye out for you. You didn't tell me where you were staying, so it took them some time to track you down . . . by that time, you were gone. When the hotel staff said you had not returned to the room that night, we knew something was wrong."

"But how'd you find out about the Monique?" Jake asked.

"From your own staff, that young Chinese fellow, Peter Wong. He had the message recording, with the time of the meeting and the reference to Monique. Our technicians compared voice prints with your recording, and came up with Erik Weigel."

"Weigel? How did you come up with him?" Jake asked. "Don't you have to have something to compare it to?"

Jacques laughed "Jolly good! . . . you're right of course, dead giveaway. Let's say we already had our suspicions, together with the fact that we had Weigel on file . . . his voice I mean. What you mentioned last week about Steinbock et al, together with some of the work that Bert Jackson and his F.B.I. colleagues started, we put a few things together. Actually, we had already been monitoring certain phone calls from the U.S. for some time . . . Weigel was included in some of them, the N.S.O. had him on file."

"N.S.O.?" the name rang Jake's alarms.

"Quite. Interpol tries to work with all police and security organizations . . . or at least as much as they will let us. When Butler's name showed up in some of the files, things started going together. Of course we can't get a word out of N.S.O., some of these chaps are pretty tight lipped, especially when it comes to covering their own ass."

"I had no idea you guys were this far involved." Jake said, surprised. "What . . ."

"Let's just say we knew it was Weigel . . . but that really didn't help us. There's still something missing . . . almost as if . . . " He stopped, shaking his head, not sure where his thoughts were taking him. "It wasn't until your office said they hadn't heard from you, then the hotel missing you, we started to get worried."

Jake interrupted again. "All that could have been handled by your staff or the local police . . . how come you're here Jacques . . . what was it that dragged you out?"

Manet paused a moment while he poured them both a glass of water. Cautiously, he started speaking. "Two things, really. First . . . the main reason I wanted to be here personally." He paused, measuring his words. "Jake . . . remember when we talked last, I mentioned about those mercenaries we were tracking?"

"Yeah . . . some middle-east group . . . the ones that finished Butler."

"That's right. When I talked to you, one group was headed for Washington, the others were on their way to Berlin from London. We were too late for Washington, you probably heard what happened there."

"Pelly?"

"Right-o. That's why I headed here as soon as we received confirmation that the other group had left Berlin and were heading to Frankfurt. By that time, with Pelly gone, we didn't figure these chaps were coming to Frankfurt to see the sights."

Jake listened to the words, but his mind was replaying the horror of the attack on the barge.

"I think I can confirm that" Jake offered. "From the way they hit us, I'd say this was most likely the same group. These guys weren't your average bunch of thugs . . . they were a well trained hit team, experienced in night fighting, and were well armed."

"Don't be too quick to jump to conclusions, Jake" Jacques interrupted, "I thought the same thing . . . until we found a body further down river from where you were found . . . no I.D., ski mask . . . looks like one of the bad guys, but I would say a Nordic blond . . . definitely not Arab, or from anywhere in the middle east."

"What?" The statement surprised Jake, screwing up their theory. "Well then, who the hell are they, and where's your mercenaries? I figure there should be at least two more bodies, unless they were still on the Monique."

"No, we found lots of blood, but it looks like all the bodies were disposed of some other way, otherwise we would have found more by now."

Jake was afraid to ask about details, but Jacques read the look on his face.

"Don't worry Jake, there was only two areas in the cabin that had blood. One was the dining room, where you said the butler did it," he laughed, trying to make light of a gruesome scene. "The other was at the foot of the stairs . . . looks like they caught one of them coming down."

Jake tried to visualize what might have happened, and all scenarios must have been horrifying to Christa. If it wasn't for Weigel's men being on their toes and the captain spotting them jump off that bridge, we would all be at the bottom of the river now. After he was shot, he could imagine the situation must have grown much worse. A thought suddenly occurred to him.

"Tell me Jacques, regardless of whether these are the original 'mercenaries' or not, how did they know where we would be . . . and when? We didn't even know until the last minute that the Monique was a river barge, yet they attacked with precise timing at a specific location where we were vulnerable."

The question bothered the Interpol agent, but it was obviously not a new one. "I don't know Jake, that's one of the questions

I've been asking myself ever since we found the Monique in Würzburg yesterday."

Jake filed the question away as something further to check. "You said there was two things you wanted to tell me."

"Yeah, this one got me out of the office and on my way. Just after Pelly was killed, we got a call from the F.B.I., a Bert Jackson . . . I think you know him."

"Yeah, good man, I mentioned I was calling you."

"Anyway, the Bureau had a request out for the Swiss Police to pick up Klaus Müller at the Zürich airport on Friday . . . actually Saturday morning . . . seems like he took off from Washington right after Pelly was killed, heading to Zürich and planning to continue on to Munich."

"Good! I'm sure he can tell you a few things about this mess."

"Not any more. When the flight arrived, Mr. Müller was dead!"

"Wha . . . how did they get to him on the flight?"

"I don't think it was them. I think Müller killed himself . . . quite accidentally. Apparently he's had a bad ulcer for years . . . living on antacids and pain killers. From what the doctors said, this was too much for him and he O.D.'d on his pills and booze, and bled to death during the flight." He paused, remembering previous cases where things were not always as they appeared. "Of course, we'll be doing an autopsy . . . just to confirm our suspicions."

"Christ! What a way to go!" Jake said, shaking his head. "All the same, we're losing too many people Jacques, too many witnesses that know something. I don't trust any of these so-called 'natural' deaths."

Becoming impatient, he stirred, moving his arms tentatively. Other than stiffness from the bandages, he felt surprisingly good.

"I've got to get out of here." he said, swinging his legs out of bed.

"Not bloody likely, Jake! You've just been shot twice and had a slug pulled out of your shoulder!"

"I feel O.K., just a little stiff."

"Right, you're on pain killers and antibiotics . . . you need more rest, let it heal."

"We've got too much to do, I can rest later."

"Ah . . . Jake, there's a little matter of the local police. It is only by special request from me that I got into here to talk to you first . . . I used the excuse of some sort of 'international emergency'."

"What? I haven't done anything wrong! I've been kidnapped, attacked, shot, and dumped in the river! My girl friend and her father have both been kidnapped! Like I said before Jacques, the only results we have are those from our own actions!"

"But you can't be that way Jake, the authorities can handle it."

"Like the way they've handled this, and everything else so far? Don't try to kid me Jacques, I'm getting a little pissed off with the 'authorities'! They always seem to be at least two steps behind the bad guys. You might be hampered by red tape and procedures, but I'm not! I'm taking off and going after them."

"But there's a little matter of the gun you had on you."

"If you were so good, you'd already know that belongs to Weigel."

"Yes, actually . . ."

"Also, if you were so damned important, Mr. Manet, you should be able to clear it with the local authorities, maybe tell them I was working with you or something . . . or just plead another 'international emergency', maybe it will work a second time. In spite of your comments Jacques, I'm not a complete amateur, I was trained in the foreign service, counter espionage and counter terrorism for a few years."

Jacques couldn't argue with the logic. He left the room to start his little deception and get Jake out of the hospital.

Chapter 38

During the next few hours, Jake wondered whether he had made the right decision. First, his bandages were changed and reinforced to help immobilize the wounds. The nurse then retrieved his clothes; now clean, but still complete with rips and bullet holes. Even with Jacque's help, getting dressed was an interesting workout, an uncoordinated ballet punctuated by stabs of pain. The sling bandage around his left arm and shoulder stiffened his entire side, making his movements awkward. From years of habit, he started to reach for his cane, realizing he no longer had it. As he continued to get dressed, he knew he would not even be able to use a cane effectively until his arm healed. He was also conscious of the bandage on the smaller wound on his right arm, but the pain was minimal. Before they left the hospital, they stopped briefly at the in-house pharmacy and medical supply shop and Jake bought another cane.

"I'll try using my right hand, it might at least help to steady myself if my leg goes again."

It was mid-afternoon by the time the paperwork was complete and they left the building. Jacques even managed to have the Sig Sauer 9mm returned to Jake, now a deputy undercover officer assisting in part of an ongoing investigation.

"My car's back at the hotel." Jacques announced as the door closed behind them. "I walked here earlier . . . didn't really expect you to be getting out. I'm staying at charming little place called the Bronnbacher, not far from here." As they started down the street towards the hotel, he added "I want to stop briefly at the local police station, it's close to the hospital, we can let them know you are leaving, you know, sort of a courtesy."

Jake nodded, concentrating on walking, not used to using the cane with the other hand. He felt a little light headed and weak as they walked towards the hotel. Once past the police station, they continued down across the Tauber River into the old town. It was much further than Jacques thought, so as they walked, his legs felt weak and wobbly from his trauma and almost three days of inactivity, and they had to stop several times to rest. He was visibly shaking and soaked with sweat by the time they arrived at the hotel.

"Like I said before Jake, you're in no condition to travel today" Jacques told him as they arrived. "I'll get you a room, we can have something to eat, and you can get a good night's rest before we leave. I have your suitcase here from your hotel in Frankfurt, so you'll have some different clothes to wear."

Jake didn't object, the immediate care for his battered and wounded body outweighed his concern and ability to find Christa. The idea of a decent meal and a good night's rest was already sounding good. The Bronnbacher Hof was a delightful little inn on the *Mainplatz*, a perfect example of old world charm and elegance. As soon as they were settled in, Jake called his office in Vancouver, just starting their week on Monday morning.

The relief was obvious in Shannon's voice as soon as she heard it was Jake.

"Jake, my God . . . how are you, where have you been? We've been frantic, worrying about you. We haven't heard from you since Friday."

Jake kept trying to answer, but Shannon kept firing the questions between expressions of concern and telephone messages from others.

"Bert Jackson has been calling . . . Frank Haywood the same." She paused, rustling some papers. Before Jake had a chance to start talking, she interrupted again. "Oh, I almost forgot! Scott Anderson is on his way to Germany . . . in fact he should be there now. Scott said he would check with the Interpol office to try to catch up with him . . . we were hoping Jacques Manet had found you."

"Shannon . . . please? Jake interjected quickly as she paused again.

"Oh . . . I'm sorry Jake, I guess I'm so glad to hear from you. I'll stop talking and you can tell me what's happening there. Alan and Peter are here, so I'll put you on the speaker-phone."

Jake then started his story again, relating the events from the time they boarded the river barge to when he woke up in the hospital. The entire account was punctuated by Shannon's expressions of surprise, with additional comments from the rest of the crew when Jake began describing the mercenary attack on the river barge.

"Do you think this was the same group that Interpol have been tracking?" Alan interrupted.

Jake didn't reply immediately as he considered the question. Again, something wasn't right, parts of the puzzle were not fitting the way they should have. Eventually, he answered Alan's question. "I don't really know, Alan, quite possibly . . . although Manet says they found one body . . . a Nordic blond . . . doesn't quite fit the image of an Arab terrorist." Jake paused again, then continued "What's more important Alan, if it was the mercenary group Interpol was tracking, how did they find us that night? Hired mercenaries or terrorists or whatever, but I'm still at a loss to explain how they knew exactly where we would be that night."

"I must say . . . it does sound rather odd . . .sounds like an inside job, as they say" Alan said slowly, also mentally reviewing the events. "Interpol didn't even know where you were . . . or us for that matter."

"Right" Jake answered, "Jacques said that Interpol didn't know the Monique was a barge until Sunday, when they found her in Würzburg. These guys knew that, plus our exact route and location that night . . . it doesn't add up." Thinking about Alan's last comment, he repeated "'An inside job', you might have something there Alan, we just have to figure out who." He remembered Shannon's earlier messages. "Shannon, you said Scott Anderson was on his way here, to Germany?"

"Yes, I talked to him on Saturday . . . we hadn't heard from you for over twenty-four hours. He was concerned with what Manet had told us . . . about those terrorists heading to Frankfurt. He had been talking with Bert Jackson about Pelly's death and was afraid they were catching up to you. I'm sure he left Saturday, so he would have arrived sometime yesterday. He said he would call Interpol when he arrived . . . to find out where Manet was."

"I've got to hand it to him, Scott will go anywhere to get his story. Knowing him, he'll be here soon."

Shannon continued "As I said earlier Jake, Bert Jackson's also been trying to get hold of you . . . the F.B.I.'s going ape over this! Frank Haywood too."

"I'll call them both now." Jake said wearily, his shoulder aching. "Then I'm having a good dinner with Jacques and I'm turning in early . . . it's been quite a day!"

"Make sure you keep in touch." Shannon said firmly. "You scared us Jake, and now that I've heard your story, I'm even more worried about you. These guys are for real! You could get hurt!"

"Yes, Mother, I'll be careful." Jake answered, laughing weakly. I'll call again tomorrow . . . let you know what's up."

Jake had just lifted the phone again to make another call when someone knocked on his door.

"Come in!" he yelled, thinking it was Jacques.

The door slowly opened, and Scott Anderson's face peeked in. "Jake?" he asked tentatively, spotting Jake sitting on the bed. "It's Scott Anderson . . . remember?"

"Scott, of course!" Jake replied, getting up and moving toward the reporter. "I just got off the phone from my office . . . Shannon said you were on your way here. How'd you find me?" He grasped the reporter's hand firmly, glad to see a familiar face.

"Not easy!" Scott replied. "Trying to get information out of Interpol is like pulling teeth. An overnight to Frankfurt, and after a few hours sleep, spent most of yesterday and this morning calling Interpol and a few other people tracking you down . . . actually trying to find this Jacques Manet in Lyon. He had been working the weekend, but had left by the time I called. I talked to their Wiesbaden office just after the time when Jacques had heard you had been found. Unfortunately, I didn't find out where he was staying until this afternoon."

"Yes, he's just down the hall . . . most likely making some calls." Jake said. "He talked me into staying a night . . . felt I wasn't in condition to carry on."

"I'm afraid I have to agree with him . . . you look like hell Jake, and the bandages complete the picture! Do you feel up to telling me about what's been happening here?"

"Come with me" Jake said as he moved toward the door. "Jacques and I are going down for dinner. You're welcome to join us, you can meet Jacques and we can bring you up to speed. You can also tell us what's going on in L.A. and Washington, and I won't have to call Bert and Frank tonight."

Chapter 39

WASHINGTON WAS CHAOTIC. BY MONDAY morning the newspapers and television stations across the country were in a feeding frenzy. The death of Senator Pelly had come as a shock, even to his worst enemies, and had almost created a panic in government offices in Washington. The news over the weekend was sporadic, but by Monday morning there had been enough information released that the tabloids and morning news and talk-shows covered the event exhaustively. The details included the usual graphic comments by explosive experts and trauma doctors explaining what happens to the human body when subjected to an explosive device at that range.

Security was tightened, restricting movement around the city and especially within government offices. The 'alphabet soup' was out in full force - the F.B.I., C.I.A., N.S.A., N.S.O., Secret Service and Homeland Security, along with a dozen other less known agencies. Mail and courier deliveries were screened, X-rayed and sniffed for anything that did not belong.

By noon Monday, someone had leaked the possibility of a connection between the Senator's death and the Los Angeles disasters. The outcry increased, with demonstrations by right wing and special interest groups demanding action, pickets by government employees for safer working conditions and guarantees of protection. By Monday evening, the President had called a called a high level staff meeting at the Whitehouse to review details of both cases. Even with the extra security, or possibly because of it, the experienced members of the press sensed something was happening and hung around, hoping to glean further information when the meeting broke. It was much later that evening when the meeting finally adjourned with only another brief press release about the death of Senator Pelly from the efforts of "a person or persons unknown at this time". No announcements were made about the not-so-subtle reorganizations, high level job losses, Secret Service task forces and new special investigative committees that had been formed to report back with better answers.

Special Agent Bert Jackson was no stranger to White House meetings, but this one felt different. Although he had never attended one of the sessions involving an international crisis, he felt this was a close match. For basically a domestic matter, it included some very high level people, and had a feeling of urgency; too many people had died and the killers were still loose, possibly still in the city. By the time he left the meeting, he knew the matter had grown into an international affair. As he walked out with his boss, they were both silent, both wrapped up in their own thoughts. He had been looking forward to going home and turning in early, but he knew there would not be much sleep tonight.

Frank Haywood's press contacts had reached him as soon as they heard about the meeting, so he made sure he was close by when the meeting adjourned, hoping to catch someone he knew. Luckily, he spotted Bert Jackson heading back to the parking lot.

"Bert . . . wait up!" he called, quickening his pace to a trot to catch up to the tall man. "It's Frank Haywood" he explained as the F.B.I. man turned, trying to figure out who it was in the darkness.

"Frank . . . what's up?" he asked, with a feeling he knew what the man was after.

"Have you heard about Jake?" Frank asked breathlessly as he caught up to the agent.

"Jake?" the answer was unexpected, diverting Bert's thoughts about the meeting. "What about Jake?" he asked.

"He and Christa were attacked . . . some terrorists or hit team with automatic weapons."

"Christ! When . . . where . . . are they all right?"

"Jake is . . . Christa's still missing . . . Stefan too. Jake's in a hospital in Germany, wounded, but O.K. Actually, he got out today . . . just called his office. He's been missing all week-end, so everyone was getting a little anxious." He continued his account, repeating what he had learned from Shannon Hall just hours ago. He briefly explained what he knew about their planned meeting on the river barge Friday night, and Jake's account of how it was attacked later that night. "He's still with this Manet fellow from Interpol . . . I think they are going after Christa and Stefan."

By this time they were standing by Bert's car. He already had his keys out, frozen mid-step by Frank's news. He motioned quickly to Frank as he reached down to unlock the car. "Hop in Frank, we have to talk . . . let's have a coffee somewhere."

Frank slid into the passenger seat, glad to have someone with whom he could discuss this latest twist. "If it's all right with you, I think I'll have something a little stronger."

They settled into a booth in an all-night diner, Bert taking out his notebook, ready to jot down some details. The place was quiet, except for a juke-box playing at the far end, fed by coins from a young couple sitting nearby. After delivering their coffees, the owner had settled down again behind the counter, reading the latest news about the demise of Senator Pelly.

"O.K. Frank, give it to me again, this time slowly."

Frank repeated his story, adding a few more details as he remembered them. "From what Shannon told me, Interpol knew these mercenaries were heading to Europe . . . probably from information from you, that is, the F.B.I.."

The news surprised Bert, mainly because he had not heard of any traces being done by the Bureau on this group.

"I don't know Frank . . . we knew there was another player in the game . . . from what we found in L.A. last week . . . information about the bombs. Both the F.B.I. and N.S.O. agreed that the second bomb was from a different source, possibly middle east, Libyan, Arab or whatever." He thought a moment, trying to recall details of his report and subsequent reactions. "I even talked to Manet on Friday, but nobody had said anything about them already tracking a group, though . . ."

"Maybe they were just keeping a lid on it."

"Even so, I'm directly involved, I should know."

Frank's impatience was starting to show, as he stirred his coffee more violently. "Jesus, I don't blame Jake for taking off . . . trying to find out answers himself! Nobody here knows what the hell is going on . . . and when someone does, they don't tell the next guy!"

Bert couldn't argue, his own anger was starting to rise as he wondered who was holding back information.

Frank interrupted again. "What I don't know Bert, is how did this hit team know where and when to find Jake and Christa? The only people in Germany that knew of the meeting was Jake, Christa and whoever they were meeting with."

"Do you know that for sure?" Bert asked.

"Well no, but . . ."

"And how about on this side of the Atlantic?"

"Just Jake's crew . . . the meeting details were recorded in his answering service."

"And who did they talk to?"

Frank reached for his own notebook, opening it to a blank page. He started writing names in a column, leaving room for comments beside each name. "First, after Jake's crew, there was Manet at Interpol."

"Yeah, I've already talked to him . . . he had his experts working with Jake's crew to analyze the message . . . the one about the meeting details." He smiled, remembering something. "Jake called me earlier that day, but didn't mention anything about the meeting. It must have been already set up, but he didn't say anything about it."

"That limits the number of people who knew about the meeting," he said, writing Bert's name on his list with an additional note. "And myself" he added. "I told George, my lawyer. We've been investigating this thing for a long time."

"Who else?"

Frank tried to remember. "I don't know . . . whoever these people told, I guess."

"Starts to get pretty vague . . . maybe the leak was on the Germany side . . . someone involved with this Weigel character . . . someone on the Steinbock staff."

"Possibly . . . " Bert mumbled, deep in thought. "I get the feeling this guy doesn't let that kind of information out to many people." He paused again, something bothering him. "After all," he added, "He had already kidnapped one person and was planning on two more!"

"You're right . . . that's why the message was a little cryptic!"

"How do you mean, cryptic?"

"When Weigel arranged the meeting . . . the message on Jake's service, he didn't mention a boat, just said something like 'Look for Monique'."

"So? What do you mean?" Bert asked, not understanding where Frank was going with this.

"Don't you see? Nobody knew that Monique was the name of a boat, some river barge. We all thought he was meeting with someone called Monique!"

Bert accepted the comment, trying to fit its meaning into the picture.

"And when did we find out it was a barge and not a person?" he asked.

"Today . . . actually Manet found out on Sunday, when they found the barge abandoned in Würzburg, full of bullet holes."

"So what you're saying is that someone learned about the meeting, but also knew it was on a river barge."

Frank nodded, deep in thought. "Yes . . . so it had to be either someone on Weigel's staff, or someone on this side that was intimately familiar with Weigel's operation."

"It appears that the only ones on this side that knew anything about Weigel was Paul Butler and Richard Pelly, both of whom were blown up!" He thought a moment, then added "And Klaus Müller, who is also no longer with us."

They both stared at each other across the table, not comfortable with the implications of Bert's last statement.

With his troublesome and destructive experience with government agents, Frank never took anything at face value.

He added "Unless whoever it was made notes, kept records of some kind . . . or, there's still someone else in the game . . . someone we're not aware of."

Chapter 40

THE NEXT MORNING, THEY ALL met for breakfast. Like the evening before at dinner, Jake headed to the rear of the room, sitting at a large table in the corner. Some decorative mirrors were mounted on both walls, giving him additional views of the entire room. "Christ, I'm getting paranoid!" he thought. As he quickly reviewed what had happened in the past few days, he didn't feel guilty about his paranoia. As the old expression goes, 'even paranoids have enemies'."

The Bronnbacher Hof was exactly as Jacques had described it, a charming little place. Scott looked around the room, decorated in European elegance, with a light colour above and dark wainscoting panels below, finely crafted wooden chairs and white linen tablecloths dressing each table.

"A little nicer than most of the places I've worked" Scott said to the other two, "I'm usually stuck in the cheapest dive in town, waiting for some military coup to take over the government."

Jake laughed, familiar with some of Scott's work. "I can imagine. Have you spent much time in Germany before Scott?" he asked.

"No. Actually, this is my first trip. Most of my work has been either Central or South America, or back in Washington to cover the political scene. I really haven't been to Europe before except for one trip to London a few years ago."

"Well," said Jake, "I hope you can enjoy some of this trip, I think you might be in for a pleasant surprise!"

Once their coffee was served, they all helped themselves at the generous *Früstück Buffet,* or Breakfast Buffet. Jake found he was ravenous, his wounds feeling much better after a good night's sleep. He kept thinking about Christa and her father, and what they must be going through, and was anxious to get on the road.

"Well, it appears our discussions last night didn't produce any answers," he said between mouthfuls, "we still don't know who's calling the shots here!"

"What do you mean?" asked Scott "I thought that this Weigel character was running the show."

"Yes and no . . . for instance, is Weigel going to order a mercenary attack on his own boat and himself?"

"No, that doesn't make any sense."

"Then who?" Who knew where we were going that night, and by what route, etc.?"

Scott mulled this over, trying to find the hidden clue. "Jacques," he finally asked. "Your people in Wiesbaden . . . or the German police or whatever, you said they've been tracking this 'mercenary' group as far as Berlin, and then you heard they were headed to Frankfurt."

"Well, yes . . . but it's not quite that simple, much of this is based on very sketchy information, rumour, a few leads from informants, you know. Then our analysts put it all together and try to picture the best case scenario."

"So what you've told us might or might not be a true person, or event."

"That's right . . . We can't always be sure." He turned to Jake. "Remember Jake, what I said about that body we found, one of the terrorists?"

"Yeah, you mentioned that he didn't appear to be from this group." Jake answered.

"When I talked to Wiesbaden this morning," Jacques continued, "the local police have found another body in the river . . . again, fair hair, blue eyes."

"So what are we talking about here . . . its unlikely these two are just odd men in the group, so are we talking about a completely different group?"

"Christ, that's a scary thought!" Scott added. "Do you think we might have two groups of hit-men running around?"

"Possibly," said Jake. "Which means that if the same ones that Interpol had traced from Berlin to Frankfurt are still coming, they should show up any time . . . or we could meet them in Bavaria."

Before long, they had all packed up and settled their bills, ready to continue. Both Jacques and Scott had rental cars, so they decided to stop at Würzburg to drop off one of the cars before they headed south.

"Just take this road up to Highway 3, then head east to Würzburg. We'll see you at the car rental office near the main train station, so as you enter the city, just watch for signs to the '*Hauptbahnhof*', you can't miss it."

Getting into the car was a painful experience as he tried to bend his lanky frame to fir the compact vehicle Jacques had rented. Fastening the seat belt was another torturous exercise as he twisted to tighten the belt and lock the buckle. Finally in, he breathed a sigh of relief as he turned to Jacques. "I think while we're in Würzburg Jacques, we should look over the 'Monique', just in case the police missed something."

Jacques nodded, then started the car. Once on the road, they made good time and within an hour they were driving across the bridge into Würzburg. They went immediately to the Hauptbahnhof rental office and picked up Scott, then headed down to the river to check the Monique.

As they drove south beside the river, they passed the *Alter kranen*, or historic old crane mounted at the side of the river bank, a site where freight had been unloaded from river barges in years past. Jake could see the familiar sight of the Marienberg fortress on the mountaintop across the river. He pointed out the famous attraction to Scott.

"If you look around Scott, you'll notice all of the surrounding hills on both sides are covered with vineyards, all producing the famous *Frankenwein,* or Franconian wine." Scott was amazed at the extent of the wine growing area.

"Bye the way," Jacques said as he drove, diverting their attention back to business, "Like I said earlier, I talked to both headquarters and the NCB at Wiesbaden this morning. They have arranged to join the local police when they approach the building at the T.U.Z. place. They've had it surrounded since yesterday, very discreetly, watching for activity. So far, nothing, not a move anywhere, not a person in sight."

"I'm not surprised," said Jake, "did you really think Weigel would take Stefan and Christa there, just walk in and have Stefan continue his research? After what has happened, I doubt it!"

"He might . . . they probably think you're dead, and nobody else knows where they are." He watched as Jake cringed at the comment. "Ah, sorry Jake, it was just an idea." He stopped again, then added "I hate being the devil's advocate on this, but actually, we don't even know if any of them are still alive."

"That's OK, Scott, I realize that." Jake said quietly.

"Well . . .where then?" Jacques asked. "Where the hell are we going now, if not to Bavaria to this special lab?"

Jake was silent, trying to think up a good answer. "Jacques, call your people again and have the local police check Stefan's house in the village of Waldbach, about sixty kilmeters south of Munich . . . they should be able to find out where it is . . . maybe they went there. It probably isn't far from the T.U.Z., as Stefan worked there."

"Good idea!" he said as he pulled out his phone to make the call.

Just then, they pulled up to the riverside mooring area where the Monique was tied up. The police had cordoned off the area to keep curious people from wandering on board to inspect the bullet holes. They parked the car and headed for the vessel.

A sense of *deja vu* came over Jake as he stepped over the bulwarks onto the deck. He almost turned to help Christa on board, suddenly remembering who he was with. His eyes glanced quickly around as he tried to place where he was on the night of the attack, where his assailants were standing, and how it all went down. He walked around the sides of the deck, explaining to Jacques where everyone was during that frightful time just a few nights ago. He could see the bullet holes from the automatic weapon as they tore up the deck towards him, how the corner of the roof had been shot off. He shivered, reliving the horrors of that night. Occasional pools of dried blood stained the decks at various locations.

Jacques had climbed up to the cabin top where the little car is normally parked to examine the area around the parking blocks. "I don't see any traces of oil or petrol, so it doesn't look like the car was hit."

Jake nodded, then looked around at the dock area beside the barge. "They probably just swung her overboard like they always do, and carried on their way."

They continued to walk around while Scott checked out the forward decks. With some trepidation, Jake entered the main cabin behind Jacques.

The scene shocked Jake. The beautiful, well appointed cabin had been transformed into piles of rubble. Fragments of flower pots, plants and soil covered the floor, mixed with shattered glass and dried blood. *Objets d'art,* fine china and paintings on the wall were either smashed or shot beyond recognition. Sheets of plastic had been taped on the shattered windows to keep out the rain and pigeons. The table setting for four still remained on the table, crystal wine glasses tipped over, a half empty bottle of Weigel's *Frankenwein* still on the table, flies buzzing around remnants of food shrivelled on the plates, mute witnesses to the events that evening.

Jake's gaze scanned it all, reliving each moment of horror, trying to see something different, something out of place. He carefully stepped through the shattered glass fragments to the stairwell to the level below, afraid of what he might see.

As they entered the main stateroom, the gun cabinet doors still remained ajar, one drawer still partially pulled out. He remembered the Sig-Sauer, and pulled open the drawer further, looking for something.

"What is it Jake?" Jacques asked behind him. "Did you find something?"

"No, sorry Jacques," Jake replied as he pulled out another drawer. "Ah, here we are!"

"What . . . what is it Jake?"

"Just a holster for that 9mm. That thing gets heavy, and it's a lot easier to carry in a shoulder holster. I thought Weigel would have one for it!" He removed it from the drawer and painfully pulled it on over his shoulder and fastened it. Jacques was disappointed, as he thought Jake had found something important.

They all walked around the cabin, careful not to disturb anything significant. Their voices were hushed whispers, their footsteps muffled by the deep pile carpet. Jake couldn't remember much about the cabin from that night, but everything seemed intact, nothing broken or severely out of place. He only remembered Christa and Monique huddling in the corner by the closet, keeping low in case of flying bullets. He walked over and opened the closet, pulling aside some clothes to look inside. Amid shoes and hat boxes piled in one corner, he spotted a small purse lying on the floor. Picking it up, he recognized it as Christa's small evening bag, the one she had with her that night. He could picture the two women, terrified, and eventually crawling into the closet to huddle in the corner while all hell broke loose above them. He showed the bag to Jacques before slipping it into his pocket. Jacques made a note of it in his book, and consoled Jake that it really didn't help them at this point.

"We already know she was here" he said, "we want to know where they have gone." He walked over to the companionway stairs. "See Jake, here's the only place down here we found blood . . . it looks like Weigel caught one of them coming down the stairs."

"Or at the top and he fell down." Jake added, inspecting the stairs closer. They continued along the hall, trying to find out where it led to. As they approached the end, a man stepped out of the darkness.

"What the . . . " Jake yelled, stepping back and reaching for his empty holster.

"Whoa . . ." yelled Scott, "It's me!" He started to laugh as he noticed what Jake had done. "What are you reaching for Jake?" he laughed.

"You scared the hell out of me!" Jake laughed nervously. "I guess this place made me a little touchy. Where'd you come from anyway?"

"There's another entrance to this end of the hall, from a little hatch on the poop-deck or whatever you call that area back there."

"Interesting . . . " Jake thought, wondering if that entrance had played a part in the battle that night.

"I think we're done here men, if that's OK with you Jake" Jacques interrupted. "Let's get on the road again."

As they left the outskirts of Würzburg, Jake directed Jacques to head south on Highway 7 towards Ulm. They all settled down for the ride, Scott enjoying it the most as they drove past old villages filled with half-timbered houses with red tile roofs, stone castles dating back to medieval times, and what surprised him the most, miles of open spaces, rolling hills, pasture and farmland so neat and tidy that they appeared to be trimmed and manicured by hand.

Jake figured it was too early to call his office in Vancouver, so he called Bert in Washington instead. His call was transferred quickly.

"Jake . . . where are you?" Bert asked as soon as he picked up the phone. "The last I heard from Frank Haywood was that you had been ambushed or something, ended up in the hospital and you had just been let out. How are you?"

"We're still in Germany, Bert, heading south to Bavaria. Thanks for your concern, I'm fine now, but we have a great story to tell the next time we get together for a beer!" He paused, shifting in the seat to ease his shoulder. "Jacques Manet from Interpol is with me, along with Scott Anderson from WCB. Scott will do anything for a story!" He continued talking, explaining the latest events to Bert, and where they were going.

"Do you know where they are?"

"Well . . . no." knowing it sounded ridiculous. "We're hoping we learn some more by the time we get there."

Bert interrupted "Remember Jake, you asked about the other agent that worked with Paul Butler?"

"Yeah, do you know who he is?"

"Not yet, nobody seems to have any files on him . . . almost as if he didn't exist, but a guy in our office knows one of the N.S.O. old-timers who knew Paul Butler in the old days. He said he has some information on his partner, so we should have something soon."

"Good! Please call me as soon as you know, and see if you can get the other agencies to follow up as well to find out what he's been up to and more importantly, where he is now. I have a feeling about this guy . . . especially now if you can't find any record of him! If he's not the missing link, he probably knows who is."

He finished the call and as he shut off his phone, and slipped it into his pocket, he thought about what Bert had told him. He was even more anxious now to learn about Paul Butler's old friend. He turned to the others and brought them up to date. Within an hour, they arrived at a big interchange north of the city of Ulm, and continued on Highway 8 towards Munich. A few minutes later, Jake pointed out the window.

"Scott, you might be intersted in this . . . the bridge we are approaching crosses the Donau River, or what you know as the Danube."

Scott watched out the window as they crossed the bridge. "The Blue Danube" he mused aloud, "It's not as big as I thought, and it sure doesn't look very blue from here."

"Not yet," answered Jake, "this is still fairly close to its source, behind us up in the Black Forest. It's much bigger later, as you go downstream, but I can't recall it ever looking very blue."

Scott took over the driving while Jacques called his headquarters as well as the NCB at Wiesbaden again. He did not stay on the phone very long.

"Still nothing moving at the T.U.Z.." he said, obviously disappointed. "I don't understand it, if they left Würzburg on Saturday sometime, even late Saturday, they've had plenty of time to get there . . . it's only a few hours drive."

"Any word yet on Stefan's house?"

"No, nothing."

"But I thought the whole reason for this exercise . . . kidnapping Dr. Schiller and his daughter . . . was to get him back to the lab to complete more tests." Scott noted.

The comment produced silence among the group. Jake was the first to speak.

"Yes and no Scott. Mainly, they wanted Stefan and his notes, most likely to protect their investment. He stopped, shaking his head. "As I said, we've been thinking too simple, or should I say, not simple enough! We've been reading too much into this. They don't need Stefan to run tests, they have other staff in the lab for that . . . they can run tests anytime. I think they just want Stefan to complete his notes, calculations and record his ideas and suggestions before it's too late!"

"Too late? . . . Too late for what?"

"Weigel knows someone is after the notes and all the data on this process, or wants to eliminate Stefan and everyone involved with it, probably both." Jake replied. "I think Steinbock . . . Weigel wants desperately to get it all recorded and secure before something happens. Obviously Stefan held back some of the critical information . . . maybe he suspected something like this."

"Which means they could be anywhere." Jacques moaned, wondering what their next step was.

By this time, many of the road signs were pointing out the turnoffs for the city of Augsburg, just south of the highway they were on. With directions from Jake, Scott continued on Highway 8, now turning slightly south towards Munich

"We'll be passing just outside Munich in about twenty minutes," Jake advised. "As much as I'd like to continue, I think we should stop just south of the city for lunch . . . maybe by then, we'll hear something from Jacques' people."

As the miles rushed by, Jake kept thinking, angry with himself for not having a better plan, for not figuring out his opponent better. Weigel was not the type to leave much to chance, so he had apparently planned this trip well ahead of time. The attack on the 'Monique' was obviously not in his plan, but once overcome, he was the type that would stick to his original scheme. He was not infallible, as the attack had shown, so he knew now that his options were becoming severely limited and he must move fast. The more he thought about it, the more Jake was convinced that whoever was behind the information leak from Steinbock, was someone within Weigel's own staff, or who at least had access to the company files and telephones. There were still big gaps in their data, and they were running out of time!

Jacques was on the phone again when they left the autobahn and changed roads a couple of times to bypass Munich and switch over to Highway 11, a much smaller road that headed almost due south into the heart of southern Bavaria. About twenty miles later, they pulled off into a small village to have lunch.

"OK," Jacques said finally, folding his telephone. "They found the listing and should have the local police do a drive-by within minutes. I asked them to be discreet, but check it out carefully."

"Good! I doubt if they will find anything, but we had to check." Jake said, knowing that Weigel would have a much better plan, something that wouldn't be so obvious.

As they entered the old Gasthof, Scott was all eyes, trying to take in the atmosphere, the furnishings and old country ambience that pervaded the place. A friendly waitress in traditional Bavarian dress soon had them seated at a large wooden table with three large, cold beers following quickly after. They studied the menu, with Jake helping to translate and and make their choice.

"I still can't figure it Jacques," Jake said, thumping the large beer mug down on the table. "Weigel had this all planned before he left Frankfurt . . . a specific destination. We know now he planned to go by barge only as far as Würzburg, then drive somewhere from there."

"Perhaps," said Jacques, but you don't know for sure, he might have even planned to go all the way, the Main river, then through the Main-Danube canal . . . but that would have taken a long time."

"But he could have had Stefan working on his notes the entire time. So he really didn't have a time restriction . . . unless he thinks someone is catching up to him." Jake offered.

Chapter 41

THEY HAD BARELY FINISHED LUNCH when Jacques' phone rang again. After listening for a brief time, he pocketed the phone and turned to the others.

"That was the Wiesbaden NCB. They've double checked all their leads from Berlin on the mercenary group . . . nothing! It appears that the intel reports about going to Frankfurt were wrong, they never made it."

They waited, hoping for additional information.

"Well?" Jake asked, "Do they know where they are?"

"No," Jacques replied, obviously frustrated. They haven't any idea. Germany's a free country, so once you're in, you can travel around wherever you want. It's hard to keep track of someone, especially if they don't want to be tracked."

Jake remained quiet, not wanting to think about where these killers might be going, or what their plans were.

The group was visibly troubled as they returned to the car and again headed south.

"Just stay on this road," Jake advised, Stefan's village is about 20 miles further, just a few miles east.

Another call for Jacques brought more disappointing news. "The local police are at Stefan's house, nobody's there, everything's quiet."

Jake nodded, not surprised. "We'll stop there anyway, it's on the way to the T.U.Z. He kept reviewing their options, trying to think about what he was missing, what he was overlooking. "Jacques, have your people checked for anything around here owned by Erik Weigel?"

"Yes Jake, that was one of the first things we did, when we got the location of the T.U.Z."

Suddenly, Jake remembered what was bothering him. It was their conversation with Weigel on the barge that night. Monique owned the barge, 'a little anniverary gift', Weigl had called it.

"Brehmer, of course!" he yelled out. Turning to Jacques, "Have them try Brehmer, Monique Brehmer. She owned the barge, so I'm willing to bet she has another little investment down here." Jacques nodded, immediately dialling his phone.

By the time Jacques had finished his call, they were turning off onto a secondary road towards Stefan's village. Familiar scenes surrounded Jake as he pointed the way to Stefan's house. By the time they pulled up in front of the house, he was choked with emotion, wishing he was visiting under different conditions.

Jake breathed a sigh of relief when he found Stefan hadn't changed the hiding place for the spare key. They entered the house, quiet and abandoned. More memories flooded back to Jake as they walked through from room to room.

"Look here, Jake." Jacques called from the bathroom. "Some cotton and bits of bandages in the waste basket, with small amounts of blood. Looks like someone washed their wounds and put on some new bandages."

Jake looked them over, sick at what they might represent.

Jacques continued "Don't worry Jake, at least they're still alive, and not badly wounded by the looks of this . . . probably only glass scratches from all that broken glass on the barge."

"Right!" Jake added, trying to control his emotions. "They must have stopped here on the way."

"On the way to where?" Scott asked. Blank faces stared back.

As if to answer the question, Jacque's phone rang again. "Yes . . . good . . . O.K., text me that address."

Jake looked at the text message, "O.K., I think I know where that is, just east of the T.U.Z., on a small road further south. Let's go!"

Scott took over the driving as they speeded up their pace. "Jake, how the devil do you know all these places around here, there doesn't seem to be any kind of sequential numbering system to the addresses."

Jake explained a little of his past history, how he and Christa had hiked and bicycled almost every road and trail within a fifty mile radius. "While I was here, I picked up another degree at the university in Munich, and I've done a little consulting for some of the firms here too. In case you're fooled by this touristy post-card ambience with fields, cows and beer-hall music, the area around Munich is home to some very high-tech companies, like *Bayerische Motorenwerke* or BMW, Messerschmidt, MAN, Rodenstock Optical Works and of course Siemens, the largest private firm around here." He paused a minute, his brow wrinkled in thought. "I just realized as we drove here that I already knew where the research facility was . . . the T.U.Z., Stefan was working there when I lived with them, but I never visited the place. I never really put the two things together until now."

They listened with interest as Jake explained the area further, the customs, the music and the history, with it colourful contrasts of past and present. The Bavarian countryside sped past the windows, the late afternoon sun casting lengthening shadows as they topped yet another hill overlooking a series of valleys below.

"That should be where the T.U.Z. is located," Jake pointed, "Down there near that far village." He was interrupted again by Jacque's phone.

Jacques listened briefly, then turned to them, a puzzled look on his face. "That was the local police around the T.U.Z." he said slowly. They're pulling back . . . ever since a S.W.A.T. Team arrived to secure the facility."

"S.W.A.T. team?" the other two echoed. Jake continued "What S.W.A.T. team?" I thought there was nothing there . . . where did the team come from?"

Jacques was on the phone again, and before long was patched into the local police squad at the T.U.Z.. He started repeating things for Jake and Scott. " . . . a team of four arrived by helicopter, ski masks, black suits, automatic weapons, radio coms . . . of course, I understand. Did they say where they were from, where they were based? . . . no . . . I thought so!"

Jacques looked at Jake, shaking his head, a grim look on his face.

"Well hello, Mr. Mercenary!" Jake offered.

Jacques turned again to the phone, his face deadly serious. "Listen, Captain, listen to me very carefully. Do not, I say again, do not engage these men when they exit the building. They are trained and very well equipped killers. Call your headquarters immediately asking for backup and a real S.W.A.T. team as soon as possible!" He hung up and immediately made another call, patching through to Wiesbaden to request support from the nearest S.W.A.T. team.

"Where the hell is the nearest team from here anyway?" asked Jake. "These local villages don't have that kind of fire-power, they might have to come from Munich."

"I hope not," Jacques mumbled, holding the phone. That'll take over an hour . . . where's the nearest airport?"

Jake thought a moment then answered. "The last village we just passed, Königsdorf, has a little airfield. Christa and I used to fly out of there with gliders, so it's large enough for small planes at least."

Jacques passed on the information to Wiesbaden then hung up.

Scott had been pushing the speed on their rented car as much as the roads would allow. As they approached the small village, the T.U.Z. became obvious, a large impressive building on a rise overlooking the valley. They could just make out some figures running around the grounds when the popping and rattling of distant gunfire drifted across the valley.

Scott stepped on the accelerator, propelling the car even faster. Conversation halted and faces became grim as they tried vainly to see what was happening in the distance. Skirting the village, they had to approach the research centre from the side, over the brow of a hill. Just as they came over the crest, a small helicopter rose in front of them, a rain of automatic fire spraying the road ahead.

"Duck!" Scott yelled as the bullets kicked up dirt along the side of the road towards them. He spun the wheel and jammed on the brakes, screeching the car sideways to the opposite side of the road as the helicopter flew low over them. Automatic fire raked across the car, exploding one of the side windows and the rear window, showering glass over the three crouching men, lacerating bare skin viciously. Scott accelerated again, spinning the wheels loudly to gain some speed and manoeuvring capability. Jacques had his gun out and was trying to turn in his seat to get a shot out the missing rear window at the helicopter. The small craft had already turned around, now coming at them from the rear. More bullets ricocheted off the pavement behind them, getting closer to the car as the shooter started to close in. Jake struggled to get his gun out, his seat belt strapped tightly across his bad shoulder. Scott started evasive actions, swerving the car wildly down the last few hundred yards towards the plant's front gate.

"I can't keep this up forever guys, he's going to nail us . . . get ready to jump!"

Finally out and ready, Jake quickly holstered his gun again to prepare to jump.

Just then, other gunfire was heard in front of them. The firing behind stopped then started again, but not at them. They raised their heads, looking ahead. One of the police officers was propped up against the fence, a semi-automatic rifle cradled in his arms. The crack, crack, crack of high velocity bullets was a welcome sound to their ears, some reason for hope. The helicopter let loose one more volley at the policeman, narrowly missing him as he kept pumping off shells towards the craft. Their job done, the mercenaries decided no further risks were necessary, and turned the helicopter away. Shaken, the three men watched the small craft hover for a few seconds, then disappear over the landscape as the T.U.Z. centre erupted in a massive explosion.

For several seconds, nobody moved. The whap, whap, whap of the disappearing helicopter was barely audible over the muffled explosions and the roar of the inferno in front of them. Room by room, entire banks of windows blew out the front of the building, showering the garden and sidewalks with glass. Suddenly more huge explosions burst forth as new fuel tanks were found and destroyed. They watched helplessly as the entire building became involved in an intense firestorm, sucking the surrounding air into its vortex.

Scott started the car again, inching slowly along the road towards the centre, closing the last few meters to the front gate. The heat became uncomfortable, even behind the windshield of the car. As the car stopped, they all got out, sickened by the sight before them.

Except for the one officer, they were all dead, the centre's security guards and the small squad of local police sent out to check the facility. The wounded officer that had done the shooting was slumped over, the exertion too much for him. They rushed to him, both to thank him and try to help stop his bleeding. Bullets had shattered a bone in his leg, but mercifully had missed the artery. They wrapped it best they could, making him as comfortable as possible as they called again for an ambulance.

"Come on guys," Scott pulled at them. "Let's get this guy out on the road, or somewhere away from this fire. We don't know what's going to blow next." Two of them propped the wounded officer between them, dragging him further away from the intense heat.

Jacques was almost in tears as deep sincere feelings for his fellow officers welled up. "I tried to tell them, I tried to tell them . . ." he kept repeating as feelings of guilt stabbed through his body.

Jake tried to console him. "Jacques, it's not your fault . . . you told them, either they didn't believe you and take appropriate action, or these guys are deadlier than we thought. Maybe we can find out more about the group from that officer, if he's up to talking." Jacques settled down on the ground beside the wounded man, both to comfort him and try to gain as much information as possible.

Jake walked along the fence that surrounded the building, trying to evaluate the situation. The entire facility was involved now, with more muffled explosions signalling the destruction of another tank of volatile material, probably fuel of some kind. From experience and what he had seen here, he knew these killers were professionals, experts at their trade, they knew exactly where and what to strike, and they were determined to leave no witnesses. Jake's thought turned to Christa and her father, wondering if they were safe at Brehmer's lodge. His next thought scared him as he wondered if the mercenaries knew about the lodge.

Chapter 42

IT WAS OVER TWO HOURS later when they finally left the site. An ambulance had taken away the wounded officer, but no other survivors had been found. Firemen still battled the blaze, but they could all see that very little of the centre would be left standing. Jacques Manet spent most of the time explaining to the local police what he knew of the situation and why they happened to be in the area when the attack happened. He finally walked away from the small group of policemen, slumped over, his face heavy with sorrow.

Jake paced the road in front of the center, trying to stay out of everyone's way. He was concerned about Christa, and where the mercenaries had gone. Not being one to waste the opportunity, Jake made a telephone call to Bert Jackson in Washington. Before he had a chance to relate the recent events, the FBI agent launched into a hasty account of his progress.

"Boy, am I glad you called!" he began. "I think I've found out who your mysterious missing agent is . . . the guy who used to work with Paul Butler."

Jake's interest was kindled, his present circumstances temporarily forgotten. Before he had a chance to respond, Bert continued.

"His name is Kurt Landau, a deadly serious and extremely skilled individual. When I say deadly, I mean deadly . . . this guy has one of the highest body counts in the business, and by the sound of it, he's still working on it!"

"OK, tell me something I don't know . . . like who is he, where's he from?"

"He's German, but was raised and schooled in the U.S., so his English is as good as any of us. His parents were German and Russian, so he learned both languages as a child. With these language skills he was trained by and worked for the N.S.O. during the cold war in East Germany and Europe. He knows how the systems work on both sides of the Atlantic, knows the right people and how to get things done."

"How come we didn't know this before, is he still working for N.S.O.?" Jake asked.

"No, not for some time. After *glasnost,* he stayed in Europe, working for various security organizations, sort of a gun for hire. He finally settled in Germany, landed a job as head of security for Sicherheit Steinbock, eventually working into general manager of the firm, reporting directly to Erik Wiegel. From what we can find out, he kept his connections with Paul Butler, working with him on this fuel thing. Kurt was the one that handled all the money transactions for Steinbock from Europe to Paul Butler to finance the project in the U.S.."

"Jeez, what a can of worms!" Jake muttered, still puzzled. "This Steinbock outfit really has some surprises up its sleeve. So what was his plan, is he the one behind all these attacks?"

"Yes and no. Between Interpol, the F.B.I. and a few other organizations, we've traced some of Landau's movements, as well as those of his hired guns. We figure there are two groups involved."

"We suspected that," said Jake, "But we didn't know how it all came together."

"We still don't know that completely, but we do know the group that hit the barge was some of Landau's thugs. He still has good contacts in the former East Germany, Soviet bloc . . . highly skilled hit men, mercenaries, whatever. These guys are trained as East German security, excellent at what they do, extremely ruthless, and very mobile."

"But that doesn't make any sense!" objected Jake. "Why would he order an attack on the barge . . . Steinbock's barge?" He paused, thinking aloud about what he had just said. "Unless he has his own agenda, maybe he's after Wiegel's job, maybe total control of the company . . . then he'd have it all."

"That's our guess too," Bert answered. "He was one of the few people in a position to know that Stefan was not on the barge, not in danger, so his ace card was still protected. Wiegel and especially you were just collateral damage, disposable. Christa would be valuable to save as a bargaining tool with Stefan, but not essential."

Jake digested the information. Other details started to fall into place.

"You said you found two groups . . . what's the other one?" Jake asked.

"Right. The other one was the group that the F.B.I. and Interpol had been tracking since this stuff first started in the States. Remember, Jacques Manet had said they had traced them to Europe, and they were on their way to Frankfurt?"

"Yes, and they lost them!" Jake replied. "I think we found them today!"

"What . . . what do you mean?" Bert asked, suddenly interested.

"I'll tell you in a minute, first, you tell me who they are, where are they from?"

"We don't know everything yet, but we do know at least two of them are middle-east, highly trained assassins, first class graduates from a Libyan terrorist school!"

"But how . . . ?" Jake started.

"Never mind how . . . more importantly, we've also gone further with the explosives, the ones that killed Butler and Senator Pelly. Forensics have traced the Semtex and the trigger device to some illicit labs they've dealt with before. I think by now, they probably know exactly which lab it was made in." He paused, the sound of turning pages audible in the phone as he thumbed through his notebook. "We are still at a loss as to who is behind it all! Another thing, these guys don't come cheap!" he added. "Someone had some deep pockets to hire this gang, especially for a multi-hit engagement on two continents."

"Oh, I'm sure they have deep pockets," offered Jake, "If my guess is right, we're talking big oil cartels here. After all, there are billions at stake, so hiring a few hit-men is no problem at all."

Jake continued to talk with Bert, explaining the recent events at the T.U.Z., and the escape of the mercenaries. It was Bert's turn to be surprised as he listened to the gruesome account of the massacre at the research center.

"Christ! these guys don't fool around!" he exclaimed.

"No, that's what I've been telling you guys! This gang has a job to do, and they go out and do it! The good guys . . . that's us . . . get so wrapped up in procedures, protocol and red tape, we can't react fast enough to catch them!" He stopped talking, thinking about what Bert had just told him. "Bert, tell me, if we have two different groups, where is this second group getting their intel . . . their information? I can understand Landau's men, they have a direct pipeline to Steinbock's head office through Landau, but what about these mercenaries, whoever they are?"

Bert laughed, "I wondered how long it would take before you asked that question. I said before you should be working for us! It took four experts almost three hours of talking and analysis before that question came up." Jake could hear more flipping of pages as Bert turned back to his notes. "When Landau and Butler were handling the Los Angeles thing, there were lots of phone calls, faxes and other communications between them . . . more than enough opportunities for the information to leak out. Since then, or rather since Washington and Senator Pelly, almost all of the communications has been in Europe, so we figure that's where the leak is."

"Leak? But where, who?"

"We're not exactly sure, but everything points to Steinbock, Landau's office."

"But from what you said, he's too smart for that! He's in charge of security for Christ sake!" Jake objected.

"Right, so it must be someone on his staff, maybe even one of his hired guns . . . someone whom he trusts, but someone who is also on somebody else's payroll."

Jake thought a moment, then asked "Other than this unknown person, this Mr. X, do you think each of these groups is aware of the other?"

"Well, think about it. If Mr. X knows, then I'm sure the other group knows what Landau's group is doing. I'm not sure if Landau knows about the other group. In any case, somebody has some very good connections here, and is using the information very effectively!"

Jake suddenly felt cold, the realization dawning on him that two well informed and well armed terrorist groups might be converging on a quiet lodge in the Bavarian Alps, the lodge where Christa and Stefan could be held prisoner.

"Bert, I've got to go . . . I don't have a very good feeling about this." He continued to explain where they were going, what he suspected might be happening.

"Jake, don't be crazy! Wait until the S.W.A.T. team arrives, you guys shouldn't be going in there!"

"Like I said Bert, if the bad guys are heading there, they won't wait. Maybe you should make some calls, call up the cavalry or something. Talk to you later."

As he closed up his phone, he noticed his two travel buddies waiting and watching him. "Scott, Jacques, let's go! I'll talk on the way!"

Dusk had fallen by the time they arrived at the little side road that lead up to Brehmer's lodge. The cool evening air had already formed small pockets of ground fog in the lower areas and surrounding fields. The pine forests of the lower slopes still perfumed the air after a day of warm sun. They could see the building through patches of trees, a few hundred meters up the driveway. It was a typical alpine hunting lodge, with woodwork and stonework built by local craftsmen. A wisp of smoke drifted up from the massive chimney at one end of the building, telling them that the building was occupied.

"That's most likely a fireplace," noted Jake, "possibly a cook-stove."

Jacques nodded. "Let's leave the car down the road a little way. we can walk back and approach the cabin slowly." They all agreed.

"Do you think they'll have a guard posted?" asked Scott.

"I doubt it," Jake said, "They probably don't expect anyone, unless they've invited someone. I think we should cover the entire area, just in case, then I'll go in to check it out."

"Bloody Hell you will!" Jacques whispered loudly. "Don't forget, I'm the only cop here, I'll do the sneaking around."

"Oh Yeah," Jake answered sarcastically, "That makes sense . . . *Sprechen Sie Deutsch?"* When Jacques didn't answer, Jake continued. "Look, they're not expecting anyone, it's dark out here now, they're inside, probably a noisy fire burning in the fireplace. I'll try to find another entrance at the back, or into the cellar. Jacques, you stay over to one side, in case I have to signal you. Scott, no matter what happens, you just stay out front here, completely out of the way . . . someone has to observe and report what happened here tonight . . . one way or the other. Also, you can watch the road for extra visitors."

Two grim faces nodded, rigid smiles trying vainly to lighten the moment as they shook hands briefly and turned toward the cabin.

Chapter 43

THE THREE MEN WALKED QUIETLY up the side of the driveway under the overhanging trees, their footsteps muffled by the grass. As they approached the lodge, Jake was surprised by its size. Counting the cellar, it was three stories tall. Like many of the old traditional farm homes in Bavaria, the main living area was built above the ground floor level, which usually housed the farm animals. Monique Brehmer's lodge was similarly built, typical of the hunting lodges and ski cabins in the surrounding country. In the modern version, the ground level was a large cellar, a storage area for extra supplies and an emergency stock of firewood. The walls of the lower level were crafted from local field stone and river rocks, with a huge chimney of the same material climbing from ground level to above the steeply pitched roof. A massive set of front stairs climbed from ground level to the main level. Jake guessed it would be much like many others he had seen before. The main level would most likely be one large room, consisting of a living area with its large fireplace at one end and a large kitchen at the other end. The dining room occupied the centre of the room. Bedrooms were normally upstairs off a long balcony overlooking the great room.

"I don't have a very good feeling about this, guys," Jake whispered to the others, "We don't have any control here . . . we have no idea what we're walking into." They both agreed, but as there was no alternative, they continued.

They had left Scott part way down the driveway while Jacques took up position on the chimney side of the house, ideally located to signal either man. Jake quietly skirted around the house, carefully keeping close to the building and avoiding the light patches from the windows. Leaving his cane behind, he kept close to the stone wall to gain a little extra support as he moved. Creeping around the house, he could hear a Mozart concerto being played inside. He found the entrance to the cellar just beyond the corner, an ornately carved wooden door with a leaded glass window.

"Only in Bavaria" he thought as he studied the door, smiling to himself. Remembering what Christa had told him about Sicherheit Steinbock and their security alarms, he carefully checked the locked door to see if it was wired. Knowing that he would never detect the alarms if they were wired professionally, he decided to risk it. He could see the door latch just inside the window. Not wanting to risk the noise of breaking the window, he took out his pocketknife and carefully peeled back the thin lead frame from one of the small panes of glass. Slowly, he bent the soft lead away from the glass until he had all four sides open and the pane was loose. Carefully, he removed the glass, bending the last of the lead back to free the glass. He reached in and turned the latch, holding his breath as he turned the door handle and opened the door. No alarms were set off. Before entering, he pulled out the Sig Sauer from the holster, racking a bullet into the chamber. He carefully lowered the hammer, readying the weapon for quick, quiet use. He quickly entered the cellar and closed the door behind him. Just in case someone investigated, he opened the door again and replaced the pane of glass, bending the lead back just enough to hold it in place. He then closed and latched the door, turning his attention to his surroundings.

The cellar was dark, only a soft glow filtered through a couple of small windows from the light at the front stairway. Empty crates and boxes were piled at one end of the room, while various provisions, cans, bottles and bags of dry goods were stacked along shelves running across the front wall. Built against the stone wall was a long set of racks full of wine bottles. Multiple rows of bottles reclined on notched boards, sorted by variety and vintage. Jake examined a few, admiring Monique's choice of wines. At the other end was a long wood pile, the cabin's winter emergency supply. A small room housed a pump and water system for the house, most likely from its own well. The air was cool, filled with mouldy smells from the vegetable bins, damp rock walls and the fragrant aroma of split pine firewood. As Jake checked the room, he could periodically hear footsteps above as someone walked from one side of the room to the other. Approaching another door near the large chimney foundation, he could hear music from upstairs. He knew he had found the stairwell up to the great room.

He cracked the door open, listening carefully. Voices and music intermingled with kitchen sounds in a melody of sounds with the crackling of the fireplace punctuating the performance. He couldn't make out anything that was being said, so he quickly entered the stairwell and partially closed the door behind him. Quietly and cautiously, he climbed the stairs, one step at a time. After what seemed an eternity, he reached the main floor level. From the position and volume of the conversations, he tried to place the location of each of the speakers in the room. Luckily, they all seemed to be near the far end. As nobody had crossed the room in several minutes, he decided to take a peek over the floor level.

The layout was identical to what he had pictured it. Almost everyone was now seated at a huge oak table in the central dining area while a man in a white apron served them dinner. Erik Wiegel sat at the head of the table with Monique beside him. Christa and her father sat at the other end, with Christa almost facing directly toward Jake. Helmut stood by the front door, too relaxed and blinded by the inside lights to be much good as a guard. The massive fireplace was at the opposite end of the room to the kitchen area, large logs crackling warmly. The room was filled with the warm aroma of traces of wood smoke mingled with cooking smells from the kitchen. Jake huddled in the stairwell and watched patiently from under the rails, just above floor level, making sure all the players were visible as the meal continued. Erik and Monique talked idly while the cook returned from the kitchen to pour more wine.

"Johann, you'd better go down and get another bottle" Erik said to the cook. Johann nodded and went to leave the empty bottle in the kitchen. Jake suddenly realized he was coming downstairs to get the wine. Quickly, he withdrew, stepping down the stairs as rapidly as he could, trying to match the sound of his footsteps with those of the cook's coming across the living room floor. In one quick movement, he was through the door and closed it behind him. He left the door only partially latched, hoping Johann wouldn't notice. He ducked back, frantically looking around for a place to hide. Not knowing what Johann's habits were, or what route he would take, Jake crossed quickly over to the small pump-house room and stepped inside just as Johann opened the cellar door and flipped on a light. Jake took a quick look around the pump house, realizing he had no further place to run if Johann decided to check. He was glad he hadn't tried to just duck into the shadows, as the bright light would have given him away. As he watched through a knothole in the pump-house door, some dust from a beam above trickled down the boards in front of him, inevitably inhaled by his nose as it was pressed against the wall. The dust sent an overpowering tickle up his nose triggering an immediate, powerful sneeze reflex. Jake grabbed his nose and mouth, trying to stifle an involuntary sneeze into a low snort. Quickly, he looked again through the knothole, ready to defend himself. Johann had not heard anything. He wasted no time, walked rapidly to the storage rack and selected a bottle of white wine after only a cursory glance at the label.

"Probably Weigel's private label," thought Jake, thinking back on their dinner on the barge that night.

His selection complete, Johann turned and headed upstairs immediately. Jake left the small room and quietly tried to clear his nasal passages of the remaining offending dust. He followed as quickly as possible after Johann, taking position again in the stairwell overlooking the great room. Johann proceeded to open the bottle and serve all around.

Stefan sat still, barely touching his food, while Christa's brow creased with concern. Her eyes were red, her hair uncombed and stringy. Jake's heart skipped a beat as he realized how much he loved her. He watched her, conscious of the pain she had suffered in the past few days. He had to get a message to her without the others spotting him. It had to be a kind of message that would be meaningless to others if it were intercepted. Crouching down, he reached into his pocket for a piece of paper. Instead of paper, he found Christa's small evening bag from the barge in Würzburg. Suddenly, he knew how he could send her a message without the others knowing.

"Helmut!" Erik called from the table. "*Kommen Sie heir, essen Sie etwas,* Come here, eat something. Kurt will be here soon enough, he said he might be a little late. You don't have to stand guard."

Helmut nodded and walked to the table, calling the cook for some food. Jake let out a breath of relief as Helmut moved away from a direct line of vision to the stairwell. Erik's words finally dawned on him . . . Kurt? Was Kurt Landau coming here tonight? Jake had an uneasy feeling, a concern that events could turn very nasty before the night was over. Already it was obvious that Erik did not know about Kurt being behind the attack on the barge. What other surprises were in store?

Before things changed again, Jake knew he had to make a move to signal Christa. Another quick trip down to the wine cellar produced a couple of corks, which he slipped into his pocket and headed upstairs again. Watching the room carefully, he moved up the stairwell a little further, making sure he was partially hidden behind a large potted plant. He pulled both the purse and the corks from his pocket and slipped the two corks into the purse. He waited until everyone was occupied by something the cook was saying in the kitchen, and lightly tossed the purse out a couple of feet onto the floor. It was very visible, but could have easily been dropped by its owner. He moved back down the stairs to watch and listen.

The dinner continued, with both Christa and Stefan only picking away at their food. Several minutes later, Christa's gaze wandered over towards the stairwell, spotting her purse on the floor. At first, a look of puzzlement crossed her face. Then it finally dawned on her.

"Wha . . .?" she started in astonishment.

The others looked up quickly.

"What is it?' they asked

Recovering quickly, Christa coughed lightly and reached for her wine.

"I'm sorry," she said quickly, "I wasn't paying attention to my eating." After a couple of swallows of wine, she coughed again, then stood up, excusing herself to the washroom. As she crossed the room, she quickly bent over and picking up her purse, continued to the washroom. Once inside, she feverishly opened her purse, not sure what she would find. She knew she had left the purse on the barge after the attack, so the only way it could have got here was for someone to bring it, someone who was on board that night but had not been here for the past two days. Then she noticed the wine corks. She never carried corks in her purse, the only person she knew who saved corks was Jake . . . he was always slipping them into his pocket "to add to his collection" he always said.

Her heart beat rapidly, "It must be Jake, but how? Maybe he wasn't dead, Oh God, let it be true!" she whispered. She thought again . . . the corks . . . if it were Jake, he must be in the wine cellar, or want us to go to the wine cellar.

A light knock on the door. "Are you all right Christa?" Monique asked, concerned that Christa had not returned.

"Yes," she replied quickly, "I'll be right out." She closed her purse and joined the rest at the dinner table, her face flushed with excitement which the others mistook for the results of her coughing spell.

For the most part, the conversation was boring. Erik and Monique continued discussing plans for their vacation, eventually turning back to Stefan to discuss his progress with the formulas.

"I'm sorry old man, but we're running out of time. You better come up with something soon, or Herr Landau won't be as forgiving as I am."

Stefan hung his head, his shoulders slumped. "*Verstehen Sie nicht?* Don't you understand? I've told you a thousand times . . . this is not just some simple mathematical problem we can solve by sitting down with pen and paper for a few hours. We must try other combinations in the lab, fine-tune the formula by experimentation!"

"But you must try again old man, not only for your sake, but your daughter's. As I said, I'm sure Herr Landau will have some ideas about that."

As if on cue, the front door opened and Kurt Landau walked in, followed directly by another man, both with automatic machine-pistols slung from their shoulders.

Chapter 44

THEIR SURPRISE AT SEEING LANDAU was doubled by the weapons the two men carried, but they were totally unprepared for what happened next. In one swift motion, Kurt stepped towards the kitchen, pulling a 9mm silenced automatic pistol from his under his coat. Before anyone could make a move, he calmly placed a bullet in Johann's forehead as he turned around, driving the cook backwards into a kitchen counter and down to the floor. He then quickly turned and deliberately did the same to Helmut as he sat at the table. Helmut's head snapped back and his hands flew up, a fork full of food scattering across the table. Like a bizarre slow motion movie, Helmut then slowly fell forward, his life long past as he went face first into his sauerkraut.

Gasps of surprise broke the shocked silence, followed by screams from Monique. In two steps, Kurt crossed over to the table, his hand whipping across Monique's face.

"Silence! I've heard enough of your whining and scheming!"

With that, Erik jumped up from the table. "Kurt! What the hell is going on? Are you out of your mind?" Kurt's gun whipped up, clipping Erik on the side of his face, tearing open his cheek as he fell across the table.

"Shut up!" he hissed, "I've listened to your miserable, weak snivelling for years, done your dirty work . . . and for what? I'm in charge now! I should have taken over long ago, before this got out of control! You don't deserve to be in charge!"

Christa froze at the first sign of trouble, vivid memories of that night on the barge playing in her mind. She clutched her father's arm, now trembling with fear for their lives.

Monique sobbed uncontrollably as she held her napkin to Erik's face, trying vainly to halt the bleeding. She could not comprehend the reasons for Landau's actions after years of faithful service, especially when so much was at stake. Erik was equally baffled.

"Why, Kurt, Why?" he mumbled through the napkin.

"Why?" Landau answered, his head snapping back and forth. "You ask me why? After years of over-riding my decisions, years of hiring idiots and expecting me to correct the problems, years of miss-management of the fuel project at the T.U.Z., ending in that fiasco in Los Angeles, then expecting me to fix it!" His face was red, his dark eyes blazing with hatred as he spat out the words toward Weigel.

Jake watched from the stairwell, feeling helpless. He watched Landau, a dangerous animal that had been cornered too long, and was now retaliating. The second man stood near the door, his hand loosely on a deadly machine pistol slung from his shoulder. A third man who had been on the front porch was not in sight. Jake wondered where the man was as he carefully pulled out his pistol, quietly cocking the hammer.

"But, Kurt, you know that wasn't all our fault!" Wiegel offered meekly.

"Then who's fault was it? That amateur *auslander?* That Prescott, a Canadian scientist that made you all look like idiots? I told you we should have got rid of him the first day, but no, you had to send more incompetents . . . and now look what you have."

"But Prescott's gone, we have Schiller and his daughter . . . we should have the answer soon."

"What do you mean 'we' Erik?" Landau snapped, "You're finished, I'm taking over! I'll get the answers out of Schiller or his beautiful daughter will suffer for it!"

Christa shuddered, gripping her father's arm even tighter. She couldn't think of what to do, how to get out of there before this madman went any further with his vendetta.

Before any more could be said, the front door burst open and Jacques Manet was flung headlong onto the floor, followed immediately by another man holding an automatic weapon.

"Look who we found snooping around outside."

"*Was is . . .?*" Several questions were quickly asked in German.

Jacques pulled himself up painfully from the floor. "Sorry old chap, never did get the hang of that language" he quipped, a pained grin on his face.

"Shut up!" the gunman yelled, shoving the butt of his rifle in Jacque's back, forcing him back to the floor. "We'll tell you when to speak!"

Landau stepped forward, waving to the first man who had come in with him. "Both of you, outside! Do a perimeter check . . . where did this guy come from and are there any more?

As both men headed outside, Jake hoped Scott was well hidden. He remembered the back door to the cellar and was glad he had locked it behind him. Landau waited patiently, his eyes darting around the room as he kept his gun trained on Jacques.

"Get up!" he finally said. "Get over there to the table and sit down!" Jacques obeyed slowly, some unseen injuries obviously bothering him. He sat down beside Stefan, nodding politely to Christa.

"Good evening Miss Schiller, I . . ."

"Shut up!"

Before long, the two men returned alone. Jake breathed a sigh of relief.

"Nothing, Kurt. All locked up, no sign of anyone else."

"Am I surrounded by idiots?" Landau screamed. "So this guy was just out for a stroll, happened to come across this cabin and dropped in for a drink?"

The others looked embarrassed, shifting uneasily in the doorway.

Landau continued, still holding his gun on Jacques. "Search him!" One of the men stepped forward, standing Jacques upright while he went through his pockets, emptying everything on the table. Kurt thumbed through the papers, picking up his wallet. His eyes opened wide, then closed to narrow slits as he read the contents. "Interpol!" he spit out, "What the hell is an Interpol agent doing here?" he asked, not really wanting to know the answer. "No gun? How is it you're wandering around here and you have no gun?" he asked. Suddenly he felt uncomfortable, his plans starting to run askew. He looked at the rest of the papers with new interest, in more detail. Train tickets, car rental papers, hotel receipts . . . "What's this?" his eyes almost burned through the paper in his hand, a hospital discharge receipt for "Prescott!" He whipped around, shoving the paper into Jacques' face. "Just what the hell is this?" he asked in English.

"Let me see . . . " Jacques grinned, looking intently at the paper, "It looks like the discharge papers for Jake Prescott." Stefan and Christa listened closely, scarcely believing what they heard. A large smile started on Christa's face, quickly controlled when she saw Landau's temper flare.

"But he's dead! My men said he was shot and went overboard!"

"Your men?" Wiegel screamed. "It was your men that attacked us that night?"

"Of course, you idiot!" Landau answered. "But as usual, I'm surrounded by incompetents! A team of supposedly highly trained commandos foiled by an amateur, two women and a couple of fat businessmen!" He turned in disgust to Wiegel, his temper barely controlled. "I lost a good friend that night Erik, all because of this Prescott! It was all supposed to be over that night . . . I was going to take over, finish the project, and we'd all make millions . . . the same millions you had planned to enjoy with your little whore here." Monique flinched as the gun waved in her direction.

Turning back to Jacques, he asked "Where is he?"

"I'm sorry old chap, I have no idea."

Kurt's gun whipped up, brutally clipping across Jacques' face, driving him over against Christa. She grabbed him, preventing him from dropping on the floor. Ignoring Kurt, she dipped her napkin in some wine, gently sponging the vicious cut on Jacques' cheek. Jacques leaned towards her, his hand on the napkin as well to shield his voice. "Downstairs," he whispered, "get downstairs!" Then he thanked her aloud.

Kurt raised his gun again, pointing it towards Christa. "Very touching, Mr. Interpol! I suggest you start to remember, or your pretty friend here will be next!"

Jake started to rise, ready to do battle, then stopped as Jacques began to talk.

Pulling himself upright, he faced Landau directly, locking eyes with defiance.

"I would suggest old chap, that you think about beating a hasty retreat, rather than worrying about Mr. Prescott. As we speak, Jake's probably got the local police or a S.W.A.T. team on the way. The only question you should worry about is who gets here first, the *Polizei* or those mercenaries who wiped out your little research centre today. I think you should hope for the police."

All heads spun around, both Wiegel and Landau barking out at the same time.

"What mercenaries? The centre . . .? What are you talking about?"

"Oh yes, didn't you know?" he smiled, enjoying the moment. He then explained about the attack on the centre, the shootings, the explosion and resulting fires. "You didn't think you could get away with cheating the oil cartels out of billions of dollars did you?"

"We're not cheating . . ."

"No matter . . . they stand to lose billions . . . that's why the centre and everyone associated with it must go. Who do you think disposed of your friend Butler in Los Angeles?"

Landau's chin dropped, his eyes skipping across the room from person to person. He suspected something like this, but had no idea who was behind it. His dream for taking over the centre gone, his enemy too close. His rage turned to something he could recognize . . . Prescott and his girl friend! He turned towards Christa, his eyes flashing, his mouth open in a scream of rage as he lifted his gun.

Jacques jumped up, grabbing the barrel of Landau's gun. "Go! go!" he yelled to Christa. He wrestled Landau to the floor, his grip still tight on the gun. Landau's accomplice started to turn, raising his machine pistol as Jake jumped up from the stairwell, his Sig Sauer firing twice. The man spun around and dropped, his weapon sprawling across the floor. Christa and Stefan were already in motion, moving across the room, crouching down to avoid the gunfire. The front door window shattered inward as automatic fire from the third man raked across the room from the front porch. Stefan stumbled, a shocked look on his face as he staggered a little and fell to the floor beside Jake. Jake turned, his weapon kicking two more times through the shattered window, spinning the man around, firing wildly as he went over the porch rail. With that he turned to help Jacques, who by the sound of it was bouncing off pots and pans in the kitchen in a desperate fight with Landau.

Christa's scream spun him around. Christa had dropped to her knees, her father's head cradled in her arms.

"Papa, no, no . . . Papa, talk to me!" she sobbed, her voice falling on deaf ears. Jake bent down, reaching for Christa, pulling her into his arms. Desperately wanting to comfort her, he knew the ordeal wasn't over yet. The room had a hazy, mystical appearance as the gun-smoke mingled with steam and smoke from something spilled on the stove. Holding Christa's sobbing face close to his chest, he looked over her head, the faint perfume of her hair a comforting contrast to the air in the room. He could barely make out the vague form coming from the kitchen. Too late he realized it was Landau, his gun raised, his face twisted grotesquely in a scream of rage. He tried desperately to push Christa away and raise his gun. She clung to him tenaciously, overcome by grief.

Like a slow motion movie, he watched Landau's gun fire, a puff of smoke exiting the barrel as it kicked upwards. Christa's body shuddered suddenly, her sobbing stopped. Jake's gun was almost level when Landau's fired again. Christa stiffened, her head rolling back, eyes pleading to Jake. She then slowly released her hold, sliding gently to the floor. Jake fired, then fired again, screaming obscenities at the smoke filled room in front of him. He couldn't see Landau as he emptied the rest of the clip in the general direction of the kitchen. Pulling the second clip from his pocket, he quickly changed it, racking the pistol for quick firing.

Tears in his eyes, he dropped to Christa, pulling her body up from the floor. "Christa . . . Oh my God, Christa, hold on, we'll get you to a hospital!" he cried, knowing it was already too late. He picked her up gently, heading for the stairwell.

He didn't get far when all the windows exploded into the house in a massive rain of automatic weapon fire. Jake knew at that moment they had lost, he knew it could only be the mercenaries returning to wipe up the final survivors.

"Jacques!" he yelled, hoping his friend was still alive somewhere. His voice was drowned in a cacophony of gunfire and explosions as a grenade landed in the kitchen, blowing pots and dishes to hell. Jake couldn't see anything across the room, now filled with smoke and debris. A dark figure moved in the distance, quickly disappearing up the stairwell to the bedrooms upstairs. A hand pulled at him, tugging him down the stairwell as the entire front wall exploded inward in a shower of glass and splintered wood. The agonizing sting of tiny daggers drove into his back as he staggered down the stairs with his grim burden.

Chapter 45

Scott crouched lower in the bush, peering out as much as he could manage without being seen. He watched quietly, at first fascinated by the arrival of Landau and his crew, then horrified by the shooting that had followed. Not long after, he watched helplessly as Jacques was captured and dragged into the building. From the way it happened, he realized Jacques had deliberately set himself up to be caught, to be part of the action inside the house. Not a stranger to gunfire, Scott's instincts normally told him to keep his head down and not get involved, only report the results. He was just about to move closer to the lodge when the two gunman came running out again, searching the area around the house, checking for more intruders like Jacques.

Scott moved closer, slowly working his way around the house to see where Jake had entered. He was almost ready to go in himself when the shooting began again. He tucked himself back into a bush, listening closing. Another car pulled into the driveway and muffled footsteps headed up towards the house, then up the front stairs. His worst fears were realized as he heard the shattering glass, explosions and automatic gunfire.

Two men stumbled out of the building, Jake collapsing to the ground with Christa in his arms. Something shifted in the trees ahead, moving towards them. Jake pulled himself up, levelling his gun at the figure ahead.

"Jake, don't shoot! It's me, Scott!" Scott appeared from the bushes.

Jake holstered his gun, turning his attention to Christa. Tears blinded him as he listened for a pulse, trying desperately to revive a spark in her lifeless body. His deep love for Christa slowly turned to anguish, then rage as he turned to the others, his jaw set, eyes burning. A deep howl started to come from within as he turned his eyes skyward.

Jacques jumped forward, clamping his hand over Jake's mouth. "No, Jake, quiet!" he whispered urgently. "We're surrounded by mercenaries!"

Scott and Jacques both kneeled down beside him, hoping to console their friend. "Jake, my friend," Jacques began, "we'll get him, we'll get him!"

Jake said nothing, his jaw locked firmly to withhold his screams of anguish. It was then he felt cheated of his revenge, he wished he had killed Landau slowly, painfully. Instead, it was all over in seconds, too fast. He now remembered the anger, the rage he felt as he pulled the trigger, again and again, sending the bullets to snuff out the life of this monster, Kurt Landau.

He shook himself, still scarcely believing that his old friend and mentor Stefan, and the love of his life, Christa were both gone in the midst of a senseless battle of greed.

As he looked up, finally recognizing the other two men. "Oh God, what a mess! Thanks Jacques, I assume that was you that pulled us out?"

"No problem, just happened to be going out that way myself!" Jacques quipped, a painful flicker crossing his face.

Scott started to say something, then stopped as he saw the dark stain spreading on Jacques' shirt.

"You're hit!" he yelled, reaching to peel back his shirt to get a better look.

"It's OK, just my shoulder . . . got it on the way out . . .hurts like hell!" He grinned at his two friends, his teeth firmly clenched. He pointed to Jake's arm "Were you hit again Jake?"

Jake tried to move his arm again, now covered with blood. "No, I think it's just my old wound opened up from all this," realizing he had carried Christa out of the building with a bad arm and a bad leg.

Jacques nodded and said "I wasn't kidding about the mercenaries Jake, I think that last little burst was them . . . I'm afraid it's not over yet old chap!"

"When the hell are the good guys showing up?" Scott asked.

"They should have been here before now . . ." Jacques said, his jaw set, "I don't know, but we can't wait, let's get out of here!"

Jake looked down on Christa, the pain of his love bringing tears to his eyes. Knowing he could not help her, he turned to his friends. Scott helped them both to stand up, partially supporting them as they headed into the woods behind the house. Two more explosions rocked the ground, blowing all the windows out of the house. They stumbled a few yards further, tripping over branches and small bushes. Climbing further up the slope behind the house, they eventually arrived at a small open area with a clear view of the house. Explosions still going off at sporadic intervals from grenades and small arms fire. Dark figures were circling the house, checking from front to back, making sure there were no survivors. As far as they could see, only three of the mercenaries were still active, down from the four that had left the T.U.Z. in the helicopter.

"Unless the fourth is still back at the helicopter, waiting." Jake said, thinking about how the mercenaries operated. "Scott," he said, turning to the reporter, "How did they arrive, did you see them?"

"I'm not sure Jake, but I think they arrived just before the fireworks started. I heard a car stop in the driveway. They were very quiet . . . but a few minutes later, they slipped by me, quiet as a mouse . . . must have had something on their shoes. I couldn't warn you because all hell had already broken loose by then."

Jake turned to Jacques, now sitting on the ground, looking pale. "We've got to get Jacques to a hospital, he's bleeding pretty bad."

"You're bleeding pretty good yourself Jake," Scott noted, "how does your back feel?"

In the heat of the moment, Jake hadn't felt a thing as the splinters of glass and wood penetrated his back. Now it was starting to hurt, like a hundred small drills, boring into his back. With this damage on top of his old wound, he knew it would get worse, but he realized Jacques' wounds were more life threatening.

The eastern sky was beginning to lighten when Scott said "Jake, look, things look real quiet down there now . . . any idea what's happening?" They all watched as smoke was coming from every window of the house. Nothing else moved, nobody was running around, no shooting or further explosions.

"They've gone . . . if they think everyone's dead, they will be heading out of the country very fast!" Jacques was already on the phone, trying to get though to the N.C.B. or the local police station. "Nothing," he finally said, pocketing his phone, "I think my batteries are too low, can't seem to get a good connection."

It was almost daybreak when they walked down the hill and past the house. As they headed down the driveway, the S.W.A.T. team arrived, followed immediately by the fire-truck and an ambulance. After a few comments about being too late, they turned Jacques over to the medics to get to a hospital as soon as possible.

"I'll go with the rest of you in the car." said Jake, not wanting to stay around the house.

"Oh no!" Scott yelled, first at the spot where they parked. "They've cut our tires!

"Damn!" said Jake as they looked at the car, sitting on four flat tires.

Jake looked around. "Where's Landau's car?" he asked.

They all looked around, but their's was the only car there.

"Those guys obviously came by car, then took off again . . . where did they come from?" asked Jake.

"Didn't you say there was a small airfield near here, a little village . . ."

"Königsdorf . . . of course! Scott, run back and tell that S.W.A.T. captain, we need a lift to Königsdorf, along with a few of his men!" While Scott went off, Jake thought about Landau's missing car. Was there a chance? Could he have missed shooting him? Could Landau have survived the attack and fire? Running quickly back, he met the ambulance just leaving. He waved for it to stop.

"Jacques . . . sorry old man, I have one quick question."

"Shoot, old chap!" he answered through sleepy looking eyes.

"What happened after your fight with Landau? Did you see him, was he killed by my shots, did the others get him . . . what . . .?"

"Don't know, we were struggling when that guy shot the window out . . . I think you shot him. The second guy started shooting and you took him out as well. That's when Landau lost it, he threw me aside like a rag doll and went after you." His eyes rolled up, his voice getting thicker.

"Jacques . . . Jacques, don't leave me yet . . . then what happened . . . can you remember?" Jake yelled.

His words came rapidly, slurred but full of conviction. "Remember? Of course I remember . . . I'll never forget. I was at the other end of the kitchen when he went after you . . . I was crawling along trying to stay low, the bullets were flying pretty heavy at that point. Then, the first explosion went off and all hell broke loose. Landau was gone . . . last I saw, he was heading upstairs . . ." Jacques finally succumbed to the painkillers and drifted off to sleep.

"Damn!" yelled Jake, "Upstairs . . . that's what I saw . . . wasn't sure." He turned to the others, his face grim. "I can't believe it! I'm willing to bet our Mr. Landau managed to get out of that alive!" His heart skipped a beat, his skin flushed in anticipation. A second chance for revenge was all he could think of, a second chance to make Herr Landau pay for his work tonight!

Blank stares looked back at him, three people who had just been through hell, only to find that the devil was still loose!

It was mid-week and there were no early morning fliers at the small field. A car pulled in from the road, drove the short distance to the edge of the field and stopped near the small helicopter. Three men got out of the car, threw their gear into the back of the chopper and climbed in.

Kurt Landau sat in his car on the far side of the field and poured himself another brandy, glad he had guessed correctly and arrived at the airfield before them. He eyes narrowed, his glance twitching from side to side as he watched the car pull up and the three men enter the helicopter.

Kurt Landau had learned many years before that personal vendettas and revenge should not enter into the business at hand. At the lodge, he had come close to losing control, losing sight of his objectives as he strived to destroy Prescott and those associated with him. He now looked on it as tying up loose ends, wiping out all those who opposed him and cheated him of his rightful reward. As he watched the three men load up, the three men who had annihilated everything that would make him a rich man, he felt he was justified in retaliating, cleaning the slate, so to speak.

Patiently, he slowly savoured his drink as he watched the machine wind up, its turbine screaming as the rotor started to turn. Before long, the small craft lifted off, hovering for a few seconds over the field, then headed off across the hills. Landau pulled a small box from his pocket and pulled out a little antenna, watching the craft climb. As it achieved maximum altitude to clear the peak, he pushed a small button on the box. The helicopter exploded in a ball of fire, pieces of flaming debris showering down on the hills below.

Landau finished his drink, a satisfied smile on his face. His twitching had stopped, as he sat there, planning his next move. He started the car, threw the little box out the window, and drove off.

Chapter 46

The buxom blonde waitress easily carried another three large steins of beer to their table, replacing the ones they had just finished. Two days had passed, and Jacques had just been released from the hospital that afternoon, his arm in a sling. After a heart-wrenching double funeral in Stefan's village, Jake had driven them further into the mountains of southern Bavaria for a few days in a luxury resort before they all headed home. Despite his personal pain and grief, he decided it was time for the group to get together for a little fun and relaxation. They were surrounded by the ultimate in Bavarian ambience, with the modern resort incorporating every cliche and caricature of the Bavarian culture into the decor of the little "beer-hall" they were in.

"Well Jacques," quipped Scott, "at least is wasn't your drinking arm that was injured!" They all laughed as they raised their steins for another toast.

"*Prost!*" Jake said weakly, his heart not in the mood. "I don't know how to say this, but I want to thank you all for your help and support . . . " he stopped, his eyes glistening. The others nodded, letting him know they understood.

Turning to Scott, he continued, trying to change the subject. "Well Scott, how's the great story coming?"

"Well, it would be fine if I were allowed to write it. The German police, Interpol and now the F.B.I. has recommended that I suppress certain elements of my story 'in the interests of national security' they say." He smiled grimly, adding "And I thought only the U.S. Government used that 'national security' excuse!"

Jacques interrupted, "I'm sorry Scott, but you know what could happen if some of the details got out. There are still people in the world who don't want any information on that secret formula to be released, and will do anything . . ."

"Even if we don't have a secret formula?" countered Scott.

"Yes!" replied Jake, "Even the idea of one existing . . . or even the possibility that one exists could create havoc. It's best the secret die with Stefan." He stopped, his face becoming sombre again.

"I know, I know," Scott said, "But you've got to admit, it would make a hell of a story!" He pulled out a newspaper from his brief-case, spreading it out in front of him. "Here's what did make it into the news, just so you know," as he started to read from the newspaper.

> "RESEARCH CENTRE ACCIDENT IN GERMANY KILLS 14 - Munich: Sources in a small village south of here report that a series of explosions and fire that destroyed the Steinbock Environmental Research Center was most likely caused by a gas leak. Advanced research done at the center involved many types of fuel which no doubt contributed to the holocaust. Steinbock officials stated later that the center would not be rebuilt, as all the leading scientists involved in the research were killed in the explosion. When asked by certain members of the press, Steinbock representatives also denied any connection of this incident to the recent disasters in the U.S.. Coincidently, the president of Steinbock and his secretary were killed in a house fire at her lodge near here."

"Of course, there's more, little details, stuff like that, but no real substance! I feel frustrated, especially after what we've all been through! There's not a word about the mercenaries, or Landau's involvement."

"The investigation at the lodge confirmed what we knew . . . Landau wasn't there. I have a suspicion he had something to do with that helicopter crash . . . the one near the Königsdorf airfield. They're checking the remnants of the explosive device that brought it down, as well as a transmitter found nearby. I'll bet it was Landau's work. They never did identify the bodies but they are trying to trace the helicopter . . . it was out of an airport in Munich."

"I think we'd all like to know who they were," Jacques offered, "Our trace was just a little slow catching up. All the stops have been pulled out now for Landau."

"I have a feeling you won't be seeing him for some time. From what Bert tells us, he's a slippery character, and will just disappear."

"I for one would be glad if he disappeared . . . permanently!" said Jake seriously, "I'm more concerned about him showing up again . . . after all, he was some pissed off with me for screwing up his plans . . . and he'll be even more angry when he finds out I'm still alive! A man like that has a long memory. He'll be back." Jake's prediction threw a blanket of silence over the group, as frightening memories of the events flooded their minds.

Scott broke the silence. "Actually, I have a lot more written for my article. I'm heading back to Washington tomorrow to meet on the weekend with Bert Jackson and Frank Haywood. They should be able to fill me in on the state-side investigations. I'm writing mainly about the bureaucratic influence and involvement in this entire affair, how our leaders and politicians were involved from Washington to California. I'm sure there will some long, drawn out inquiries over this. Very little will be mentioned about the actual research part in Germany . . . that will be secondary to the main theme."

"Looking forward to seeing it Scott," Jake commented, "What are your plans after that?"

"Well," he started, "I'm getting tired of the dirt, poverty and corrupt dictatorships I normally cover." Looking a little flushed, he continued "As soon as I'm back in the U.S., I'll be calling Linda Seymour . . . see if I can talk her into a European trip."

"Jolly good!" said Jacques, raising his stein for another toast. "I suggest we all meet back here for some fun . . . or better still, come to France . . . to Lyon, and I'll show you all a good time!"

"Sounds good to me, we'll keep in touch." Scott turned to Jake, not sure how to ask the question. "Jake, what are you planning now?"

Jake answered slowly, each part of the answer painful. "I think I'll stay over here for a few weeks . . . haven't had a real vacation for years . . . I have to clear up some of Stefan's affairs."

Scott turned to Jacques, trying to take Jake's mind off his problems. "And you Jacques . . . what are your plans?"

"Well chaps, some of us have to work for a living! I'll rest up here for a few more days while the final investigation is being completed, then it's back to Lyon and back to work. Of course we'll be trying to find out more about this so-called mercenary group, but I'll be concentrating on Landau . . . I want to find out more about him, where he's been, where he's going, the whole thing. We have to catch him while he's regrouping, before he's had time to build another organization."

"You're assuming he doesn't already have an organization," Jake said, "from what we know about him, he's already planning his next move."

"We'll be following the money route . . . we know he has accounts in Zürich . . . that's probably where he'll show up first."

Scott spoke again, speaking to Jacques. "Tell me, there's still a few things not clear in my mind."

"We're all a little confused Scott," answered Jacques, "But go ahead, what's bothering you?"

"Was Landau working for himself . . . or was he part of a larger organization?"

"Now that's a scary thought! We're really not sure . . . we think he was just fed up with Wiegel and wanted to run Steinbock for himself. When Stefan's catalyst idea looked like it could make them all millions, he wanted to be part of it, preferably all of it! With his connections with Paul Butler, Klaus Müller and others in America, he was in a position to do it! He didn't count on Jake getting curious and getting involved with his buddies . . . otherwise, they could've covered that disaster up, and eventually carried on with their tests."

"So how did this other group, these mercenaries, get involved?" Scott asked, a puzzled look on his face.

"That's more of a puzzle." Jacques answered slowly. As I've said before, we're really not sure who they are, or when they became interested. Our guess is that these people are always watching research groups like Steinbock. In some cases, they are actually funding, or helping to fund the research. That way, they can keep their finger on the pulse, so-to-speak, they know exactly what's going on and when. This time, it went too far. From what Stefan told us, Steinbock should have stopped when their first accident happened . . .back in the lab. They didn't count on Landau, Müller and Butler going ahead with the U.S. tests, especially with Senator Pelly pulling the strings. Because of that and the subsequent disaster, everyone involved had to be silenced . . . can't have bad press you know! That's when the big guns were called out . . . a specialized hit team designed to obliterate all knowledge of the product."

"Don't remind me!" Scott said, knowing how close they all came to being eliminated.

"Erik Wiegel was a shrewd and sometimes ruthless businessman, and really didn't deserve this. He knew he had an excellent market potential in Stefan's catalyst, and was willing to go a long way to get it out there. Unfortunately, he hired the wrong man to run the organization, a man that had bigger ambitions than he did, but also had the deadly skills to go with them." He paused a moment, then added "Actually, Erik had no idea he was threatening the oil cartels, no idea of the risks he was taking. I'm sure that even if Landau wasn't involved, Erik still would have ended up the same way . . . dead!"

Jake interrupted the discussion. "That's it! No more doom and gloom! Time for another round and a good meal . . . all on Prescott Industries!"

The evening improved as the food and drink flowed freely, weeks of tension and pain slowly erased with the benefit of friendship and goodwill.

Jake watched his friends, thinking about how different this evening might have been. He was overwhelmed with emotions, his love, his grief, but overall, his hatred for the man responsible for it all. Throughout the evening, Jake kept thinking about Kurt Landau, and when he would see him again.

The End